GET BACK IN THE GAME

Terry Leiden

SAVANNAH RIVER PRESS

AUGUSTA

Get Back in the Game
By Terry Leiden
A Savannah River Press Book/2008
Savannah River Press is an imprint of Harbor House.

Copyright 2008 by Terry Leiden

For information address:
HARBOR HOUSE
111 TENTH STREET
AUGUSTA, GA 30901

Jacket and book design by Nathan Elliott

Library of Congress Cataloging-in-Publication Data
Leiden, Terry.
Get back in the game / Terry Leiden.
p. cm.
ISBN 978-1-891799-45-7
1. Businessmen--Fiction. 2. Cancer--Patients--Fiction. 3. New York (N.Y.)--Fiction.
I. Title.
PS3612.E3556G48 2008
813'.6--dc22
2008006489

Printed in the United States of America
10 9 8 7 6 5 4 3 2 1

Cover photo
Courtesy © Joseph Mander/Photosport
Taken at April's Finest
Senior Softball Tournament
Charleston, South Carolina
April 9, 2006

This book is dedicated to all my fellow prostate cancer survivors. We come from all walks of life: we are mechanics, carpenters, electricians, pipe fitters, food service workers, soldiers, sergeants, generals, senators and mayors. We have all suffered, endured and hopefully, gotten on with our lives.

A special dedication goes to all the Agent Orange prostate cancer survivors. While doing their duty in Vietnam, they were unfortunately, and unwittingly, exposed to chemical contamination. For these men, especially, this book recognizes their service and welcomes them home.

Acknowledgements

DR. RAY FINNEY first diagnosed me in 1996 and provided excellent advice. This book would not be possible without the medical prowess of the skilled medical practitioners of the Georgia Radiation Therapy Center at the Medical College of Georgia. My thanks go to Dr. Arlie Fiveash, Dr. Jerry Howington and Dr. Byron G. Dasher. In addition, I do not want to overlook the people who assisted me at the Georgia Radiation Therapy Center: Tammy Street, the office manager; Terry Rogers; Tommy Jordan; and Barbara Peavy. Additional thanks goes to Dr. Russell Burgess at the Medical College of Georgia. There I was put in contact with Dr. Gordon L. Grado, then practicing at the Mayo Clinic in Scottsdale, Arizona. All of these skilled physicians and their staff members provided me with the treatment that removed the prostate cancer from the picture and laid the foundation for me to get back in the game.

Because I was exposed to Agent Orange in Vietnam, a large part of my follow-up treatment for prostate cancer has been performed at the Charlie Norwood Veterans Administration Medical Center in Augusta, Georgia. To the personnel at this facility, I am grateful.

Getting back in the game was the first step, but keeping an old senior softballer competitive in that game was the unenviable job of Dr. David Gambrel and Dr. Jewell Duncan of Sports Medicine Associates of Augusta. Broken ankles and fingers and torn hamstrings and muscle pulls were treated for a prostate cancer survivor without a moment's hesitation. To them and the physical therapists who assisted me, I say thanks.

Ten years after the first draft and getting innumerable rejection letters, Carrie McCullough of Harbor House expressed interest in my book. She turned me over to Peggy Cheney who is my editor. I had much to learn, and she took the time to teach.

Most important was my wife, Sara, who suffered through the initial diagnosis, my denial of the initial diagnosis, the medical treatments, and the follow-up testing over several years. I know the problems were an emotional turmoil for her, and for my sons. I give my gratitude for their support. In addition, Sara was an astute proofreader of many drafts. To all the readers of this book who have received a diagnosis of prostate cancer or are relatives of one, read about your fellow patients. Good luck, God bless, and get back in the game!

Terry Leiden
Augusta, Georgia

CHAPTER 1

NEW YORK

LEO CLICKED OFF the radio alarm and got out of bed. He walked over to the window and stared out as the city was coming to life beneath a blue sky. Pigeons fluttered between the buildings while people walked along Fifth Avenue on their way to work. The first car horns could be heard faintly. "A glorious day," Leo said. He walked to the shower humming a Beach Boys' tune. It would be the last carefree shower of this period of his life.

Bonnie watched the bathroom door close, wondering where her husband, thirteen years her senior, got his energy. Lured by the scent of fresh coffee, she put on her robe and slippers and went to the kitchen. The automatic coffee maker was percolating merrily. From the cabinet, she took out a pair of glasses and then poured orange juice.

Leo walked in wearing a towel, smelling of soap and talc. "Coffee ready?"

Bonnie, tying her hair back, glanced at Leo. "In a minute," she said.

"How about some orange juice?"

"Here." Bonnie handed him a glass. "Leo, your happy morning-person routine ruins my day. Couldn't you be miserably unenergetic every other day?"

Leo ignored Bonnie's remark. "I've got to look sharp, really sharp today. I'm meeting with Mr. Williams. He's picking the new chief operating officer. That wimp Patterson said that his wife was sick. He's going to retire so he can take care of her. Where is that man's loyalty? He's been paid by the company for thirty-five years. He wasn't CEO material anyway."

"And you are?" said Bonnie.

"You bet I am, and COO is one step closer. I've been president of my division for five years. I have earned it and I deserve it," Leo said, pushing his finger into her ample bosom.

"Here's your coffee, COO," she said as she slapped his finger away.

"Where's the suit I had tailored in London last year?" asked Leo.

"The cleaner didn't deliver. And I forgot to get it," said Bonnie.

"Damn it, Bonnie. Mr. Williams is fussy about the officers presenting the right image. He'll spot an off-the-rack suit in a flash."

"Take it easy, Leo. It will be okay," said Bonnie.

"Pick out a great tie for me," said Leo.

"Okay, okay." Bonnie walked to the cedar-lined walk-in closet and selected a monogrammed cuffed shirt and a maroon power tie. Pricey, but understated.

"Hey, I can't wear these," said Leo.

"What's the matter?" said Bonnie.

"The elastic in these boxer shorts is shot," said Leo.

"Who's going to see your shorts?" said Bonnie.

"I have a doctor's appointment this afternoon," said Leo.

"What doctor?" asked Bonnie.

"The urologist," said Leo.

"You didn't tell me anything about that," said Bonnie.

"When I was there last week he said I had to come back for the test results," said Leo.

"Damn it, Leo! It's one thing to put up with a perky morning person, but if you have contracted some social disease, I'll divorce you in a minute. I don't need medical problems," said Bonnie.

"C'mon, Bonnie, give me a break. I haven't been running around," said Leo.

"You better not have. I want to see a copy of that report," said Bonnie.

"For Pete's sake, Bonnie. Worry about the doctor's report later. The first priority is the meeting with Williams and becoming COO." He studied his image in the Cheval mirror.

"Your tie is just a tad crooked. Here, let me adjust it." Bonnie fixed his tie and gave him the perfunctory kiss. The intercom squawked. Bonnie pressed the button. "What is it?"

"Tell Mr. Able his limousine has arrived," said the doorman.

"He will be right down." Leo hurried out the door to the elevator. "Good luck," she yelled after him.

In the lobby the doorman opened the door to the street and followed Leo to the waiting limousine, which whisked Leo quickly through the springtime Manhattan traffic to the front door of the QRX building. QRX is a large American conglomerate, which initially built radios then expanded into computers, auto parts and sports equipment. The walls of the lobby reflected visual images of the different divisions. Leo headed the largest, the Radio and Computer Division. He looked with pride at the exhibit that contained his picture and informed visitors his division had had one and a half billion dollars in sales the previous year. Leo got into the elevator, noting with satisfaction that he was five minutes early for the seven-thirty meeting. He got off the elevator at the forty-eighth floor and was greeted cheerfully by the receptionist.

"Good morning, Mr. Able."

"Morning," mumbled Leo as he ran into his office to pick up his papers. His personal secretary, Rita, was already there. Aware of the importance of this meeting, she greeted Leo with his presentation folder.

"Mr. Williams' secretary called. They are waiting for you," said Rita.

Leo rushed back to the elevator, rode up to the fiftieth floor and walked briskly into the CEO's large walnut-paneled office. Mr. Williams was seated not behind his desk but in the more informal conversation area next to the window. Tom Reeble, the CFO, was sitting on a sofa. Both stood as Leo strode toward them, hand extended.

"Good morning, Mr. Williams," Leo said. Mr. Williams shook his hand rather tentatively.

"Good morning, Leo. Good luck to you in the future."

That was a little unusual, thought Leo.

"Leo," Mr. Williams said, "we called you here because it has become necessary to discuss a sensitive issue."

"Is it about a promotion?" asked Leo.

"We were considering you for COO"

"Has there been a change?" asked Leo.

"Leo, I will come directly to the point. We just received a report from your doctor. You have prostate cancer. He recommends you go to the Mayo Clinic as soon as arrangements can be made," said Mr. Williams.

The color drained from Leo's face and he sat down in the chair. "How do you know this?" he asked.

"If you're going to be promoted, you have to pass the physical. The doctors called us, naturally," explained Mr. Williams.

"How can you know before I do? Isn't there a patient-doctor privilege?" asked Leo.

"Come on, Leo. When the company pays your medical bills, you give us a right to look into your medical records. You know that. You devised the system," said Mr. Williams.

Tom Reeble said, "Remember the corporate pilot who had the heart condition? He concealed it because he feared he'd lose his job."

"Right," said Williams. "If the S.O.B. wants to have a heart attack on his own time, it's okay, but he's not going to have one flying our corporate jet with me in it."

"We have access to all employee medical records," Reeble said. "The corporation pays the doctors and the doctors know it. You need to go over to the doctor's office this afternoon."

"You knew about the appointment, too?" said Leo.

"Of course," said Williams. "Go to the doctor's office, make arrangements with the Mayo Clinic, and tell Bonnie. The doctor says that if you move fast, the procedure can be scheduled in about a month."

"And then what?" asked Leo.

"Then nothing," said Williams. "Don't worry about your job. You're going to continue on salary. There will be no changes whatsoever. Make arrangements to have your subordinates pick up your work. When you come back from the Mayo Clinic, I'll have a complete report on your medical condition. You tell me whether you want to continue to work," said Mr. Williams.

"Of course I want to continue to work," said Leo. "I have a loyalty to this corporation."

"I know you do," Williams said, "and we appreciate it. Thanks for all the work you've done for this corporation. You took Radio and Computer Division from four hundred million to one and a half billion in sales. Believe me, this corporation will remember your effort and loyalty."

Williams shook his hand. Reeble shook his hand and looked at Leo head to toe, like an undertaker measuring him for a casket.

After Leo left, Williams turned to Reeble. "There goes a real business shark. Aggressive, knows how to go for the jugular, with lots of competitive spirit. Mean as hell to his staff. I'll miss him."

"Our competitors won't," said Reeble.

"That's what worries me," said Mr. Williams.

Leo, in a daze, walked slowly back to the elevator and returned to his office. Rita studied his expression. "I'm sorry about your illness. I know that you and Bonnie will get through this."

"Damn it, why didn't you tell me?" asked Leo.

"The report came in late yesterday afternoon, but I was instructed not to tell you," said Rita.

"By whom?" shouted Leo.

"Ms. Novak," answered Rita.

"Unreal! She really wants my job," said Leo.

"Now, Mr. Able, bad language is not helpful. There are more important concerns at this time. Don't you think you should tell Bonnie?" asked Rita.

Suddenly very tired, Leo walked into his office and closed the soundproof door. He stared at the phone. I wonder if they're taping my phone conversations. Damn that Rita. She knew about this before I did.

Leo sat in his chair. Cancer. How long do I have? I sure don't want one of those long lingering illnesses. Maybe I should just jump out of my office window. No way, that is definitely not an option. That exec on the fortieth floor tried it. He broke his collarbone but the inch-thick glass is still intact.

Why me? Thought Leo. Kids are all on their own. My career was going great. Bonnie is a great wife, not like Cybil, that alimony-hungry ex. I must call Bonnie.

His hand trembled as he punched the number. Bonnie answered cheerfully. "Bonnie," Leo said.

"Yes, Leo, how did the meeting go?"

"It's over," said Leo.

"What happened?" said Bonnie.

"The good news is I don't have a venereal disease," said Leo.

"That's good," said Bonnie.

"Did you know about this too?" demanded Leo.

"Know what?" asked Bonnie.

"Nobody told you anything?" asked Leo.

"Leo, what are you talking about?" said Bonnie.

"Mr. Williams just informed me that I have prostate cancer," said Leo.

"He said what? Leo, is this a sick joke?" Bonnie asked.

"I'm going over to the doctor's office this afternoon. They're going to schedule a biopsy and treatment at the Mayo Clinic," said Leo.

"You are serious," said Bonnie. "I want to be with you, I will meet you at the doctor's office."

"My appointment is at two o'clock. How about coming around three o'clock and I'll go home with you. Bring a fifth of Chevas Regal," said Leo.

"In the Buick?" asked Bonnie.

"Yes, and with two glasses. I am not drinking it out of the bottle like some wino," said Leo.

"I'll be there at two o'clock," said Bonnie.

ATLANTA

A bright May sun warmed the Atlanta senior citizens softball diamond. Fifty and sixty year olds scampered around the softball field like children dismissed from school early. The hot, sticky weather of summer had not yet descended on the city. The fifty year olds were playing the sixty year olds. Larry Nedil was playing right field.

"He's coming your way," shouted Pat, the second baseman. "This guy always hits to the opposite field. Watch out." The pitcher threw the ball, and the right-handed batter hit a rope of a line drive to right field. Larry reacted instantly. The ball hit the ground fifteen feet in front of him. But as he gracefully reached to scoop it up, the ball hit a sprinkler head, ricocheted off and smashed into his groin. He quickly retrieved the ball and threw it to the relay man before slowly collapsing to his knees. Larry's suntanned face paled. Pat trotted out to check on his teammate.

"Hit ya in the family jewels, did it?" said Pat.

"It sure did," moaned Larry. Beads of perspiration dotted his forehead and face.

"That's stopping it the hard way, Larry," said the right center fielder as he jogged over. "Why didn't you use your glove?"

"He couldn't," said Pat. "The ball bounced off that sprinkler head. When it does that you never know where it's going."

"I should have worn a cup," said Larry, "but I thought I was safe in the outfield."

"Hell, there ain't more than one in ten of us that wears a cup. When you get older it doesn't hurt as much," said Pat.

"That's a crock," said Larry slowly rising to his feet.

"You okay?" Pat asked again.

"Yeah," said Larry, "you know how it is. It goes away in about five minutes." He adjusted his glasses in an effort to keep his hands from clutching his crotch.

"Yeah," said Pat, "but it hurts like hell for a couple of seconds, don't it?"

"You got that right," exclaimed Larry.

"Play ball!" shouted Pat. The senior citizens scampered on.

After the game, Larry drove toward home. He was still hurting as he stepped gingerly out of his car at Mom & Pop's Convenience Store.

"Hi, Larry," yelled a bald-headed Pop.

Larry walked in about ten feet, stopped, looked around, and yelled to the hard of hearing owner, "Hey Pop, where's the chewing tobacco?"

"It's here, under the counter," said Pop.

"It used to be over there next to the marijuana rolling paper," said Larry as he pointed.

"You mean the tobacco rolling paper," said Pop.

"Yeah, sure. How many kids buy strawberry-flavored paper so they can roll Bull Durham cigarettes?" asked Larry.

"I get a great profit markup on that paper," Pop said.

"Better than the pot dealers get?" asked Larry.

"Hey, lay off, Larry, these are New York Stock Exchange companies that make the paper," said Pop.

"Is that right?" Larry said as he looked at the name of the company that manufactured the rolling paper.

"Right," said Pop, "my mutual fund has got shares of that company."

"Interesting, my teacher's retirement fund owns a half a million shares of a company that makes rolling paper for marijuana cigarettes," said Larry.

"Hey, Pop," a young girl said, "where are the condoms?"

Larry saw a girl who looked to be twelve years old follow Pop's hand over to the gum rack. She picked up two packs of three each.

Pop asked, "You're really going to need six?"

"Yeah," she said, "my boyfriend's coming home this weekend. How much?"

"Three dollars and seventy-nine cents." The girl paid and walked out the door.

"That girl looks about twelve years old," said Larry.

"Don't worry," said Pop, "I know her, She's fourteen."

"Okay," said Larry as he put two packs of chewing tobacco on the counter.

"That's five dollars and forty cents, Larry, and I have to see your I.D. card," said Pop.

"Pop, I'm fifty-eight years old. I need an I.D. to get chewing tobacco?"

"That's right," said Pop.

"That fourteen-year-old girl walked out of here with six condoms. You didn't ask to see her I.D.," said Larry.

"Hey, take that up with Congress," said Pop.

"Isn't that statutory rape?" asked Larry.

"Not with congressional approval," said Pop.

"How do you get congressional approval?" asked Larry.

"Use a condom," said Pop.

Larry muttered to himself, collected his change, walked to his car and drove home. He pulled into the driveway and limped through the side door. His wife Sarah was used to the strains and pulled muscles of the would-be major leaguers.

She shook her head. "One of these days, Larry, you're going to come home with your own broken leg under your arm instead of a softball bat."

"The ball hit me in the groin. I'll mow the grass, have a cool beer and it will just go away like always," said Larry.

"Why don't you take some Tylenol?" asked Sarah.

"Tylenol is for strains," said Larry.

"What did you do, pull a thigh muscle?" Sarah asked.

"No, Sarah, a ball ricocheted up and hit me right in the groin," Larry repeated.

"I always wonder why you men go on so when you get hit there. You moan and wince like mad. You'd think you were in labor! I just don't understand," said Sarah.

"You would if you were on our side of the gender index." Larry kissed her and went out to mow the grass.

The next day Larry told Sarah, "I am going to the doctor after I get through at school."

"It must really be bothering you," she said. "You won't go to a doctor unless you're half dead. It's a good idea. You haven't had a checkup in a year or two anyway."

Monday afternoon, Larry was in Dr. Korn's office.

"What's the matter, Larry? You don't look one hundred percent."

"Well, Doctor, I was out playing softball—" said Larry.

"You still playing softball, Larry?" said Doctor Korn.

"Give me a break," said Larry. "I'm still young. Last Saturday I was trying to field this ball and it bounced up and hit me in the groin."

"Weren't wearing a cup, I bet," said Doctor Korn.

"If I had been wearing a cup, I wouldn't be here visiting you," said Larry.

"Okay, Larry, just drop your pants and shorts and let's have a look." Larry did as the doctor directed. "There are no bruises, swelling or anything. You just took a good lick. I'm looking through your medical chart. You haven't had a complete physical in two years."

"I don't need all that," said Larry.

"Hey, you're already here and it's covered by the teacher's medical insurance. Just let me give you an examination. We'll take your blood pressure and a blood test. Since you already have your pants off, let me give you a rectal examination." He pulled on the rubber gloves.

"Geez, Doc, do you have to do that?" said Larry.

"Larry, don't be such a wimp. All I do is put a gloved, well-lubricated finger into your anus. Bend over and put your hands on your knees. It only takes ten seconds." With that the doctor took out the rubber glove and performed a digital rectal examination.

"Hmm," said Dr. Korn. "Okay, hop up here and I will complete the examination. I am going to have my nurse come in and draw some blood for a PSA test."

"What's that for?" asked Larry.

"We just want to check on everything. It won't take a minute. After she takes the blood sample, I want you to take it down to the laboratory on the first floor. Come back in half an hour and I'll have the results of your examination. What more could you ask for?"

"Believe me, Doctor, I would have asked for a lot less and been a lot happier." The nurse drew his blood into a small vial, and he took it downstairs to the laboratory. After Larry waited patiently for a half hour, a lab tech handed him an envelope that he delivered to Dr. Korn's receptionist. About ten seconds later, Dr. Korn walked quickly out to the waiting room and motioned for Larry to come into his office.

"Larry, I'm sorry to have to tell you this, but you have prostate cancer," said Doctor Korn.

"What!" Larry's face paled even more than when he had been hit in the groin by the softball.

"You've got to be kidding." Once again little beads of perspiration appeared on his forehead. "How can you be sure?"

"Larry, when I did the digital examination, I noticed that there was a lump on one side of your prostate. Without having to go in for exploratory surgery, we just use a blood test. Your PSA was nine. We will perform a biopsy, but I'm sure you have prostate cancer."

"Am I going to die?" said Larry.

"Larry, I don't know. I seriously doubt that this will be terminal. The lump appears to be very small. We caught it before it reached any significant size. That softball bouncing off your groin is the best thing that could have happened. If you had waited two or three years, it could have been too late. I am not an oncologist. My suggestion would be to get a second opinion."

"I am not rich! This sounds serious," said Larry.

"No," said Dr. Korn, "don't take that approach. You have medical insurance. I'm sure that the school will give you sick leave."

"Why me, Doc? What did I do?" said Larry.

"Larry, you did nothing. Every man is going to have this sneaky cancer. It is a one hundred percent certainty. In most cases, men die of something else first. Every eighty-year-old man walking around has it, he just doesn't know it."

"How come you don't read about it like breast cancer for women?" said Larry.

"I am not going to comment on that. It would not be politically correct," said Dr. Korn.

"Why don't you go home, discuss it with Sarah, and make whatever arrangements are necessary to get some medical treatment. There are several options."

"Is this going to affect my work?" asked Larry.

"Probably not, but I strongly recommend that you follow up on this," said Dr. Korn.

"Should I go back to work?" asked Larry.

"Sure," said the doctor, "it's late in May. How many more days of school are left?"

"About eight days," said Larry.

"Finish up the year. Make your arrangements to get medical treatment in the summer. Promise me, Larry?" said Dr. Korn.

"Yeah, I definitely promise that," said Larry.

Larry drove home slowly, incurring the wrath of other rush hour commuters. What will I tell Sarah, he thought. How will she hold up? Should we tell the kids? Do I have enough life insurance? Why am I so scared? I know I'm going to die; I just wasn't planning on a fast forward like this. Maybe the doctors can do something. A sudden loud truck horn brought him out of his daze just in time to make his I-75 exit. In a few minutes he pulled into the driveway. Sarah was waiting at the door.

"What did the doctor say?" Sarah asked.

"He said I have prostate cancer," said Larry.

"Oh," said Sarah, putting her hand to her mouth. "It's serious?"

"I guess it is. Most people don't consider it a laughing matter," said Larry.

"I know that," she said. She walked into the kitchen and started nervously peeling potatoes. "What are we going to do about it?"

"I am going to finish teaching the semester. The doctors are going to lay out the appropriate treatment," he said.

"I have heard all about that. There are several treatments: radiation therapy, and chemotherapy and then there is one where they just go in and surgically remove everything." Sarah brandished her knife and cut a chunk out of the potato.

Larry put his hand to his groin. "Cut everything out! Hey, those are my private parts!"

"Don't be such a baby. They'll just go in and remove the bad stuff and that's it," said Sarah.

"That's it? How do you know about this?" said Larry.

"Wives talk about it at aerobics all the time. Some of the wives have husbands with prostate cancer. We hear their stories about how sometimes they're impotent and have to wear diapers," said Sarah.

"Oh thanks, Sarah. That really makes me feel better." He said.

"That could never happen to you, Larry!" Sarah looked at the blooming flowers and azaleas in the yard. Such a contrast to Larry's disease. "Why did you get it?" said Sarah.

"I don't know. The doctor said some Vietnam veterans who were exposed to herbicides developed cancers," he said.

"Doesn't that make you angry? You're serving your country and they're dousing you with a dangerous chemical," she stated.

"No, it doesn't," said Larry. "If the Air Force hadn't dumped herbicides on us, the foliage would have been so thick the V.C. snipers could have come close enough to shoot me. Then Mrs. Nedil's pride and joy would not have returned and you would have married that guy with the big nose."

"His nose wasn't that big," she said.

"Doctor told me to see an oncologist and go to some place like the Mayo Clinic," he said.

"The Mayo Clinic? Can we afford that?" she said.

"He said the teacher's medical insurance will cover it. We have to pay the airfare and accommodations," he replied.

"Won't that be expensive?" she asked.

"It will give us someplace to go this summer. Let's look at it as our vacation—make the most of a bad hand? Of course, it'll ruin my soft-ball season," Larry grumbled.

CHAPTER 2

THE MAYO CLINIC rises majestically from the desert floor in affluent Scottsdale, Arizona. The clinic sits on the flat Sonoran desert plain surrounded by Saguaro cactus against the background of the Gold River Mountains. The building is an architect's adaptation of a Navaho Renaissance edifice, with earth tone colors.

The first-time visitor is perplexed by no visible parking lots. A small unobtrusive sign points to an underground parking area. Like desert animals that burrow underground to escape the sun's heat, the patients hide their cars in the underground parking cavern. Patients walk from the dark parking area into the sun, squinting like a ground hog emerging from his burrow.

Next patients walk through a huge reception area with Remington prints and other original art. Navaho rugs adorn the walls.

The prostate oncology reception area is stark, painted light green with no decoration on any wall. Chairs in the area are formed plastic with chrome legs. The reading material consists of information regarding external beam therapy (X-ray), radical prostatectomy (surgical removal of prostate), seed implants of radioactive elements, chrytherapy freezing of the prostate and estrogen injections.

Larry sat in the oncology waiting room impatiently thumbing through the medical information on prostate cancer. Suddenly the reception area door burst open and Bill Kibler, a lean six-footer wearing neat carpenter overalls, stumbled up to the receptionist desk.

"Hi," he said. "I'm here for my appointment at nine o'clock. I'm late. I landed in Phoenix last night and I figured I could get here in about ten minutes. But this city is about as big as four counties in Tennessee. It took me a while to get here."

"No problem. Please sign in, Mr. Kibler," said Nurse Carrie. "The doctor's not ready yet."

Bill looked around at the other patients; no one acknowledged him, so he went over to a chair and sat down.

A few minutes later voices could be heard coming down the hall.

"Damn it, Bonnie, I'm ten minutes late. I was supposed to be here at nine. You and your makeup. You're going to make me late for all these appointments. I don't know what the hell you came out here for anyway," said Leo.

The door opened and Leo and Bonnie walked in. Leo was dressed casually in some Gucci loafers, pressed pants and a Polo shirt. He had a handsome, suntanned face, framed by gray hair at the temples. The men looked up and Bonnie immediately caught their eyes. She had a small waist and long blond hair and was big-breasted. Leo had traded in his first wife, Cybil, for a younger wife he could parade in front of other executives. If you want to have the proper corporate image, thought Leo, it doesn't hurt to have a knockout of a wife. Besides being a good wife, she was a smarter, more intelligent woman than Leo had realized.

Leo walked up to the receptionist desk. "I'm Leo Able. I have a nine o'clock appointment."

"Yes, Mr. Able," said Nurse Carrie. "Won't you sit down. I'll tell the doctor you're here."

Carrie opened the door to the chief oncologist's office. Dr. Gee looked up. "They're not happy campers," sang Carrie.

"That's normal," said Dr. Gee.

"But they're reee-ly not happy campers," said Carrie.

"Carrie, have we ever had happy campers? They're all concerned about themselves, their wives, their futures, and their life expectancy. I should think they would be concerned," said Dr. Gee.

"You're the doctor. They're waiting for you," said Nurse Carrie.

"I'm going to treat them as a group. One patient may ask questions that another one would be afraid to ask or forget to ask. And there's always group dynamics. Are they all here?" asked Dr. Gee.

"Yes," said Carrie. "Mr. Kibler was late because he got lost. Mr.

Able was late because his wife, who looks like a movie star, was putting on her makeup. I'll get them all together." She walked out to the waiting room and announced, "Would the following patients please come to conference room four: Leo Able, Larry Nedil, Rev. Allen Kilpatrick, Bill Kibler and Michael Yret."

Five men immediately got up and walked into the conference room. There were looks of concern on their faces as they were called in. They had not expected a group session.

Dr. Gee came into the conference room. "Gentlemen, I'm in charge of the Oncology Department. You came here with a diagnosis of prostate cancer and you're going to have a surgical procedure for the implanting of radioactive isotopes. I'm going to submit a short questionnaire which I request that you fill out. I'll be back in a few minutes to talk to you."

Leo spoke up. "Hey, I paid for private treatment here. I expect that if I pay top dollar, I'm not going to participate in group therapy."

"Give this a chance," said Dr. Gee. "Since all five of your prostate cancer conditions are similar, it might be beneficial if you worked together. Problems are a little easier when you talk them over. Does anyone have any objection to continuing in this manner?"

Leo grumbled, "No." The other four shook their heads. The doctor left. Leo continued to grumble, "Group therapy? Who does he think he is, Oprah Winfrey? The whole world is a support group, transactional therapy or some such crap. I'm an executive of a Fortune 100 company. How could any of you provide support for me?"

"Maybe your fellow executives could be a support group for you," suggested Bill.

"Are you serious?" Leo replied. "My fellow executives would cut my throat. If I don't get this cancer cured quickly, my career is down the drain."

Larry asked incredulously, "You mean your colleagues would publicize your cancer so you'd be fired and they could be promoted?"

"You bet your sweet ass they would," said Leo. "When you're in a Fortune 100 company, it's a jungle. A misstep, a wrong decision, and you're out. If anybody gets the idea that you're sick and it could affect your decisions, you'd have a corporate tombstone on your face in a minute."

"Wow, that's a little rough," said Rev. Allen.

"He's correct; he can't get any help from his co-workers," Michael added. "I'm an accountant for a large company in Amarillo. When you're alive and in good health, they'll stab you in the back. If you have bad health, they'll just nail you to the cross."

"Who's got bad health?" asked Rev. Allen. "All I've got is a little cancer that they tell me they can cure in a minute."

"Hey, Reverend," said Larry, "we all know we're in trouble. We got a diagnosis of prostate cancer. We're not out here for a vacation. We're here because our doctors have all told us we have to have this operation, or the shit's gonna hit the fan."

"You mean that I have the same cancer that you people have?" Leo asked.

Rev. Allen countered, "What do you mean by 'you people'? Are you saying that your cancer is only for white people? Are you suggesting we black people have got a lower class of cancer? Sounds like a racist comment to me!"

"Hey, hey, hey, Reverend, take it easy," said Larry. "Cut him some slack."

"I say again, sounds like racism," said Rev. Allen.

"He's just saying that we're a bunch of plebeian slobs," said Larry. "Every one of us is wondering why the hell we got it and somebody else didn't. You hear this stuff about women—one in eight is gonna get breast cancer, right? When it comes to men, five out of ten are gonna get prostate cancer. What's the big deal? Women have all kind of support groups. The other day I saw where some famous model had bared her breasts on television, reminding women to have breast cancer examinations."

"Do you think Sylvester Stallone will expose his nut sack to remind us men to go have a prostate cancer examination?" asked Bill.

"Not on prime time television," commented Michael.

Leo, Bill and Larry laughed loudly. Everyone relaxed a little. Even Leo seemed a little less hostile.

Dr. Gee came back. "Have any of you answered the question-naires?" They hadn't. "Okay, we'll get the questionnaires later. All of you are worried and you should be. Medically I will do all I can. Your chances are good, but even if the procedure is a success, you will never be the same. Some friends will desert you. Don't be upset. They are running from reality, not from you." There was dead silence in the room. "My nurse is going to come in and talk with you." The doctor immediately left the room.

Carrie walked in, and she announced, "We're going to talk about self-catheterization."

Rev. Allen said, "I don't know what catheterization is."

The nurse very politely continued, "I know you're going to be a little squeamish about this. Let me explain. After you have the operation, sometimes the opening to the urinary bladder swells, and you can't void your urine."

Bill turned to Michael for a translation.

"It means you can't piss," whispered Michael. Bill nodded.

Carrie, undaunted, explained that after the operation there would be a Foley catheter temporarily inserted in the penis. In about five percent of the cases, there could be a problem with emptying the bladder. "In order to release you from the hospital, but to prevent you from having to go to an emergency room and wait two or three hours, we're going to teach you the process of self-catheterization," she said.

"Now, to do this you use a catheterization tube, which can be placed in a bag or even right into a commode." She held up a catheterization kit, which consists of a hollow plastic tube about one-eighth of an inch in diameter and eighteen inches long ending in a clear plastic bag. "You take the tip of the tube, put a little Vaseline or K-Y Jelly on it, insert it into the penis and ease it up to the urinary bladder—"

"I'm gonna what?" Larry asked.

"Bull!" Leo exclaimed.

"No way," said Michael.

"Like hell," Bill said.

There was silence for about three seconds, and then Rev. Allen added, "Screw that!"

Everyone in the room looked at the Reverend. Rev. Allen realized the effect of his language and blanched slightly. "I'm sorry," he said.

They all took a deep breath and yelled, "We ain't doing that!"

Undeterred in her duty, Carrie handed out the catheterization kits. She then told the men that they were to step into the adjacent dressing rooms and that she would be around to assist each one of them on an individual basis.

Bill said, "You mean I'm going to take my pants off in that room. And you're going to come in and see if I do this right?"

"Yes." Carrie nodded sweetly.

Bill immediately reddened from his neck to his ears. "I'll j-just go in and see how this is done."

Leo said, "I hope you got a tube that's at least eighteen inches long because I will require that much."

Rev. Allen brought him back to earth. "The only way you're gonna need eighteen inches is if you stick it in your ass."

Michael and Larry laughed. Carrie stifled her laughter. Leo reddened considerably and went into the dressing room.

Nurse Carrie went into Larry's room. Larry was clearly heard yelling, "Hey, that hurts."

"Do it carefully," said Carrie.

"You can bet on that," said Larry

"Now you've got the idea," said Carrie. "Use a little more K-Y Jelly and work it up slowly and carefully. That's good."

Carrie walked to Leo's room, "Ouch, damn it," said Leo. "Why do I have to do this?"

Carrie heard him and walked in. "Would you like someone else to just ram it up there?" asked Carrie.

"No, I'll do it," said Leo.

"Real easily," said Carrie, "like porcupines making love."

Leo laughed. "Okay, I think I got it."

"All right," said Carrie.

Rev. Allen shouted, "I hope there aren't any video cameras in here. Medical reason or not, how would I explain this to my congregation?"

Carrie walked over to the next dressing room. "Mr. Kibler."

There was no answer. "Mr. Kibler," said Carrie, a little louder.

"Yes, ma'am," came Bill's voice.

"How are you doing in there?" said Carrie.

"I'm doing my best," said Bill.

"I've got to come in and see how you're doing." She eased into Bill's dressing room.

Bill was almost in tears. "I just can't do this," he said.

"Look, Mr. Kibler. I know you're very squeamish about this, but you have to work it through. If you don't, we won't be able to let you out of the hospital for three or four days. Now you don't want to stay in the hospital for three or four days, do you?" said Carrie.

"No, ma'am," said Bill.

"Okay. Now put the jelly on the end of the tip and very slowly ease it into your penis. It doesn't hurt," said Carrie.

"Do I really have to do this?" said Bill.

"Yes," said Carrie, "you do, or we won't release you from the hospital. Now, just do it slowly but steadily."

Bill made a serious attempt, and he was successful the first time.

"You see, Mr. Kibler. The problem isn't doing it. The problem is worrying about doing it," said Carrie.

"Yes, ma'am. Thank you very much," said Bill. "You won't tell the others will you."

Carrie smiled. "No, I won't tell the others."

"Mr. Yret, how are you doing?" Carrie asked.

"I'm doing okay, ma'am. Once you get by the thought of doing it, it's really not that much of a problem," said Michael.

"Please show me Mr. Yret," asked Nurse Carrie.

"Really do I have to?" said Michael.

Carrie walked into Michael's dressing room. "Mr. Yret, you haven't taken the catheter out of the package."

"What's the use—I'm not any good at this. I wasn't able to take care of my wife. Illness frightens me. I am totally inept when it comes to just dispensing aspirin!" Michael said.

"Mr. Yret, you have to do this. The tube is strange and it will tingle, but it doesn't hurt. Just use the jelly and insert it. Notice the tip is not pointed; it's round. Now please try it," urged Carrie.

"Yes, ma'am." Michael carefully inserted the tube and worked it to the bladder. "May I take it out now?"

"Of course, then do it one more time, Mr. Yret, and you're through," said Carrie.

After about fifteen minutes, everyone dressed and returned to the conference room.

Carrie said, "That wasn't as hard as you thought, was it? Actually, it's fairly easy to accomplish. All of you should be proud at how easily you learned to catheterize yourselves."

"That was not on my list of life's goals. I'm not going to do it to anybody else," snapped Leo.

Rev. Allen, anxious to take affront at anything said, "Oh, does that have some kind of a meaning?"

Larry spoke up. "Hey, Reverend, do you wanna do it to him?"

The Reverend immediately responded, "Hell, no."

"Then it doesn't mean anything, does it?" said Larry.

"Calm down," Nurse Carrie ordered. "Look, we're only talking about self-catheterization here. It appears that you've all been married, and there is no sexual preference issue here."

"You got that right," said Bill.

Michael said, "One thing about prostate—cancer, women don't get it. It's one of the few things we have all to ourselves."

"Yeah, I got some ball-busting female executives at work who would like to take my job. I'd be glad to give 'em my dose of it," said Leo.

Carrie cautioned them that the doctor would be in to see them shortly. If they wanted to have any discussions about their cancers, they were to feel free to talk to each other. She left the room. There was a silence for a few minutes, then Michael asked, "Bill, how did you find out that you had cancer?"

"I'm a carpenter, and been doing framing work on houses for about thirty years. About four months ago I would go to work, and after two or three hours, I'd be tired. Finally I went to a doctor. You know how doctors are. After they get through with everything else, they pull on that big rubber glove, lubricate it with Vaseline, and shove it up your butt." He indicated with his hand.

"I know how that is," said Larry. "I've gotten to the point where I go into a physiological pucker when anybody walks by me with a rubber glove on 'em."

"Anyway, after that examination, the doctor said I had a mysterious lump and they found it was cancer. Then I ended up here. One day, I was tired but happy—next day, I was tired and scared to death."

"I didn't have any problem with loss of energy," Leo said. "I went to the company doctor for a physical so I could be promoted. The S.O.B. told my boss I had prostate cancer before he told me. I'm worried they won't promote me because I have cancer. I hope this doctor is good."

Rev. Allen spoke up. "I sure got a surprise. I went in to take a physical for a credit life insurance policy for a building loan for our church. I went in as happy as could be. After the life insurance physical I found out I had cancer. Now the bank won't make the loan. They're afraid that if I die, the congregation will go to other churches and the tithes will go down. It has really been a shock."

"I was playing softball and got hit in the groin," said Larry. "I went to see the doctor and they gave me the great glove with the Vaseline treatment. They called me later and said I had cancer, but it wasn't caused by softball. If it wasn't for softball, I never would have discovered it. I go back to teaching school in the fall with two years to retirement. I enjoy teaching. What about you, Michael?"

Michael sat quietly listening to the other people's problems. "I went to the doctor to get a blood test for a marriage license. The doctor also did a PSA test. He told me I had cancer. A biopsy confirmed it."

"Wow, did you tell your fiancée?" Larry asked.

"Yes," said Michael, "and she canceled the wedding."

"What the hell would she do that for?" asked Leo.

"She said she had buried one husband, and she didn't want to lose another," said Michael.

"She actually said that?" Larry asked.

"How does she know that?" asked Bill. "Are we really in bad trouble?"

"Do you really think the doctors are telling us straight?" Leo asked.

"I told my fiancée that the doctor said it was treatable," said Michael. "She said even if you don't die of cancer, you'll be impotent and incontinent."

"What's incontinent?" asked Bill.

"Incontinent is when you can't hold your water and it drips all the time and you have to wear diapers," said Michael.

"What causes that?" asked Bill.

"Sometimes it's the operation," said Leo.

"The one that we're going to go through here?" Bill asked.

"That's right," said Michael.

"I have enough problems just getting older. I don't want to complicate it even more," said Allen.

"I don't think impotence will be a problem for me," said Leo.

"I don't know," said Michael. "It was quite a shock to go from planning a wedding to changing my will."

A silence fell over the room.

"Do you think I'll have these problems?" asked Bill.

"The purpose of this radiation implant is to avoid the surgical removal of the nerves which cause impotence and incontinence," said Larry.

"Sure hope these doctors are right," said Leo. "What's the use of having a wife if you're impotent. Do you think they'll stay married to us? Hell, sex brought us together. It's the glue that keeps us together."

"It would ruin my self-esteem," said Rev. Allen, "but I will always love and support my wife and she will always be there for me."

"It's too late to worry about it now," said Bill.

The silence was broken when Dr. Gee walked in. "Gentlemen, if you will, complete these questionnaires. You will have your radiation implants tomorrow at seven, eight, nine, ten and eleven. After you wake up, you will experience some mild discomfort."

Bill said, "I heard that before when I broke my hand."

"We will give you an appropriate painkiller as necessary to relieve some of the discomfort. When you wake up, you'll have a catheter inserted in you. You will remain in the hospital overnight and be discharged about ten the following morning. You'll all meet back here in this room around one p.m., two days from now. We will review everything with you."

They all shook hands with each other.

Forty-eight hours later, all five returned to the conference room. Leo introduced Bonnie to Larry and Sarah. Allen presented Lisa. Bill introduced Sylvia. The wives looked a little haggard, as none of them had gotten much sleep. The men were happy. They were alive, sedated and relieved to have completed the ordeal.

The five men treated each other as old comrades who had come through a war experience. Bill said, "I'm sure glad that's over with."

The men, as giddy and exuberant as they could be, perhaps due to pain killers, began to exchange information.

Leo said, "I want to go back to work. I hope to become chief executive officer now that this problem is behind me."

Larry said, "I'm going back to teach. I have about two more years to retirement."

"My congregation is waiting for me, and I'll be busy building the addition on the church," Rev. Allen said.

"As soon as I'm able to do the hard labor, I'm going back to being a carpenter foreman," Bill said.

Michael said, "I'm going back on the job."

"I hope everything turns out well with your fiancée," said Larry.

"Thanks," said Michael. "My first wife died and I don't have any children. It looks like Susan is not going to marry me, so I'm not even going to have stepchildren."

"Don't give up on it," said Leo. "It's our dreams and ambitions that keep us alive and vital. If we give up on our dreams, we give up on our lives."

Rev. Allen stated, "One of my dreams has always been to lead a civil rights march of one hundred thousand people. I'm just a small-time minister. The pinnacle of my career would be leading a march that made a change."

Bill said, "One of the things I want to do is to build Houses for Humanity, for people who can't afford them. All my life I've worked on framing houses for rich people. I want to build houses for people who don't have the money."

Leo said, "I want to go back to work and become the CEO of a corporation and make something happen." He turned and said, "Who's the president of General Motors?" The other four men in the room said they didn't know. He asked, "Who is the president of Chrysler Corporation?"

Bill, Michael and Larry answered, "Lee Iacoca."

Leo corrected them. "No, he hasn't been president for fifteen years. People remember him because he was the president of a corporation and made an impact on the auto industry. I want to be on the cover of *Fortune* magazine." Leo turned to Larry. "Larry, what's your dream?"

"I've done as much teaching as I can. I'm going to retire. The students come in every year. It's like an assembly line. They sit down in

September, I teach 'em the course, and they leave in June. I've been doing that for thirty years. Education from the teacher's perspective is an assembly line of people to whom we give information the same way that they sew upholstery buttons on an automobile. What I'd like to do is play softball. I want to play in a world championship game and contribute. But I'm not good enough. I don't think the cancer is going to make me any better," he groused.

Dr. Gee came into the conference room. "Your operations and surgeries appear to have gone very well. You will have to return in sixty days for evaluation. If the radiation implants were successful, the cancerous tumors will have shrunk. I'll see you then."

They all sat quietly after he left. Rev. Allen approached Leo and said, "I hope to see you back here. I hope you get the promotion."

Larry turned to Bill, "I hope that you can get back on your feet and keep up the work. I don't know what I can do about helping you on the Houses for Humanity, but I wish you the best of luck."

Bill said, "Larry, good luck on your job of school teaching. After you retire you'll be able to put a team together." They shook hands firmly and then Michael spoke to all of them.

"Look, gentlemen," said Michael. "I'll see you all again in sixty days. I know all of you have families, but I don't have anyone. If something happens to me, I wish you'd remember me." said Michael.

"Don't worry about that," said Leo. "It's going to be okay."

Bill said, "Mike, don't worry. We'll be there for you."

CHAPTER 3

LEO STEPPED OUT of the marble lobby of his opulent Fifth Avenue co-operative as the uniformed doorman opened the door and motioned for his limousine. Wearing an immaculate dark blue Hickey Freeman tailored suit and carrying a briefcase, Leo ordered the chauffeur, "Take me to the office." He'd risen early this morning to be in the office at seven-thirty. The limousine pulled up to the office building, and he immediately took the express elevator to the forty-eighth floor.

On his floor were the presidents of the different divisions of QRX Corporation. With growth and conglomeration of assorted enterprises, the corporation had decided that in order to attract public interest, it would put a "Q" in front of its name. It would have "inquisitive attractiveness" to investors on the New York Stock Exchange.

The elevator bell rang for the forty-eighth floor and Leo walked out. Even at that hour, a receptionist greeted him quite spiritedly. "Good morning, Mr. Able. There are messages on your desk."

"Is Rita here?" he asked.

"Yes, she is. She knew that you'd be in early this morning. She'll bring you up to date."

Rita, his forty-two-year-old administrative assistant, was waiting for him.

"Good morning, Mr. Able. You've got a lot of messages on your desk. Mr. Williams wants to see you at nine this morning. He'd like an interim report on the operations of your division, your assessment of the future potential in this division and a list of promotable subordinates who have potential for larger, more fulfilling jobs within this division," said Rita.

"Thanks," said Leo.

Rita added, "The CEO realized that you were out of town last week, but he wants your input today."

Leo was not perturbed. His staff had made all the computations and had estimated future projections. He was expecting this call. The presidents of the divisions were on the forty-eighth floor. The forty-ninth floor held the three higher executive positions of chief operating officer, chief financial officer and chief management officer. The CEO had the fiftieth floor to himself. Mr. Williams had been president of the same division as Leo. Leo's next step would be either chief management officer or chief operations officer.

Leo commented to Rita, "If the COO wants to go home and spend time with his wife he, can do so. He doesn't deserve to be in the corporation anymore. If that's the way he feels, he ought to be let go and I'm certainly willing to step in and assume that position."

Rita, who had been Leo's administrative assistant for about fifteen years, said, "It would be nice to share a floor with only two other officers."

Leo glanced in the mirror. "I'm going in to read all the messages and reports."

The only flaw in his presentation was the list of promotable subordinates within his division, which accounted for approximately $1.8 billion worth of revenue, of QRX's total of $5.9 billion. The president of a division that accounted for one-third of the corporate revenue was certainly an indispensable man. Leo, who had operations experience in one-third of the company's enterprises, would be a logical candidate for the chief operations officer. The other six divisions consisted of the Automotive Parts Division, Hand Tool Division, Machinery Division, Trucking Division, Textiles, and the smallest of all, the Leisure Division.

As he reviewed his subordinates, he realized that if he were to be promoted to the chief operations officer, he wanted a good and loyal friend as president of the Radio and Computer Division. Technology in the radio, television, computer and satellite products was evolving so rapidly it was hard to predict what the future was going to be. Going to

Las Vegas and playing craps is not quite as risky as being involved in this Radio and Computer Division. You didn't know what the Federal Communications Commission was going to do. You didn't know what your competitors were going to do. Just when you thought you had a good market share, someone came out with a better chip. He had encouraged the growth in this area by supporting a new, updated computer. One of the vice-presidents in his division, that Wharton MBA Margaret Novak, had argued that the company make no changes to its products, sell all of its inventory, and wait three years for new developments. She had gotten a hearing from the Chief Financial Officer, Tom Rebul, who was afraid of the aggressive, good-looking MBA.

Leo had been successful in suppressing her ideas. He decided that to eliminate any future problems with her, he would suggest her reassignment to President of the Leisure Division. It only had one hundred million dollars in sales, obviously a dead-end job for her. He would not have a disloyal subordinate. He could count on Stan Lunk to continue the Computer Division in the same vein.

Leo chuckled to himself as he thought about transferring that conservative Margaret to be president of the Leisure Division while he was promoted to COO. He snorted to himself, "As long as I am COO, she will be at that Leisure Division, and she will never get out. If she is going to get promoted, she is going to have to do it at another company."

Smiling to himself and smug with his decisions, he was interrupted by Rita. "Mr. Able, you're meeting with Mr. Williams in five minutes." He gathered up his papers, checked himself in the mirror and walked briskly to the elevator. Within fifteen seconds, he emerged on the fiftieth floor and said good morning to the receptionist.

She answered brightly, "Good morning, Mr. Able. Go right in. Mr. Williams is waiting for you."

Leo strode confidently into the open office. Mr. Williams was sitting not at his desk, but at an adjacent burled mahogany table in his spacious office. It was a table for twelve people, and gathered around it were Mr. Williams; the Chief Financial Officer, Tom Rebul; his vice-president, Stan Lunk; and the tall, willowy Margaret Novak.

"Good morning," said Mr. Williams. "I appreciate your coming up here." He extended his hand. He was cordial and polite as always. He hadn't obtained the job of Chief Executive Officer of QRX without brains, savvy and aggressiveness. He had the demeanor of a snake oil salesman and the silver tongue of a politician. "Nice to have you back. How do you feel?"

"I wasn't a happy camper but I'm okay now."

"Good, glad to hear that. I'm always glad to see that our executives have a chance for an occasional weekend off. This rat race gets to you after awhile. Did you prepare those reports that I requested on your division?"

"Yes, sir, I did. I have the reports here for the last six months, an interim report for this quarter, my projections for the remainder of the fiscal year and my projections for next year."

"Thank you, Leo. I appreciate your work," said Mr. Williams as he pointed to a chair. Leo sat down obediently.

"Thank you, that's no problem. My staff worked on it this weekend, and I had an opportunity to review it this morning," said Leo.

"Leo, are these reports accurate?" asked Mr. Williams.

"I can tell you that I have researched these records. I am happy with them. I think the projections we make are realistic. I don't think you'll have any questions from the New York Stock Exchange brokers, or the Securities Exchange Commission. If we operate aggressively, we can meet these projections. If these projections are met, it would mean at least one additional dollar of earnings per share, assuming that the rest of the divisions operate the same as they did in the past. I'm optimistic about this, and I think that the company should do well. I think our division has done exceptionally well."

"Yes, it has," agreed Mr. Williams, "but is there anything you're not telling us about the Mayo Clinic?"

"No." Leo looked a little perturbed. He wondered what prompted the question. If he was being promoted and the Chief Financial Officer was there, why was Margaret there? "I was under the impression that the Chief Operations Officer had decided to retire because his wife was ill. It's my position that if that happens, I should be next in line for that job. I can increase the corporate profits throughout the other divisions, making the corporation more profitable in the future."

"Yes, I think you could, but what reports do you have from the clinic?" asked Mr. Williams.

"I've received radiation and external beam therapy and radioactive implants. As you can see I'm perfectly healthy today," said Leo.

"Are you going to be perfectly healthy tomorrow?" questioned Mr. Williams.

"I have to go back in sixty days for a routine follow-up," said Leo, "but the odds are nineteen out of twenty, I'll have no further problem. Once a year I'll have an ultrasound—that's a follow-up procedure—but I've been assured by my doctor that there's been no real problem—nothing that will impact upon my job performance."

"Or even your family life?" Mr. Williams asked.

"Definitely not, sir," Leo said with a smile.

"Leo, this is the toughest thing that a Chief Executive Officer has to do. I've got to look out for the company. I've reviewed this situation, and I'm going to make a change. The company has a lot of time and investment in you, and you have amply rewarded the company's investment many times over. Still we must be prepared. The brokers on the stock exchanges don't care whether an executive is sick or well, happy or unhappy,—all they want to know is how much profit this corporation is going to make.

"I know," said Leo.

"Here is the position that we're in. With a $1.8 billion division, I would be remiss in my duties and subject to admonition by the Board of Directors if I didn't take into consideration the fact that you have cancer. While nineteen times out of twenty you would have no problem, at this point I must inform you that I'm going to make a reassignment."

Leo sat silently waiting for the other shoe to drop.

"Now Leo, don't worry. Even though your responsibilities will be decreased significantly, there will be no decrease in your base pay. You will get the bonus that would be coming to you from running your division. I am going to announce a reassignment for personal reasons, and you will be assigned as the new president of the Leisure Division."

"What!" exclaimed Leo. "The Leisure Division has less than one hundred million dollars in sales, and my division has done $1.8 billion. I have put this division on track for $2.5 billion worth of revenue in the next twenty-four months if you follow the program that I have laid out. You're putting me out to pasture!"

"Now, now, Leo," counseled Mr. Williams. "Your subordinates will realize that you are a fine, dedicated corporate employee who, even though he has cancer, is willing to come to work every day. One of your subordinates, Margaret Novak, will be the new COO. And I'm sure you've trained her with the business acumen, aggressiveness and jungle savvy necessary to succeed in this business. This company owes you a debt of gratitude. Everyone in the company will understand that you have stepped down, on a short-term basis, while this medical problem is being resolved."

"What about my salary?" said Leo.

"You're not going to lose any money," said Mr. Williams.

"No," said Leo. "But I'm not going to get any more either. I'm going to be frozen because no matter what I do in the Leisure Division, I can't increase the revenue like I can in my division."

"Leo, I'm sorry. My decision is final. I hope you will think this over and agree that this is in the best interest of the company. Please reflect on my comments. In a calmer, more deliberate time, you'll agree that I'm correct. I'd like you to come back and talk with me in about one week. And, Leo...thank you very much." With that Mr. Williams stood up and shook his hand and patted Leo on the shoulder.

The Chief Financial Officer, Tom Rebul, shook his hand once again with the look of an undertaker who was sizing him up for a casket. "Very, very sorry to hear about this," Rebul said in a way that sent chills through Leo's bones.

Unbelievable, Leo thought, Tom Rebul thinks I'm going to die within the next seven days. Margaret rose to shake his hand. "I'm sorry, Leo." He shook her hand, then, quickly removed his and stormed out of the office.

Fifteen seconds later he burst into his office. Rita looked up expectantly, "Did you get the promotion?"

"No," he said, "I got demoted." Leo slammed his office door with a deafening thud.

About two minutes later there was a knock on the door and Stan Lunk came in. "Leo, are you okay?"

"Stan," he said, "what am I going to do? I'm the president of the Leisure Division. It has been a home for incompetent, brothers-in-law of executives and directors. The only thing it has is a golfing subsidiary, which provides a business reason for the executives to fly all over the

United States to watch golf tournaments at company expense. What a demotion. I don't know what I'm going to tell Bonnie."

"She will understand," said Stan.

"I don't," said Leo. "Do you want to come with me? We've been a team for almost twenty-five years."

"Sorry, Leo, I've been appointed the new president of the Computer Division, and I think I deserve it."

"You certainly do," said Leo. "I told Mr. Williams you were my first choice."

"That's not what Margaret said. She claimed she was your first choice."

"No way would I have recommended her for promotion. She was last choice," exploded Leo.

"Thanks, Leo," said Stan edging to the door. "If I can help you in the future let me know." Rita walked in, allowing Stan to get out of the way of Leo's wrath.

"You've been with me for fifteen years, Rita. What are you going to do? There's still going to be an assistant's job in the Leisure Division."

Rita smiled sweetly. "No, I'm going to stay here. I know this division, and I'm going to be the secretary for the new COO."

"In that case, you'll have to work for that uptight Margaret Novak. Mr. Williams appointed her COO."

"Oh," she said, smiled sweetly and walked to her desk.

He stayed in his office another five minutes. He told Rita, "I'm going to have a drink and go home."

"But Mr. Able," she said, "it's only 10:15."

He walked out the door.

Immediately after he left, Rita picked up the phone. "Miss Novak, please. Miss Novak, this is Rita. I'd just like to tell you that Mr. Able left early today. I told Mr. Able that I would be staying on with the new COO."

"Thank you, Rita. I appreciate your loyalty in this regard. If it wasn't for you, no one in the corporation would have known that he had cancer. I will definitely recommend that you get a very large bonus for the work that you have performed for the corporation this year," said Margaret.

"Thank you," cooed Rita.

"How did he take the demotion to the Leisure Division?" said Margaret.

"He was absolutely outraged. He couldn't believe it."

"Do you think he'll quit...get out of the company forever?"

"I don't know. When I hear from him, I'll let you know," Rita answered.

A slightly drunk Leo walked into his Fifth Avenue building at approximately two o'clock. It was imperceptible in his walk, but the doorman knew he'd been drinking from the overly friendly manner in which Leo greeted him. Leo opened the door to his co-operative and walked into a very large, spacious living room.

Bonnie, who was on the phone, hung up and walked over to him, "You've been drinking. Were you celebrating the promotion?"

"No," he yelled, "I got demoted. They think I'm going to die of cancer. When I asked Rita if she would go with me, she said no, she was going to work for the next COO. The next COO is going to be Margaret Novak. Can you imagine that?"

Bonnie, who had more street sense than Leo, said, "How could you be so dumb! If Rita is not going to go with you, she made a deal with Margaret before this thing came up. How can you be so naive! What are you going to do?"

"What can I do? I can't deny that I have cancer. The corporation is afraid that I'm either going to be incapacitated or die. They don't want me in charge of a very valuable division. They've put me in the Leisure Division."

"You always said that thing was a Humpty Dump division and they ought to sell it off," said Bonnie.

"Now I'm in charge of it," said Leo. "They said they wouldn't cut my salary. They would give me my bonus for my share of what I've done this year. In the future my bonus will depend upon the Leisure Division profits," said Leo.

"The Leisure Division doesn't have profits!" Bonnie exclaimed.

"I know, but there's nothing I can do about that now except go have a drink," said Leo.

"You've already had several drinks," said Bonnie.

"I need several more," said Leo.

"What are we going to tell our friends?" asked Bonnie.

"When I go back to the company I'll see if I have any friends," said Leo.

Bonnie gave him a hug. Leo tried to walk away but Bonnie just held on tighter. "We can survive this, the cancer and everything else that is thrown at us...together, Leo."

"Easy for you to say. I got the cancer," snarled Leo as he disengaged from Bonnie's embrace.

"This is just like the computer chip fiasco," said Bonnie.

"What are you talking about?" asked Leo.

"Remember when the first one hundred thousand QRX System 7 computers had those bad chips? Everyone at the company wanted you fired. You said to replace all the chips or give the consumers their money back. The CFO, Reeble, wanted your head on a platter. Mr. Williams said it was your funeral," said Bonnie.

"I remember," said Leo smiling. "We replaced all the chips at a cost of seven million dollars. We sold 550,000 more computers because customers knew we would stand behind them."

"Exactly. You turned a costly problem into a PR bonanza and made the CFO look bad. He never forgave you. He had a chance to get even today and he took it," commented Bonnie.

"I'd like to get even with him," said a grinning Leo.

"That's not the way," said Bonnie. "Some other company may offer you a job."

"Who would offer me a job?" said a disgusted Leo. "I suppose you'll leave me, too."

Bonnie rushed over and hugged Leo. "No! No! I love you. God knows you can be the most exasperating human being that ever lived, but there is a charming little streak of good in you which I find irresistible. You have been working for lean corporate pirates whose only allegiance is the bottom line. They think that employees are just an inconvenience to the bottom line."

"Ease off the liberal crap," shouted Leo.

"Face the situation—you have cancer. It's in remission; get on with the rest of our lives!" shouted Bonnie.

The room was quiet. Finally, Leo said, "I'm sorry," then he smiled. "When my pay goes down, so does Cybil's alimony check. I know she will scream."

"I'm going to punch her in the mouth!" exclaimed Bonnie.

"Not while I am alive. She will sue me," said Leo.

"Shall I start typing up a resume for you?" asked Bonnie.

"Not yet. I've got to call the kids and tell them I have been reassigned. I don't want them to read it first in the *Wall Street Journal*."

One week later, Leo walked into Mr. Williams' office on the fiftieth floor. He dreaded going, but just in the few days he'd had off, he appreciated the relief from some of the office politics. He didn't have to be nice to his fellow presidents. He didn't have to lick the boots of the Chief Financial Officer. He didn't have to ingratiate himself with Mr. Williams as he had done in the past. He could be straightforward and honest.

"Leo, have you looked over the reports on the Leisure Division?" said Mr. Williams.

"Yes, I have. I've been with this company for almost thirty years. I was not happy when we purchased this company fifteen years ago. We've used this division as an excuse for officers, executives and important shareholders to watch golf tournaments and play golf courses at corporate expense," said Leo.

"Easy, Leo, the Board of Directors would not like to hear that," said Mr. Williams.

"I think the Board of Directors is well aware because they have used, or even abused, that privilege," said Leo.

"Okay, Leo, I understand. It's true that the division hasn't made much profit because four or five million dollars in plane and transportation expenses is charged to that division each year."

"Is that going to continue in the future?" asked Leo.

"Why do you ask?" said Mr. Williams.

"If those corporate expenses are going to be charged against my division, then it won't show a profit. Five million dollars of golf excursion expenses on a one hundred million dollar company is five percent of revenue. If the Leisure Division is going to be used as a corporate fringe benefit, then the expenses should be charged to the corporate headquarters or spread uniformly throughout the divisions."

"Leo, we can't do that. If we do that, the Securities and Exchange Commission will be down here investigating us," said Mr. Williams.

"All right, sir," Leo said, "It's a problem for me because it means that the first five million dollars of profit is really going down the drain. I would like to see a change made in this area."

"That's not your decision to make. That's the way that division has been run for the last fifteen years. That's the way it's going to be run in the future," snapped Mr. Williams.

"Yes, sir."

"All right, have you looked at the division?" asked Mr. Williams.

"Yes, sir. The Leisure Division has a lawn chair company, a sportswear company and a metal division which makes golf clubs, baseball bats and gloves that we sell throughout the United States." said Leo.

"Leo, I want you to set up your corporate staff in Atlanta, Georgia," Mr. Williams said.

"You mean I'm to relocate from the corporate headquarters?" Leo asked.

"One of the division procedures was to keep the executives up here so that we could keep an eye on them. I feel it would be best if you would locate at the division headquarters in Atlanta. You'll have to relocate, but living expenses in Atlanta are cheaper than in New York. Your pay will stay the same. Your bonuses will be proportional to the profits of your division. I realize that's going to be a severe drop. I wish you the best of luck," said Mr. Williams.

With that Leo got up. He was leaving the headquarters. He turned at the door. "Mr. Williams, my plans for the Radio and Computer division predicted that if the company were going to make money, it would have to expand into the new products. I strongly recommended that the corporation expand its research."

"I've talked that over with Margaret Novak. She feels that we'll make more money this year if we don't put any money into upgrading a computer and take our chance for the future with an entirely new product."

"But Mr. Williams, if we don't put aside money for research for the following years, we'll have no market share two years from now," said Leo.

"Leo, that decision is final. It is not a concern of yours at this time," said Mr. Williams.

Moving executives from one headquarters to another was a common event in the QRX Corporation. Moving and relocating Leo to

Atlanta was accomplished in twenty-eight days.

In two weeks, the relocation service had previewed, for Leo and Bonnie, about seven houses in Atlanta, in the five hundred thousand dollar price range. They were quite happy with the third house they found in the Buckhead area. Compared to New York prices, Atlanta properties were a steal.

Without the traffic congestion of New York, he could drive from his home to the division headquarters in approximately fifteen minutes. He began to appreciate the freedom of not living in New York.

The division headquarters consisted of a textile company, which bought T-shirts and imprinted sports logos on them, and the sporting divisions, which sold running, jogging, biking and mountain shoes and baseball and softball gloves to the general public, high schools and colleges.

The company manufactured composite metal shafts, added rubber grips from a company in Akron, Ohio, and shipped them to golf club manufacturers. As always Leo was involved in R&D. There was a small R&D laboratory in Atlanta involved in metallurgical testing on golf equipment.

On his second visit to the R&D lab, the metallurgical engineer, a Georgia Tech grad, was working on a new composite golf club shaft. "Mr. Able, this is the most fantastic composition metal shaft we have ever made."

"What is it made of?" said Leo.

"It's an alloy of titanium, depleted uranium, and reprocessed tritium with a three dimensional carbon-graphite weave," said the engineer.

"Isn't it radioactive?" asked a skeptical Leo.

"No, it's depleted."

"Is it expensive?" asked Leo.

"No, since they're dismantling nuclear war heads, there's plenty around," explained the engineer.

"Does it explode?" Leo asked.

"Just against gold balls. An average person can put this shaft on a metal driver and knock a golf ball about five hundred and fifty yards."

"With a regular golf ball?" asked Leo.

"Yes, any standard golf ball; this new metal shaft is unbelievable," said the engineer.

"We could sell that to every golfer. It would be a great product," said Leo.

"No, sir, we can't."

"Why not?" asked Leo.

"The golf courses and balls are all regulated by the golfing associations. This new composite metal shaft with this driver would blow the game of golf away. You can hit five hundred and fifty yards with it and the golfing associations won't permit it."

"What the hell good is it then?" asked Leo.

"I don't know. We've come up with a great invention but we can't use it in golf. Baseball is all we can use it for," said the engineer.

"You can't use it in baseball. The major leagues use wooden bats," said Leo.

"Yes, sir, but the big market would be hardball bats which are all aluminum from peewee league all the way up to college baseball, and of course softball bats," said the engineer.

"Have you made any softball bats?" Leo asked.

"No," said the engineer.

"Are you sure that we can't use this metal in golf clubs?" Leo asked.

"I'm dead sure. The use of this metal driver in golf clubs would change golfing—you'd have to have eight hundred yard par fours. It's easier to outlaw the golf clubs than it is to change all the golf courses," said the engineer.

"Yeah, good point. Keep working on it for baseball and softball bats and see what develops," said Leo.

"Sure thing, Mr. Able. We'll try to have one on your desk in about a week," said the engineer.

As Leo went home he reflected on the month and a half since he'd been to the Mayo Clinic. In two weeks he'd be on his way back. He felt like an All-American football player who suddenly was forced to sit on the bench. He enjoyed the calmness, although he definitely wanted to get back into the game.

He got into his car, singing to himself as he drove home through the suburban Atlanta traffic, which would be considered light by New York standards. He reminded himself that he had to return to the Mayo Clinic.

CHAPTER 4

LARRY AND SARAH lived halfway up the block in a suburban Atlanta neighborhood. They had moved into the one-and-a-half story house when it was a brand new neighborhood. For many of the young couples in the neighborhood thirty years ago, this had been a starter home. They had since moved on to the more fashionable northern suburbs. Some had moved into pricey homes with security gates in the next county.

But, Larry and Sarah loved this neighborhood where they had raised three children. All had graduated from college and two had received graduate degrees. Larry and Sarah were proud that none of the children had to borrow money to get through college.

After the kids moved away, Larry and Sarah had thought about moving, but inertia set in. The neighborhood refilled with younger families, and soon they were the only couple in the neighborhood over fifty.

Larry and Sarah prided themselves on being active. Both jogged or walked the neighborhood, although it was hard for them to find neighbors with whom they could jog. Larry was getting old and couldn't keep up the pace with his younger neighbors. Sarah walked a good bit. When she walked with the other neighbors, the conversations spanned at least one, if not two, generations.

They contentedly thought about the grandchildren, Larry's retirement in two years, and of course, Larry's mania for senior softball. All of the sons had grown up on baseball and then softball. Larry had enjoyed ball all his life. There was a fifteen-year hiatus when he wasn't able to play, as he was involved with coaching his sons' T-ball, little league, junior and senior league ball teams.

Larry fondly remembered the time spent coaching or watching his sons play ball. He also enjoyed the senior citizens who could run, hit and throw a softball. Sarah tolerated it with smug amusement. After all, it certainly wasn't a bad activity and it cost about one-tenth as much as the neighbors who spent around eighty dollars for a round of golf every Saturday.

When they got back from Arizona, there was a notice from the Board of Education for Larry to report for teacher orientation. He had already performed the obligatory revision of lesson plans, safety rules, and certification forms that were required in order to teach students the history of the United States.

The first semester covered 1492 to 1860 and the second semester from 1860 till present day. Larry commented that they'd split American history at the Civil War, presumably, he remarked to Sarah, "because they didn't want Americans fighting over the Christmas vacation break."

He showed Sarah the Board of Education letter, and Monday morning he went to the school where he taught.

The class was entitled "History of the American Frontier." It was known among the students as "Cowboys and Indians".

He began by coordinating tasks (he had some lessons plans) with his teacher's aide. When that was accomplished, he started cleaning up the classroom and getting it dusted off from the summer layoff—readjusting all the pictures and projection equipment and seeing that the new computer was installed.

He told his aide, "If I put a television set in the room and told my students to watch it, some parents might be upset. But if I put a computer in the classroom, connect it up to the World Wide Web and it shows the same movie that was on television, that's education."

The principal's secretary burst into his classroom. "Mr. Nedil, Mr. Nedil."

"Yes." He looked up in mild amusement. The principal's secretary made a trivial announcement sound earth shattering.

"The principal wants to see you in his office right away."

"Why?" he asked.

She shrugged her shoulders.

Larry walked into the principal's office. "You wanted to see me?"

"Yes, I did. Please sit down. Larry, how do you feel?" the principal asked.

"Fine," said Larry.

"No problems?" the principal asked.

"No, sir," said Larry.

"Do you get tired from time to time?" said the principal.

"Well, sure I get tired from time to time. I'm fifty-eight years old," said Larry.

"Do you think you're up to teaching seventeen year olds again?" said the principal.

"Absolutely," said Larry. "I'm up to lecturing them about American history, and hopefully I'm up to motivating them. I know I can make them learn. Most of the kids who come here are interested in education, and it's usually pretty easy."

"Larry, I've got a report here that came from the board's office. You've been out to the Mayo Clinic. The bills are coming in from the oncology department. In order to teach, you have to pass a physical. What is the problem?" demanded the principal.

"I've been diagnosed with prostate cancer," said Larry. "I've had radiation implant procedure. I'm supposed to go back in two months for a checkup. According to the doctors, ninety-five percent of the time there's no problem and it's going to be okay for the next ten years."

"You have cancer and you still intend to teach?" asked the principal.

"Well, sure. What else am I going to do? I've got two more years before retirement," said Larry.

"Now, Larry, you've taken almost no sick leave the last twenty years. You have all kinds of administrative leave. You've been a superior teacher. If you have cancer, why are you going to teach? You could take sick leave for the next two years, get the same amount of pay as if you were working, and then still retire on your regular benefits," said the principal.

"Well, what would I do?" said Larry.

"Of course if you're on sick leave you can't go out and work, but at least you wouldn't have to come here every day," said the principal.

"Is there something the matter with the way I look?" Larry asked.

"No," said the principal.

"Am I able to walk?" Larry asked.

"Yes," said the principal.

"Is there something feeble about my appearance?" asked Larry.

"You have a mustache," said the principal.

"Do you think the students could look at me and know that I had cancer?" Larry asked.

"No," said the principal.

"Are the comments I've made over the years about the teaching profession serious enough that I would be fired?" said Larry.

"Just between you and me, I agree with what you say," said the principal. "When it comes to education, I paraphrase Winston Churchill. 'Never in the history of human events have so many educators with so much money accomplished so little in the education of children,'" said the principal.

"What is the problem? Give me some semblance of a logical explanation!" demanded Larry.

"People have a tendency to view cancer as if it's contagious. You scare people when you say you have cancer," said the principal.

"It's not that I have AIDS, you know," said Larry.

"I know it's not like AIDS. If you had AIDS we couldn't take any action against you. But hell, this is cancer. The board can do anything it wants," said the principal.

"What does the board want?" said Larry.

"The board wants you to go on medical retirement for the next three semesters. At that time you will have put in thirty-two years and get the maximum retirement benefits. I wish I could have the deal that you have. Quit work right now. In three semesters come in and pick up your thirty-two year ring and a full pension. You're the luckiest man on earth," said the principal.

Larry left the principal's office and went home anxious to discuss the latest bombshell with Sarah.

"What are you concerned about? You're going to get full pay, and in three semesters you retire. You were planning to retire anyway," said Sarah.

"But I can't work anywhere else if I'm on sick leave," said Larry.

"Just take it," said Sarah.

Larry walked outside. He thought about retiring now even though he wouldn't get full pay. At least he'd be able to get another job and have something to do. He thought about finishing the final semester and then his dissertation for his doctoral degree. What difference does it make if I get it? Nobody is going to hire me anyway. I can't even get a job as a substitute teacher.

On Wednesday morning he visited the local president of the Teachers' Federation. He explained that he was being forced to retire. After relating his story, the local president looked at him. "What's your complaint? When you started teaching you used to have five courses with thirty kids in them, right?"

Larry said, "Yes."

"And now you have four courses with twenty students in them."

"Yeah," said Larry.

"The number of kids you teach has dropped from one hundred and fifty to eighty."

"Yes," said Larry, still not comprehending.

"The Teachers' Federation got you additional pay, medical benefits and retirement benefits and reduced the number of students approximately forty-five percent. Isn't that correct?"

"Yes," said Larry.

"In addition you have a teacher's aide to move all the chairs, handle the projectors and even grade the tests if you gave true-false or multiple choice tests," said the federation president.

"Most of the time I give essay tests because that's the way students learn to write and to comprehend," said Larry.

"Yes, yes," said the federation president, "but if you gave true-false or multiple choice tests which are furnished by the book manufacturers, you wouldn't even have to do that. If you give true-false or multiple choice tests, it reduces cultural differences."

"I doubt that. I thought that a student should learn to read, comprehend and write," said Larry.

"When it comes to getting students to learn, that's not our job," said the federation president. "That's up to the Board of Education. My job is to see that while you're teaching, you have the minimum number of students, for the maximum amount of pay and benefits. Teaching the students, that's up to the Board of Education. You've got a golden deal. I wish I could take sick leave for the next three semesters and retire with maximum benefits."

Larry sat there, thunderstruck. *It's times like this I wish cancer were contagious.*

Larry realized that he could not buck city hall. He went back to the school, met with the principal, and said, "It appears you're right. There's nothing that I can do."

The principal shook his hand, "You're going to thank me for this. You don't realize what a great deal you've got."

Once again Larry thought, *I really do wish cancer were contagious.*

"Do you have a teacher to take over for me?" said Larry.

"You don't have to worry about that. Take the rest of the afternoon to clear out your personal stuff. Go to the Board Office, turn in your materials and retire. Come back and see us from time to time." Larry was chilled by the coldness of his comments.

The principal extended his hand. Larry shook it, and then he walked out of the school. There was no great feeling of nostalgia as he left. He got into his car and drove home. He had a feeling of aimlessness as he walked into the house. "You're right, I just got fired," he told Sarah.

"You didn't get fired, Larry," said Sarah. "You just got a three-semester vacation and then complete retirement. Look on the bright side. You don't have anything to do."

"That's exactly right, I don't have anything to do," said Larry.

CHAPTER 5

REV. ALLEN AND Lisa arrived at the congested O'Hare International Airport in Chicago. They limped off the airplane and went to baggage pickup, where they were met by two elders of the Mount Moriah Baptist Church.

"Glad to see you, Reverend," said Elder McIntyre. "We missed you last Sunday. That young replacement minister you suggested, Arthur Deon, did a credible job. He's good with the youth groups, the church choir liked him, and he's got an amazing charisma. He and his wife are quite gracious. We're very happy that you recommended him to us."

"Thanks," said Allen. "I thought that you would like him. He shows potential. I would certainly like him to be our next full-time minister, should it come to that."

"Now don't you go worrying about that," said Elder Watkins. "You've been our pastor for almost eighteen years, and I just can't speak highly enough of you. When I think of all the young children that you've taught through Sunday school and youth groups, who have gone on to graduate from high school and college, I'm just so thankful. You've been a credit to our church," said Elder McIntyre.

"Thank you, Elder," said Lisa. "That's very nice of you."

"I really mean it. All our congregation is looking forward to seeing you on Sunday morning for the ten o'clock service."

"Is there anything I can do for you, Rev. Allen?" asked Elder McIntyre.

"No," said Allen. "I'm tired, it's been a long day, and I'd like to go home and get some rest. Could you please help me with our luggage?"

"Same for me," said Lisa. "These are long trips."

"We will be glad to help with your bags," said the Elder.

The Elder wheeled through the airport traffic to the expressway.

"I see," said Allen, "the traffic congestion in Chicago hasn't changed a bit."

Allen turned to Lisa. "We've seen a lot of changes in the thirty years that we've been married. When I was young, we used to go down to the University of Chicago on summer evenings to tutor the nine and ten year olds from that rough neighborhood. I wonder what's happened to them?"

"If they didn't get hooked on crack," said the Elder, "they probably turned out fine. Any ten or eleven year old that wants some extra tutoring in the summertime is a motivated youngster."

"You're right," said Allen. "I wish that we could just keep track and see what happens to them."

"You've changed," said the Elder. "You never seemed to be worried before about what became of people you met in the past."

"No," said Allen. "I've always wondered about it. I probably just never put it into words before. Did the Board of Elders meet with the architect on the addition to the church?"

"Yes, they did," said the Elder. "We had a lengthy discussion, not only with the architect, but with a lending officer from the bank. He wanted a record of our contributions for the last five years and a projection for the next five. The bank was very interested in making a church loan and is concerned about fulfilling its requirements under the Federal Community Reinvestment program."

"I would think that homes would be the best investment. People are going to make their house payments," said Lisa.

"That's not what the banker said. They have to make loans in our area, and they feel the church, with twenty cosigners on the mortgage, is a better risk than ten houses," said the Elder.

Allen arched his eyebrows. "Twenty cosigners on the mortgage?"

"Yes," said the Elder. "The banker specifically stated that you, Lisa, and the entire Board of Elders would have to guarantee the loan. Otherwise, they couldn't lend a half million dollars for our church addition."

"How much would the monthly payments be on a half million dollars?" asked Allen.

"With principal, interest and insurance, the banker said the payments would run about thirty-five hundred dollars a month," said the Elder.

"Our church congregation could easily afford four thousand dollars a month for the additions to the building. We've got almost eight hundred members," said Rev. Allen.

"Yes," said the Elder. "I think that we can work this out. We'll have you in front of your house in another five minutes."

"Not soon enough for me," said Lisa. "I'm bushed."

The Elder pulled the Ford van into the driveway of a one-and-a-half-story brick home. It was on a small lot very attractively landscaped with azaleas and a manicured boxwood hedge. The parsonage was furnished by the church. Allen and Lisa had lived there comfortably for seventeen years while raising all their children.

The Elders helped Allen carry in the luggage, shook Allen's hand and left.

"How do you feel," asked Lisa. "You look tired."

"I am tired," said Allen. "I'm going to bed. I think I'll sleep in tomorrow and then have a meeting with the Board of Elders tomorrow night concerning the architectural changes and the banker's recommendations." Allen picked up his bag and went off to bed, leaving Lisa the chores of collecting the mail, sorting out the newspapers, and getting the house cleaned.

Allen slept past eleven o'clock the next morning. He would have slept longer, but Lisa gently shook him.

"Wake up," said Lisa. "You're going to sleep your life away."

"Ohhhh," groaned Allen. "What time is it?"

"It's almost eleven-thirty," said Lisa.

"In the morning?" said Allen.

"Yes," laughed Lisa. "It'll be time for lunch in a half an hour. How do you feel?"

"I took a couple of those pain pills last night, and I guess they knocked me out," said Allen.

"You were dead to the world, and you snored like a freight train," said Lisa.

"Sorry," said Allen.

"It's all right," said Lisa. "I'm leaving now. I've got some shopping to do. There's orange juice in the refrigerator, croissants on the table, and a fresh pot of coffee brewing. Get yourself something to eat. Take a shower, and I'll be back from the store by the time you're through."

"Thanks," said Allen.

Allen went downstairs and got something to eat. He leisurely read the morning paper and finished his breakfast, and then Lisa came bouncing in.

"Are you still eating?" said Lisa.

"Yes, I am," said Allen. "Should I mow the lawn and then take a shower? The lawn needs mowing and my spirit is willing, but the flesh is weak."

"You'd better get over to the rectory and get prepared for the meeting tonight," said Lisa.

"Right," said Allen, and he went upstairs to take a shower. Two hours later he arrived at the church rectory. His church was one of the most successful in south Chicago. Allen was a hardworking, energetic pastor. He lacked the charisma of some of the other pastors, but he had avoided many of the problems which seemed to be the downfall of other southside ministers. With a genuine Christian style and a humble manner, he had gently influenced his congregation.

For the past three years, the morning and evening Sunday services had been standing room only. Allen had hired an excellent choir master and had given up a portion of his own salary to keep him from being hired by another church.

Whenever there was an election, candidates would come to the church pulpit to talk about God, civil rights and his congregation's votes. Eight years ago, he had tried to organize a march against the zoning policies of the city of Chicago. He'd worked hard. When it came time for the march, he was bitterly disappointed to see only twenty members of his congregation show up. Politicians who had come to the church over the last ten years suddenly were called out of town on other important business. It was a harsh lesson for Allen. He shrugged off that memory and got himself prepared for the meeting with the Board of Elders.

At seven p.m., Allen met with the Board of Elders of his church.

All ten were there in the church fellowship hall.

"Welcome back from Arizona," said the Dean of the Board of Elders.

"Thank you," said Allen. "You can't believe how happy I am to be back."

"I had a friend who had a prostate cancer operation, and he was laid up for about twelve weeks. I can't believe that you're walking around in fewer than three days," said the Dean.

"Chalk it up to God, with a little help from medical science," said Allen.

"Let's call this meeting to order. Everyone's here. Allen, we've had a meeting while you were in Arizona, of the Board of Elders, the bank's lending officer, and the insurance company," said the Dean.

"What insurance company?" asked Allen.

"The life insurance company," said an Elder. "You have to have a medical examination in order to get life insurance. It was the bank's position that the success of this church was due to your efforts, Rev. Allen. They were concerned that if something happened to you, the church tithing would fall off. The life insurance company has declined to cover you. If this church is going to depend upon the minister, the minister has to be insurable. In short, Allen, if you are the only minister at this church, we can't get the loan."

"Wow," exclaimed Allen.

"I've talked this over with other members of the board. Many of them have been members of this church their entire lifetime, and five of them for over fifty years. You've done a tremendous service to this church. If the church is going to grow, we have to get a loan. The banks will not lend us money if you are the only minister. Consequently, the Board of Elders has offered the full-time ministry position here to your protégé, Arthur Deon."

"He will make an excellent minister," agreed Allen.

Another member said, "We appreciate your recommendation. We think Rev. Deon fits the plans we have for this church," said a second member.

"And," a third member stated, "you will continue on a part-time basis. We are requesting that you conduct one Sunday service a month at our church. You will be free to perform other services throughout the Chicago area. Most of the churches will give you a love offering for each sermon, and it's expected that there would be no substantial change in your salary."

"When is this to start?" asked a surprised Allen. "I've been the minister at this church for over seventeen years, I leave for one week, and a part-time minister is now the full-time minister. I'm to preach one Sunday a month?"

"Don't take it so hard," said the Dean of Elders. "We want you to continue on here for the next two months. Rev. Deon has commitments to other churches. He won't be free for a full-time ministry for two months."

"This is a little sudden," said Allen.

"We know it's sudden," said the Dean. "It's as sudden as your cancer. What are we to do? We have to provide a minister for the congregation. We have to provide for the expansion of the church."

"And," interrupted the second Elder, "we have to meet the requirements of the banks and the insurance companies in order to get the money to build the addition."

"It's nothing against you," said the third Elder. "We have to assure the future of the church and our obligation to God."

"That's right, Allen," said the Dean of Elders. "Here's what we want you to do. For the next two months, things are going to go on just as they always have. Rev. Arthur Deon will make an appearance at least once each week in the next two months. He will conduct the Wednesday evening services."

"At the end of the eight weeks we will pay you for an additional year," said the Dean of Elders. "You can live in the parsonage. You will have to turn in both the van and the Oldsmobile, as those will be needed by the new minister. When the year is up, you'll know if your cancer has been cured, in which case you can easily get another ministry."

The Dean of the Board of Elders had spoken so seriously and with such a straight face that Rev. Allen was stunned by it. "You mean I've got another eight weeks here, and then I'm dismissed?" he asked.

"Oh Reverend, in every time and place people get old. They can't continue on anymore. That's a harsh reality. If you died, you know we'd have to get someone to replace you. We're just doing it a little bit ahead of time. You're certainly welcome to preach here, and to minister to the congregation as an assistant, but you understand that we must have a younger man. Go home. Talk it over with Lisa. You'll find that you'll agree with us," said the Dean of Elders.

Allen drove home thinking, *What'll I tell Lisa? I've done a good job for the church. Why did God do this to me? Only bad people get treated like this. I've done nothing wrong. Isn't there any justice? There must be a reason but I don't see one.* He turned into the driveway. Allen slowly got out of the car and went inside.

"How did the meeting go?" asked Lisa.

"Terrible. I got fired," said Allen

"Just like that?" said Lisa, snapping her finger.

"They're continuing my contract for another year as assistant minister, but we have to turn in both cars," said Allen.

After Lisa's initial surprise, she became practical.

"Do we get to live in this house?" Lisa asked.

Allen said, "Yes, for the next year."

"What'll we drive around in?" said Lisa.

"I don't know," said Allen.

"How soon do we have to turn the cars in?" said Lisa.

"In about eight weeks," said Allen.

Lisa started to cry. "How could they do this to us?" She caught herself. "How could they do this to you?"

"The board was afraid that if they borrowed a half million dollars and I died, that there would be no way to pay off the loan on the church," said Allen.

"Weren't they supposed to put a life insurance policy on you so in case you died that..." said Lisa.

"No insurance company will take that risk," Allen snapped.

"You told me there was a ninety-five percent chance of success."

"Yes, I did," said Allen.

"The insurance companies don't think so. The board doesn't think so. Is there something you're not telling me?" demanded Lisa.

"I'm telling you what the doctor said to me," said Allen.

"Why is everybody doing this to you?" asked Lisa.

"I don't know. What are we going to do?" asked Allen.

"We're going to continue on and in eight weeks, we're going back to Scottsdale, Arizona," said Lisa.

CHAPTER 6

ON FRIDAY MORNING, Bill reported to the Boatwright Construction Company, where he had been employed for the last fifteen years. Originally Boatwright Construction had specialized in commercial construction. The affluence of the American economy of the 90s had created a market for second homes. They were nestled in the foothills of the Allegheny Mountains about thirty miles from the Blue Ridge Parkway. Rich summer visitors from Charlotte, Spartanburg and Atlanta purchased recreational homes from Boatwright Construction to escape the summer heat and enjoy an early vision of the fall leaf colors.

He went in to see Mr. Boatwright.

"Good morning, Bill," shouted Mr. Boatwright.

Mr. Boatwright was a robust and congenial sixty-five-year-old man. "You ready to go back to work, Bill?"

"Sure am, Mr. Boatwright."

"We're between jobs for the rest of the week. Come back tomorrow and look at some new blueprints. We've got three houses to be framed. That will keep you busy for the next six weeks for sure. If we build a couple more, you'll be working all winter."

"That's the best news I've heard, Mr. Boatwright. What time do you want me to come in?"

"Come in at about ten o'clock, after I get the other crews going. I'll go over the blueprints with you. You can check with our draftsman to see if there are any changes. Once the public sees how it looks, I think we're going to be real busy."

"That is really good news. I've got some chores to do around the house. I'll be back at ten o'clock," said Bill.

Bill got in his rusted Ford F-100 pickup and drove home. He walked in the door and Sylvia noticed immediately that he felt good.

"You look happy," Sylvia said.

"I am. I talked with Mr. Boatwright. He's got some new houses that they're working on from rough-hewn logs. We're going to have work for the next six weeks. If they get buyers on these spec homes, we'll be busy the rest of the winter." Bill pitched in and started helping Sylvia prepare dinner.

Bill arrived early at the office and asked the draftsman, "Got the plans for the houses in the Creek Subdivision?"

"Sure do. They're over there on the table," said the draftsman.

"It's something like my grandfather would have been familiar with," said Bill.

"Or even your great-grandfather, Bill. This is a modern use of old construction methods, adapted with modern amenities," said the draftsman.

Bill busied himself studying the floor plans, the elevations and a wooden model. Mr. Boatwright came in.

Mr. Boatwright called, "Bill, come on in to my office." Bill walked into the office. "Take a seat, Bill."

"Thanks," said Bill.

"How are you feeling?" asked Mr. Boatwright.

"Fine," said Bill.

"How's the family?" said Mr. Boatwright.

"Fine. Sylvia's in good shape, and the kids are all doing well," said Bill.

"Bill, is there anything you want to tell me?" said Mr. Boatwright.

"No, Mr. Boatwright. I'm feeling good. I'm looking forward to being the construction foreman on these new houses. I like this heavy-hewn construction."

"I've got a problem. Our medical insurance and our workers' compensation company are the same. I got a call yesterday morning from the workers' compensation adjuster. Your medical insurance claims agent has been receiving bills from a urologist here in Tennessee and an oncology doctor. Bill, do you have cancer?" asked Mr. Boatwright.

Bill paused, and then slowly answered, "Yeah. I have been treated for about four months. In sixty days I go back for follow-up to see if it is cured."

"Bill, the workers' comp adjuster was very concerned about you working as a supervisor if you have cancer. He's afraid that you're going to do something, lifting, bending, and you're going to hurt yourself, leaving them liable for a workers' compensation claim," said Mr. Boatwright.

"Mr. Boatwright, I've worked here for fifteen years and I've never lost a day," said Bill.

"You've been one of our best workers," said Mr. Boatwright. "But the workers' compensation agent feels that you are an unnecessary risk. I've got to go along, or pay a much higher premium, or even change companies. I can't change workers' compensation insurance companies without changing the medical insurance. I've got to stay with this insurance company, not only for you but for the rest of us. If I change medical insurance you won't be able to be covered. My wife won't be able to be covered. If I stay with the medical insurance, I've got to stay with the workers' compensation insurance. If the workers' compensation insurance says you've got to go..." And Mr. Boatwright shrugged his shoulders.

"Did they tell you to fire me?" asked Bill.

"No, but my hands are tied," said Mr. Boatwright. "I can't use you as a working supervisor or as a carpenter. You've been a loyal employee. I checked with the insurance company. You can work in and around the office. You can be my man Friday. You can pick up parts, but you can't load anything over twenty pounds on the truck. You can clean up the yard and mow the grass. I'll work out an appropriate pay scale. I'm not going to fire you."

"Thanks," said Bill.

"I don't want you to lose your medical insurance. I don't want you to leave the office grounds," said Mr. Boatwright.

"No problem," said Bill.

"I don't want you to go out to that Creek Subdivision next week," said Mr. Boatwright. "Go back into the draftsman's office, become completely familiar with what has to be done. Brief the new man. Tell him all the pitfalls, but under no condition can I send you out there. I don't want you sneaking out there. If you get caught, I get caught. The insurance company cancels the medical insurance on all of us. It's not worth it, Bill. I wish it wasn't this way, but it is."

"Mr. Boatwright, how will I support myself and Sylvia? Sounds like a cut in pay to me," said Bill.

"Yes, it is," said Mr. Boatwright. "You were making fourteen fifty an hour as a carpenter, and twenty dollars as a supervisor. I'd thought about raising you to twenty-two dollars an hour. Best I can offer you is ten bucks an hour. If you're mad at me, I understand. If you want to see if you can find something better, that's okay, too."

"Mr. Boatwright, you know I can't do that," said Bill. "I've got cancer; I need the medical insurance. If I lose my insurance, the medical bills will bankrupt me. I'll be back on Monday morning."

"Bill, I figured you'd do it like that," said Mr. Boatwright. "I want you to brief the new man. He doesn't have your experience. He's going to need your supervisory skills to get this done. If you help me out on this, we'll work out a bonus around Christmas."

"Yeah, it's all for the best, I guess," said Bill.

"You've got twelve weeks' disability pay if you need it for medical treatment and convalescence," said Mr. Boatwright.

"I didn't know that," said Bill.

"I just found out. It's in the policy," said Mr. Boatwright.

About six o'clock, Bill walked into the house a little crestfallen. "What's the matter?" asked Sylvia.

"I've been demoted," said Bill. "I'm the chief lawn mower."

CHAPTER 7

MICHAEL GOT OFF the airplane in Amarillo, Texas, alone and discouraged. He picked up his two bags, walked outside and hailed a cab.

The cabby scooped up his luggage. It was a quick trip to home. He went in, sat down and turned on the television, feeling very tired. He looked at the picture of his wife, dead four years, and began dusting off some of the tables. Then he walked into the kitchen and looked at his empty refrigerator. He grabbed a handful of breakfast cereal and swallowed it. He missed his dog, Scruffy, that he'd put in the kennel before he'd made the trip to Scottsdale, Arizona. Scruffy was a gray mongrel with a lot of long hair and a very happy attitude.

He really would have enjoyed Scruffy's company. He knew he couldn't pick her up tonight. Tomorrow he would go to the kennel. He didn't intend to go to work until the afternoon. He wouldn't be missed. After the recent amalgamation of the corporation, there were plenty of accountants, and there was not enough work to go around. Of the twenty-two accountants in the manufacturing corporation, he was number three in seniority and enjoyed job security. It was unlikely that they would do anything to him. He dragged himself off to bed and went to sleep.

Early the next morning, he got up, drank some orange juice and ate some more breakfast cereal. He felt some pain but felt better as the Texas sunrise began to peek through the kitchen windows.

At eight thirty he was at the kennel to pick up Scruffy. She was a caring, loving, affectionate thirty-pound bundle of energy and was happy to see him. Obviously, any dog who had spent a whole week in a two-by-three-by-three-foot cage was going to be happy to see her master.

He switched on the radio, turning to a classic seventies radio station and drove back to his two-story stucco house. It had a nice stand of grass which needed to be cut.

He took Scruffy to the back yard, unlocked the gate and let her go. She was happy to be in her own familiar surroundings, which consisted of a lot approximately ninety feet wide and a hundred feet long. She knew every nook and cranny. As soon as she was loose, she sniffed every tree trunk and fence post in the yard as if she expected to find a scent from another dog. "Don't worry, Scruffy," he told her. "I've been true to you." Scruffy seemed satisfied, and he left her alone.

He made a list of things he had to do: going to the store, putting the garbage cans out and other household chores. He finished up by eleven thirty, took a shower, dressed, and at one o'clock went to his job. He walked in and was immediately questioned, "Hey. How was Phoenix, Mike?" It was nice to be among, if not friends, at least acquaintances, some who were really glad to see him, and others who were just being agreeable.

He walked over to his cubicle and found that there had been some work put on his desk. He found the routine monthly and quarterly reports which he had been doing for several years.

Sitting on his chair was a small square box wrapped in paper with a big ribbon. He picked it up and saw the card underneath it. He opened the package first. He hated to open up a package when the person who gave it to him was standing there. He was always afraid that if he didn't like the gift, it would show on his face and he would hurt the person's feelings.

He pulled the package apart and inside were two tickets to a Dallas Cowboys football game. He was shocked by the gift. The tickets probably cost ninety dollars each. He grabbed the card, and inside was a note that said, "Dear Mike, Welcome back. We missed you. Please come and see me." The note was initialed "WL." This was a note from Will Link, the operations manager for the plant.

He called Will Link's secretary and informed her, "This is Michael Yret. I'd like to see Will."

The secretary said, "No problem. Come right up. He'll be expecting you."

Will was sitting at a leather-covered desk, with a big Texas longhorn head behind him on the wall. Michael laughed to himself.

Will told him, "Sit down, Mike. You've had two vacations. You've gone out to Arizona on a working ranch, and I envy you. I've gotten a call from our medical claims people. We're getting bills from the Mayo Clinic Oncology Department. Do you want to tell me about it?"

"Frankly, Will, I don't," said Michael. "I think some of these things are just better left alone."

"I know that's the way you feel. There are support groups that can help. Since your wife has died, you're alone with no children. This work is not fulfilling for you," said Will.

"How do you know that?" Michael asked.

"I look at your work. Five years ago, you used to blast this work out by Thursday and take a three-day weekend every week. I never complained because you did as much work in four days as half the people around here did in five or six. I have some accountants who ask for overtime, and they're not doing as much as you did in four days," said Will.

"There was always an incentive when Carol was alive, to get things done quickly so that we could have a long weekend. There's no incentive now," said Michael.

"Have you thought about a second career, a change in paths, so to speak?" said Will.

"No, I hadn't mulled it over," said Michael.

"I've got twenty-two accountants. You're number three in seniority. We've got eight more accountants than we need. Sooner or later headquarters is going to tell me to fire eight. I'd like to cushion that as much as I can. If I do it by seniority, then I'm going to knock off the eight youngest people. Most of them have wives, kids and mortgages," said Will.

"So?" said Michael.

"You don't have a wife or any children to support. I imagine the mortgage on your house is small," said Will.

"It's paid off," said Michael.

"Here's the situation. You could stay around here for another five or six years if your health permits it," said Will.

"Do you think my health is not going to permit it?" Michael asked.

"I know what oncology doctors do. I just don't know how bad it is," said Will.

"I've got about a ninety-five percent chance of another ten to fifteen years," said Michael.

"Do you want to spend your last ten years working here?" asked Will.

Michael said nothing.

"Why don't you retire early and get a chance to see the world?" asked Will.

"Will, are you firing me?" asked Michael.

"No, Mike, I'm not. I'm going to make you an offer you can't refuse," said Will.

"What do you mean?" asked Michael.

"Here's the situation. You're fifty-seven years of age. In five years you'd be sixty-two. About that time you'd retire anyway. So here's the deal. We'll give you five years' credit toward your retirement plan. You can retire now and get the same retirement benefits you would get at sixty-two. When you turn sixty-two, you can apply for Social Security. You can have a second career. You've been here crunching numbers for almost thirty-three years. Wouldn't you like to do something else?" asked Will.

"It's not boring if you have an interest in it. The enthusiasm for work is gone since Carol died," said Michael.

"Go to the Personnel Department. Look at your retirement benefits. With a second career you'd be getting more money than you're making now, plus you'd be adding to the Social Security benefits you'll have," said Will.

"If I quit now, my pension benefits would be frozen," said Michael.

"That's right. You've got to take the bad with the good. The retirement pay is going to be seventy-five percent of what you're taking home now. You can get yourself a second career if you want," said Will.

"I don't want to go out and work at some convenience food store," said Michael.

"I'm not suggesting that, but I know there are plenty of jobs out there," said Will.

"If I apply for a job and I tell people I have cancer, what are the chances of getting hired?" asked Michael.

"Mike, you know the company medical plan goes with you until you turn sixty-five. Then you get Medicare and the company pays the supplement."

"How do I know the company will be here?" said Michael.

"Mike, none of us knows the future. I'm concerned that I'm going to have to work until I'm seventy and then drop dead at seventy-one. I almost wish I had your—" said Will.

"Cancer. It's okay, you can say the word. It's not like swearing," said Michael.

"Okay. You've made your point," said Will.

"I'm going back to my office," announced Michael.

"No," Will said. "You go to Personnel right now, I'll tell them you're coming." Will reached for the phone.

Wow, thought Michael, they're really giving me the bum's rush here. He walked down the hallway to Personnel. He met the sprightly forty-year-old personnel evaluator and pension formulator.

"Hello, Mr. Yret," she said. "I understand you're here to review your potential for a pension, assuming the company would give you credit, as if you had worked to age sixty-two."

"Yes," said Michael. "If I retire today, will I get the increase in wages that I would have gotten if I had worked here five more years?"

"No, you won't," she said. "If you retire today, you'll get pension benefits based upon your salary today, and instead of thirty-one years of service, you'll be credited with thirty-six years of service. The benefits will not be reduced by your Social Security benefits, or a second job. You'll love having a second career; you can make more money."

He thought, the hell with it. The job's not that good. I'm really not as interested in it as I should be. Maybe I do need a second career. He went back to his desk and thought more about it. Later that afternoon he called Will. "I'm going to take you up on that proposal."

"Okay, I want you to get everything on your desk cleaned up in six weeks. We'll throw you one helluva retirement party," said Will.

"Thanks, Will," said Michael. He went back to work, noting that in six weeks he had to go back to the Mayo Clinic. He went home that night, saw Scruffy at the door and said, "Hey, Scruffy, guess what's happening. We're going to retire in about six weeks. We're going to have a second career."

He told her, "I'm going to take some classes on finding new jobs. It's kind of like Job Hunting 202 for us senior, mid-level executives. I didn't like interviewing for a job thirty-two years ago, but they're going to give me courses on it."

Michael went to the phone and dialed Susan's number. Her oldest boy Karl answered. "Hi, Michael. Do you want to speak to my mom?"

"Sure do. Can you get her for me?" said Michael.

"Hold on," said Karl.

A few seconds later Susan got on the phone. "Hi, Michael. How did it go in Phoenix?"

"All right, I guess. I called you from the airport, but I couldn't get hold of you," said Michael.

"We were on the ball field. It's T-ball season," said Susan.

"Can I come over?" said Michael.

"Not tonight," said Susan. "I've got half of the T-ball team here, and I've got my hands full."

"Sounds like you need a man to come over and help you out," said Michael.

"No, Michael. I don't think you should come," said Susan.

"What's the matter?" said Michael.

"It's what I told you before. I'm not putting my family through these health problems. You should be getting the engagement ring in the mail tomorrow," said Susan.

"You mailed back my engagement ring?" Michael asked.

"I've only got so many lives to live and so do my kids. We already buried one husband and father, and I'm not going to bury another," said Susan.

"You're going to have to bury somebody eventually," said Michael.

"I'm not up to it in the next two or three years," said Susan.

"The doctors say that I've got a ninety-five percent chance of being in good health and living another ten or fifteen years," said Michael.

"I'm thirty-eight years old. Even if you live ten years, I'm only going to be forty-eight. It took me three years to get over my first husband. I'm not going to marry another man and spend five years nursing him with cancer and five years grieving over him after he dies. I'm sorry. I sent back the engagement ring," said Susan.

"Just like that?" said Michael.

"It's less painful if you make it quick and firm. You're a fine man. I'm sorry about your medical condition, but I'm bringing this to a halt. We'll always be friends. Let's give each other a chance to move on. I wish you the best of luck in the future." Susan hung up the phone.

Michael walked over to a chair and collapsed. He looked at Scruffy. She raised her head. "You know, Scruffy, I've lost Susan, I've lost my job, and all I've got is you. If I lose you, Scruffy, they could make a country and western song out of this." Scruffy got up, put her two front paws on his knees and reached up and licked his face. "Hey, cut that out," said Michael. "Just because you're my only friend, you don't have to slop all over my cheek." Scruffy slid back onto the floor and wagged her tail.

Two weeks later, Michael showed up at the Executive Placement Program for executives who were "early retired" or "downsized." He walked in wearing his normal business attire, which consisted of khaki pants, a tie and a frayed white shirt.

The training master was a blond-haired, handsome, thirtyish man who told him, "Mr. Yret, my job is to review interviewing skills to get you a good job. Interviewers want to see a person who is well groomed and appropriately dressed and indicates a willingness and ability to adapt to a new job.

Michael nodded.

"Recruiters realize that an individual who is your age has a lot of life experience. The jobs that will be offered to you will be entrance-level pay positions. They will ask why you were terminated."

I wasn't terminated. I retired early," said Michael.

"In this era of corporate downsizing, that's not a stigma," said the training master. He instructed Michael about details that he'd never even thought about. "You must demonstrate positive body language. You must look receptive. You must dress appropriately. Your shirt collar is old and frayed. A recruiter would think, 'That shirt indicates an individual who's got some old ideas.' That tie, of course, is ridiculous. We'll have someone work with you on accessorizing your wardrobe. Your fingernails are a little long. They need to be meticulously groomed."

"I've dressed like this for years," protested Michael.

"Only because you felt you had a secure job," said the training master. "I want you to watch this videotape. This tape shows you how to walk, look people in the eye and shake hands and different types of interviewing techniques."

The training master let him watch a videotape of different interviewing faux pas, which showed a man who had failed to zip up his fly and another whose socks didn't match. The video showed one man who sat alone in the interviewing room and picked his nose while others watched him through a two-sided mirror. Michael was upset at that scene. He watched videotape of the one-man interview, the two-man interview, and the three-man stress interview.

"I've watched the videotape," said Michael as he walked out of the video replay cubicle.

"I want you to go home and come back dressed in appropriate business attire. We're going to go through posture and comportment tomorrow," said the training master.

Michael looked at him. "I'm not studying to be a ballerina. I'm looking for a job as an accountant."

"Trust me on this," said the training master.

Michael went home, looked at his suits and realized they really were out of style. Since Carol had died, he hadn't had any help in clothes selection. His co-workers thought he was partially color blind. "I'm not really color blind," he said to Scruffy. "I just lack discriminating taste."

He went to a men's store and put four hundred and fifty dollars on his charge card for a new suit, six pairs of socks, three brand new T-shirts and shorts. In one of the faux pas of interviewing, the recruiter had asked the job seeker if he wanted to play handball. They'd taken him down to the gym. When he took off his new suit and shirt, he had holes in his underwear. The man was turned down because of his underwear. Michael would never make that mistake. He had the store manager pick out three ties to go with his shirt. He began to feel pretty good. He practiced his comportment, walking in front of the mirror, extending his hand, giving a firm handshake.

He returned the next day. As he walked in, he heard a titter from the secretary. She was laughing at his shoes. Michael was crushed. This twenty-four-year-old secretary had just buried his ego.

Dressed in his new suit, he saw the training master. He said, "Those shoes are just inappropriate. Did you buy a new belt yesterday when you got the suit?" Michael shook his head; he had forgotten about the leather.

"You made an improvement," said the training master. "I'm quite happy. Tomorrow we'll work on some more improvements. I like the way you walked in today. I liked your composure," said the training master. "I want you to come back tomorrow with new shoes, well shined, and a belt."

"I will get this right," said Michael.

"Today, we're going to talk about job offers and what you do in response." Michael and the training master went back and forth practicing interviewing. "All right, Mr. Yret, we kind of like what we see here. We're going to make a salary offer that's low. Even though you had years of experience in another concern, you haven't had experience here. We want to offer you a job starting at twenty-five thousand dollars a year."

"I'll take it," said Michael.

"No, no," said the training master, "you just sit and listen."

"A twenty-five thousand dollar job would be good with my retirement," said Michael.

"Listen to me. I'll do it again." The training master went through the whole speech, but this time lowered it to fifteen thousand dollars.

Michael said, "I'll take it."

"Listen, and remain composed no matter what the offer is," said the training master.

"Okay," said Michael. They went through the practice interview again. After he was offered a job at twenty-five thousand dollars, Michael said, "That's an interesting offer. I like the quality of your company. Let me review this, and I will get back to you."

"Much better," said the training master. "All these job offers are normally going to be contingent upon your taking and passing a medical exam. Under the Americans With Disabilities Act, they can't ask you anything about any types of medical conditions during the interviewing process. After they've interviewed you, they can offer you a job contingent upon passing the medical exam. Many companies have a drug-free workshop, and they may ask you to take a urine test. Are you on any prescription medicine?"

"Yes, I am," said Michael.

"If they ask you to take a medical, don't forget to take your prescriptions. If you tell the doctor what prescription medicines you're taking, you'll have no problems. Do you have any medical condition that would be a problem?" asked the training master.

"Oh," Michael said, "didn't anybody tell you?"

"Tell me what?" asked the training master.

"I had prostate cancer," said Michael.

The training master looked upset. "Nobody told me about that."

"I have prostate cancer," said Michael.

"Is it being treated?" asked the training master.

"Yes, it is. I'm going back to the Mayo Clinic for an evaluation."

"What's your life expectancy?" asked the training master.

"Oh," Michael said, "probably just like yours. Nobody knows for sure, but ninety-five percent are cured. The survival rate is excellent."

The training master listened and a scowl came over his face.

"What's the matter?" Michael aksed.

"Nothing," he said. "Come back tomorrow with a new belt and shoes."

Michael walked out. He went twenty feet down the hallway, looked at his belt and returned. He asked the receptionist, "I noticed when I came in you laughed at my belt and shoes?"

She said, "I'm sorry, I didn't mean to do that."

Michael said, "Would you help me select a belt and shoes any fashion counselor might deem acceptable?"

"Sure," said the receptionist. "You're one of the few who, when criticized, tried to make corrections."

"I would like to get a job," said Michael.

She said, "Stay here a minute. There's a men's clothing catalog on the training master's desk. I'll make some Xerox copies for you." The receptionist walked over to the copy machine. Michael heard some loud voices in the next room. At once he recognized the voice of the training master.

"Geez, Jack," he overheard, "you ought to see the guy that company sent over, Michael Yret. I thought he had potential. We'd get a nice fee for out-placing for him. He tells me he's got cancer. I could get him fifty job offers. They're all going to be contingent upon a medical. We're wasting our time with this guy. Why did his company even send him over? They wouldn't let him be a bookkeeper at the American Cancer Society. I'm not going to waste any more time. We've got people we can find jobs for, but we're never going to get one for him."

The secretary walked up. "Mr. Yret, here are the pages that show the belts and shoes that you should wear."

"Thank you ma'am," he said, and Michael walked to the elevator. As he got into the elevator his eyes started to tear. He walked into the parking lot, got into his car and really broke down and cried.

He'd been there for a minute when a security guard came up and knocked on the window. "Hey, mister, you all right?"

Michael opened the window. "Yeah, sure," he said. "Yeah, I'm okay."

"You look upset," said the guard.

"I went to an eye doctor and I've got some drops in my eyes," said Michael.

The security guard said, "You'd better stay here a few minutes and wait till they clear up. Don't want you to have an accident on the way home."

Michael looked at the guard. "You really mean that, don't you?"

The guard looked startled. "Yeah, take it easy. Don't get hurt on the way home."

"Thanks," Michael said. "That's the nicest thing I've had happen to me today."

The guard, about sixty-five, put a hand on his shoulder. "You got some bad news, didn't you?"

Michael said, "Yeah."

"This building is full of middle-aged executives hunting jobs. You got some bad news about a job, right?" said the guard.

"I'm probably not going to find a good job at my age," said Michael.

"I know how you feel. I didn't find a very good job at my age either," said the guard. "At least you've got your health."

AN ASIDE

DO NOT QUIT reading now. This is the bottom of the well. You now sense the frustration of many cancer survivors. Even though they are medically recovering, they are struggling.

Hold on, read on, as you, your family, friends and the characters in this book get you back in the game!

CHAPTER 8

LEO AND LARRY walked into the oncology conference room of the Mayo Clinic in Scottsdale and reluctantly sat down. Michael, Bill and Allen came in about five minutes later. All shook hands, hugged each other and began rehashing events.

Then, a silence descended upon the group. Leo picked up a magazine and shuffled the pages. They were all worried. After about one minute, Michael said, "I got early retired."

"I'm sorry, Michael," Bill said. "I got demoted from supervising carpenter to maintenance man. After fifteen years, I now supervise a broom and a rake."

"I've been put out to pasture," said Allen. "I'm the assistant minister. I used to have a big congregation. Now I come in every other week and help out with Sunday school. I really feel useless."

"I got released," said Larry. "They gave me early retirement and told me not to clog up the hallways of the school."

They looked at Leo. Leo said nothing. "Anything happen to you?" asked Larry.

At first Leo boasted, "I've been made the president of the Leisure Division." He paused. "Frankly, guys, I got demoted. I was the president of another division which generated about $1.8 billion a year. Now I'm the president of Leisure Enterprises, sales about one hundred million. It's a farce so executives can write off their expenses to golf tournaments."

"What does Leisure Enterprises do?" Larry asked.

"We make lawn chairs, and we sell baseball gloves, golf clubs and golf grips."

"When I get a little older and can't play softball, I'm going to take up golf," Larry said.

"What do you mean, 'when you get older,'" said Michael. "You really think we're going to get much older?"

"We'll know in one more day. What else has happened?" asked Allen.

"One of the big problems is just takin' a piss," Bill said. "With all the pills they've given us, I have a tough time hitting the commode."

"Don't you raise the lid?" asked Leo.

"Hell yes I do," said Bill. "You know how women are. They yell at you to raise the lid and they yell if you don't put it down."

Michael said, "I know what you mean. I live alone. A couple of times I had to go to the bathroom in a hurry and it just sprayed all over the place."

Larry said, "I had a couple little accidents like that and sprayed all over the bathroom floor. My wife accused me of being drunk."

"That happened to me," said Bill, "when my little grandsons, three and five, were in the house. I blamed it on them. My wife yelled at the grandchildren. I knew they were innocent, so I took them to McDonald's. It cost me twenty dollars just because I felt guilty for blaming them. Now I don't leave the toilet seat down. I always keep it up in case I'm in a hurry. I got into problems with that, too. The other night my wife went to the bathroom about three a.m. with the toilet seat up. She fell right in the commode and got water all over her butt. Boy, did she yell." Bill paused. "I laughed like hell."

Leo turned around. "That happened to you? I didn't get any water on the floor but I did leave the toilet seat up. Bonnie fell into it. She yelled and took a cup of water out of the toilet bowl and poured it on my head while I was sleeping. Hoo! Is that a wake up."

"Did any of you take those pills that ease painful urination?" asked Allen.

"I did, for three days," said Larry, "but the pills turn your pee red and it stains everything—toilet seat, your shorts and T-shirts. What a mess."

"Did the same for me," said Bill. "Sylvia was doing the laundry and thought the red stains were blood. Scared her to death. I had to tell her about the pills. When a wife has to wash those shorts, the honeymoon is over."

"Speaking of honeymoons, Michael, did you and your fiancée work out the cancer problem?" asked Larry.

"She sent my engagement ring back in the mail," said Michael.

"In the mail!" exclaimed Larry. "Bummer."

"I'm sorry," said Allen.

"Ah, women, you can't live with 'em and ..." Bill said.

"Yeah, and I can't live without 'em," Michael said.

Dr. Gee walked in. A silence hung in the room. "Gentlemen, once again I want to talk to all of you. If any one of you doesn't want to go through this as a group, you don't have to. You've all been through radiation treatment and seed implants together. Does anyone have any objection?"

"Hell no," said Bill, "it's interesting talking with everybody to see if they have the same problems."

"Okay," said Dr. Gee. Two other doctors came in, immediately walked over to the counter and began putting on the rubber gloves.

"Oh, no," said Larry, "do we have to assume the position?"

"You know the exercise," said Dr. Gee. "All of you step back, undress and put on your dressing gowns. I want you to come out here, put your hands on your knees and bend over."

"Hey, Doctor," said Leo, "don't you get tired of being mooned all the time by your patients?"

Dr. Gee laughed. "Don't give me that. Undress, come on out and assume the position."

Allen turned to Michael. "I wonder how doctors decide to specialize in prostate cancer?"

"I don't know," said Michael. "Maybe it's people with the longest middle fingers."

"You really think so?" asked Larry.

"Sure," said Leo. "Women have short fingers. You ever see a woman prostate cancer doctor?"

"I guess not," said Bill.

They undressed, returned and formed a line, with their dressing gowns covered in front but with a separation in the back. The three doctors came along with their rubber gloves and their Vaseline and said, "Bend over, Michael. Bend over, Bill. Bend over, Reverend." Then they changed gloves for the next two inspections of Larry and Leo. "Gentlemen, it looks like there's been a significant reduction in the malignant growth. We still have to proceed with the ultrasound of the prostate this afternoon. That will be on an individual basis."

"What's an ultrasound?" asked Bill.

"That's the equivalent of having a flash light shoved up your butt," said Larry.

"It's a device like radar that measures growth inside the body," said Michael.

"You'll take the ultrasounds and the X-rays, and we'll all be back here to talk with you tomorrow," said Dr. Gee.

The next day, in the conference room, Dr. Gee walked in.

"Good morning, gentlemen. I have a colleague of mine from a national cancer institute. He's reviewed the findings of the ultrasounds. He'd like to meet with you all, and of course he'd like to have a digital inspection. Gentlemen, while we're doing this, you don't have to put on your dressing gowns. If you will, just drop your trousers and shorts and assume the position with your hands on your knees."

They all complied. Down the line came the cancer doctor. Putting on a fresh pair of rubber gloves and a huge slob of Vaseline for each patient, he digitally inspected them all. He told them to sit and said, "Thank you for the opportunity to meet with you." And he left.

"Wow," said Michael. "That doctor never shook our hands."

"If that's how he meets people for the first time, I don't want to shake that guy's hand," Leo said.

Dr. Gee addressed them. "Gentlemen, I want to give you the results." The room was instantly silent.

"We do X-rays to determine the size of the cancer when we first discover it and X-rays and the ultrasound at the time we do the radioactive seed implants, and then two months later to see if the growth of cancer has stayed the same, shrunk or expanded. When the radioactive treatment kills the cancer cells, the growth should shrink. Ultrasound measures the prostate."

"Am I cured?" asked Leo.

"I can't tell now. You will have to be monitored with regular PSA tests. Your next review will be here in six months. If everything goes as we hope, it'll be one year examinations until the fifth year. Five years of remission usually indicates a cure. For heaven sakes, don't get killed in an automobile accident, because you'll mess up my studies," said Dr. Gee smiling.

"No way," said Leo. "I don't have to drive in New York anymore. I've moved to Atlanta."

"Really?" said Larry. "I didn't know that you moved to Atlanta."

"Yeah," said Leo.

"Gentlemen, I have to see some other patients, but you're free to talk here in the room for an hour or so. Do whatever you want to do." He left the room.

"We just dodged a bullet," said Bill.

They all sat quietly. Finally Michael said, "That's a relief. I really don't have anything to do. The only one of us that has a real job right now is you, Leo."

"I don't really have a job," Leo said. "I'm head of a nothing division. The profits are being used up to support golf course fees, fishing, bass boats and executive yachts. If the company would operate it as a business, it could be profitable. I guess that'll never happen. The government regulators aren't even interested. I feel like the whole world dumped on my head."

"Larry, what are you going to do?" asked Allen.

"It's a beautiful day. I've got a couple of softballs and three or four gloves. Does anybody want to play some softball?" asked Larry.

"You're nuts," said Michael. "I'm too old to play softball. What am I going to do—go out there and break my neck?"

"Yeah, and ruin Dr. Gee's study? You know he wants everybody to be alive for five years," said Bill.

"I hope he's right," Allen said.

"We've got nothing else to do," said Leo. "We played forty years ago when we were kids. Let's go try it."

The five of them went up to the receptionist's desk. Larry asked, "Hey, is there a field that we can use to play a little softball?"

The receptionist looked a little skeptical. "You gentlemen are going to play softball?" she asked.

"It's not like we've all got jobs anymore," said Michael.

"Mr. Able, aren't you the president of a company?" said the receptionist.

"It's a leisure time company, and I'm going to take some leisure time. As a matter of fact, we make softball equipment. I've got a bat in the trunk of my car. Let's go out and hunt up a diamond," said Leo.

The receptionist phoned Dr. Gee. "Doctor, all five of them are going to play softball. Is that okay?"

"They should resume their normal activities," said the doctor.

"Should I tell them where a complex is?" she asked.

"Yes, and have Angelo go with them. He can help them out," said Dr. Gee.

The receptionist walked over to a maintenance man. "Angelo, these five patients have a cancer like you. Dr. Gee wants you to go with them. They're looking for a softball field."

Angelo said, "These gringos are going to play ball? What do they know about ball?"

"Anyway, go with them," ordered the receptionist.

Angelo shrugged his shoulders.

As the five of them were walking out of the waiting room, another patient came up to them. He had no hair on his head. He was wearing a baseball hat that came down to his ears. He used a cane.

"I understand that you're going out to play softball," he said. "I used to play a little myself. Can I come with you?"

Leo took one look at him. "Naw, we're going to go out and really try to play. It may be a little too strenuous for you, fella."

Bill put his hand on the man's shoulder. "I think, old timer, that it's not for you."

Angelo came up to them. "Dr. Gee says that you're looking for a softball diamond."

"Yeah," Larry said.

"He told me to show you the way. Come out to the parking lot, and follow my car. I'll take you to the ball diamond," said Angelo.

"Thanks. What's your name?" said Larry.

"My name is Angelo."

"Okay, mine is Larry. His is Leo. This is Allen, Bill and Michael."

As they were walking out the door, Allen turned to Bill. "All of us got fired because everybody said we had cancer and couldn't do anything."

"Yeah," said Bill. "And we just told that fella he couldn't watch us because he had cancer."

"We don't like the way people treated us but we just did the same thing. Let's go talk with him," said Allen.

Larry had overheard the conversation. "What goes around, comes around."

The three of them walked in. "Hey, old timer, do you want to come with us and play some softball?" said Bill.

"Yeah."

"What's your name?" asked Larry.

"My name is Bobby."

"How old are you?" asked Allen.

"I'm sixty-one," said Bobby.

"Geez. You're only three years older than I am," said Larry.

"Yeah, I didn't get an early diagnosis like you did," said Bobby.

"Wow! What's going on with you?" asked Bill.

"I'm taking chemotherapy," Bobby replied.

"Why don't you come with us. It's no problem," said Allen.

"My wife is out in the car," said Bobby.

"We'll walk out with you," said Larry.

The three of them walked Bobby to the car and told his wife they were going to play softball and to follow them.

The men got in their separate automobiles and followed Angelo. The wives were surprised when they were told, "We're going to go play softball."

When they got to the diamond, Angelo, Larry, Allen, Bill, Michael, and Bobby got out of the cars. Leo made a call on his cell phone. The wives—Bonnie, Sarah, Lisa, Sylvia, and Bobby's wife, Joan—went over and sat in the stands. They introduced themselves.

"You'd think there would be more important things for them to do on a day like this," said Sylvia.

"Yes," said Bonnie, "the malls are open. I don't see why they didn't go shopping."

"A minister's salary doesn't permit all that," said Lisa.

Sylvia suggested, "Maybe they're just counting the daylight hours, because they're afraid they don't have that many."

"Hah, no way," said Joan. "Even though Bobby appears to be the worst of them, he has hopes."

"How come Bobby appears to be..." asked Lisa.

"Sicker than the rest?" said Joan.

"Yes," said Lisa.

"His wasn't discovered early, so instead of having some radiation treatment, he's had chemotherapy," said Joan.

"Is he going to be all right?" asked Bonnie.

"I don't know. We just take it one day at a time," Joan said.

Out on the diamond, Larry said, "Let's warm up a little bit."

"We can't play much ball with just four gloves," said Allen.

"We can have one person pitching, one person hitting, and three in the field."

"What about me?" said Angelo. "I'm pretty good."

"In order to play on this team, you got to have cancer," said Allen.

"I had cancer, señor," said Angelo.

"Show us," said Michael.

Angelo said, "How can I show you I had cancer?"

"Simple. Just show us the black tattoo marks they put on your hip so that the X-ray machine would be calibrated at the same spot every time," said Bill.

"They put white tattoo marks on me," said Allen.

"Yeah," said Leo. "They put that little tattoo on your hips. We can spot it in a minute."

Right behind home plate, Angelo dropped his shorts, and everybody inspected to see if he had tattoo marks on the right and left hips.

"He's got the tattoo marks," said Leo.

"He's had the treatment. Okay, you can play on our team," said Larry.

The wives sat there watching Angelo. Bonnie asked, "Why is he taking his pants down? Why are our husbands looking at him?"

Sylvia just shook her head. "Men don't grow up and boys will be boys."

Sarah said, "Men! You can't live with 'em..."

The rest chorused, "And you can't live without 'em."

The men walked out on the field. Angelo was pitching; Larry, Allen and Bill were in the field; and Leo and Bobby were supposed to be the batters. Leo hit a few balls through the infield that were handled miserably.

"Okay," said Leo, "what we'll do is everyone will take ten swings and then we'll rotate and see how good we are." Leo had ten swings but only hit one ball out of the infield on the fly. After Leo had his swings, he turned to Bobby.

Bobby struggled up to the plate, but he could barely hold the bat. Angelo threw him three pitches; on the last he couldn't even get the bat off the ground. Angelo said, "Hey Bobby, I think you ought to take it easy today, because you might get tired."

Joan ran over, and Bobby walked back. There were tears of frustration in his eyes.

Joan turned to Leo and Angelo, who were the only ones within hearing distance, and said, "You know, he played a lot of minor league ball and even was in the major leagues for about three months."

"Really," said Leo. "This must be a real blow to him."

"You know it is. And I want to thank you all for letting him come out here," said Joan.

"No problem. Just let him take it easy for a while," said Leo.

Joan looked around. "Do you see where there's a rest room or a port-o-let?"

Leo said, "No, and that's a concern for all of us."

A delivery truck from a sporting goods store drove up. The driver said, "I'm looking for Mr. Leo Able."

Leo said, "That's me."

"My boss said that you're the president of Leisure Enterprises. I'm to bring you two dozen softballs, six gloves and a couple of bats."

"That's right," said Leo. "Just drop them right here."

"Who's going to sign for these?" the driver asked.

Leo took a pen out of the driver's shirt pocket, handed him his card and signed the invoice.

The driver looked at Leo's card. "Yes sir," he said as he got in his truck and drove off.

Larry said, "Wow! That's a couple hundred dollars' worth of stuff."

"It's no problem," said Leo. "It probably only cost us about sixty-five dollars." Leo handed out the gloves.

All of them batted, and only five balls got to the outfield on a fly. They took a rest. The seven of them sat down.

"Did you see that one I snared?" said Bill.

"Yeah," said Larry. "That was a good play."

"We're not doing too good," Allen said.

In the stands, the wives had witnessed this spectacle of softball incompetence. Sylvia said, "Our husbands need help."

Lisa said, "They're not too good."

"Larry's got a fairly decent arm, but he can't hit," said Sarah.

"Bill can hit," said Sylvia. "He just has a time bending over for the ground balls. They only played about twenty-five minutes. They'll probably be stiff as boards tomorrow."

"Better they play softball than chase women," said Sarah.

"I wouldn't worry about them chasing women," said Bonnie. "They couldn't catch a woman unless she was handcuffed to a telephone pole."

"Hey," said Lisa. "Don't be so harsh."

The patients hustled back on the field and surprisingly, with the new equipment and a little more experience, they did a lot better.

After another twenty minutes they called a halt. They walked over and told their wives, "Hey, that was fun! We're going to do this tomorrow."

The wives looked at each other. "What about going home?" said Sylvia.

"Go home to what? None of us has a job," said Allen. Michael and Larry nodded.

"You have a job, Leo," said Bonnie.

"It's a beautiful day. I don't need to be in my office. I am going to chalk this up to research and development."

CHAPTER 9

THE NEXT DAY, the patients returned to the softball diamond. The wives followed to monitor their husbands' behavior and sat dutifully in the stands.

Sarah remarked to Sylvia, "They have so much fun when they come out here. It's fun watching them. But I wish the sun weren't so bright. It really burns my neck."

"Yes, I have to wear a very good sunblock; otherwise, I really get burned," Bonnie said.

"Here come the police. I wonder what's up," said Lisa.

Two police officers got out of their cruiser and walked to the diamond.

Leo shouted, "How about unlocking that men's room over there. Please don't forget the ladies' room."

"Okay, we just got off duty for lunch, but we'll take care of that." The police officers walked over and unlocked the restrooms. Having nothing better to do, they decided to sit down.

Angelo was pitching. Everybody was a little stiff; they were getting better. Leo hit five balls into the outfield, and Larry caught them. Allen, who claimed he'd been a shortstop, was throwing the ball back and forth to Bill at first base. The police officers looked on in amusement and commented that no one on the field showed potential.

The police officers watched them for a while. One walked over and picked up a bat. "I'll hit some to the infield," he announced. "You infielders need the practice."

The other cop said, "I guess I could hit some to the outfielders."

Fifteen minutes later they took a break. Leo limped over to his limousine and brought out two brand new bats and two golf clubs. "Gentlemen, you know I head Leisure Enterprises, which is going nowhere. They spent over ten million dollars developing a new composite metal driver for golf clubs. This club could propel the ball over five hundred yards. Needless to say, the golf associations outlawed its use."

"No way," said Michael.

"Here, I'll show you. See that old guy over there chipping golf balls. "Follow me," said Leo, picking up the clubs. The players and the two police officers walked toward an elderly man chipping some golf balls.

Standing next to the golfer was a physical therapist. The therapist looked up and told the golfer, "Hey, it looks like some of your army is coming over here."

"I'm just out of the Mayo Clinic. I'm here recuperating. I'm not sure that I'm up to conversing with all my fans," said the golfer.

"It doesn't look like you can hide," said the therapist. "They're coming right now. They're carrying ball bats and gloves."

"They don't look like golfers, do they?" said the golfer.

"No," said the therapist.

"Hey," said Leo, extending his hand, "we saw you golfing, and we wondered if you would hit a couple of golf balls for us."

"I'm not sure I'm up to it," said the golfer.

"Hi," said Larry, "are you a patient at the Mayo Clinic?"

"Yes," said the golfer.

"You got prostate cancer?" said Allen.

"Yes," the golfer said, "I just had an operation last week."

"A radical prostatectomy?" Bill asked.

"Yes," said the golfer.

"Oh, that's serious," said Michael.

Angelo crossed himself.

"We're all prostate cancer patients at the Mayo Clinic ourselves," said Leo. "I head a company that was trying to make a new golf club. It's made out of a new composite titanium depleted-uranium and a reprocessed tritium shaft."

"I've heard about them," said the golfer, "but I think they hit the ball too far."

"That's right," said Leo, "so I've turned that technology into softball bats. I wanted you to demonstrate for the softball players the effect this metal has on a golf ball."

"Interesting," said the golfer.

"Yes," said Larry. "We want you to hit a couple for us. We don't have any golf balls. Do you mind using yours?"

"You guys all have prostate cancer?" asked the golfer.

"Yes," said Michael, "we're recovering now and we're starting a softball team."

"That's nice," said the golfer, "but why don't you take up this game? It's a little less strenuous."

"No problem," said Larry. "When I get to be seventy years of age, I'm going to take up golf. But while I'm young, I thought I'd continue to play softball."

"There's a lot of young people who play golf," said the golfer.

"Hey," said Allen, "you look familiar to me."

The golfer smiled a little bit, and Michael blurted out, "Yeah, did you used to be in major league baseball?"

The golfer's face changed. "No," he said.

"Anyway," said Leo, "I've got a two iron here and a metal driver and I wondered if you'd hit the ball to show us how far it will go."

"I don't know," said the golfer, "I'm supposed to take it easy, but I could give a little swing here for you. Hand me that iron."

Leo handed him the iron, and the golfer shook it a little bit. "It's kind of flexible," he said.

"That's right," said Leo. "It's got some give in it. And then it whips back."

"Take a swing at it," said Larry. "See what it does for you."

The golfer lined up the ball and stroked it with the two iron, and the ball sailed out of sight. "Wow," said Bill, "looks like it went about a thousand feet."

"No," said the golfer, "I estimate that would be about four hundred and twenty-five yards."

"Are you sure?" said Allen. "How can you make an estimate like that?"

The golfer looked at Allen. "I used to judge distances for a living."

"Really?" said Bill. "Are you a land surveyor?"

The golfer nodded. "I've surveyed a good bit of land and grass."

"Okay," said Leo, "you did a nice job with that iron, now try this driver."

With that, the golfer extended his arms, wiggled the end of the driver and brought it back. There was a solid thwack, and the golf ball bounced against the side of the Mayo Clinic, about two thousand feet away. "Hey," said the golfer, "can I take another swing with this driver?"

"Sure thing," said Leo. "Help yourself."

Another thwack. The ball smashed a third-story window in the Mayo Clinic.

"Wow," said Leo.

"Nice hitting," said Allen.

"Way to go," said Larry.

"How far do you think that is?" said Bill.

The golfer shook his head. "I know you're going to find it hard to believe, but that's almost six hundred yards. I can see why they outlawed this club. A good golfer could reach a par five green with a two iron."

"I told you, it's a heck of a good piece of metal," said Leo. "We appreciate your giving us this demonstration." As Leo walked away, he turned to the rest of the players. "That's what this metal can do. There's a sixty-eight-year-old duffer after prostate cancer and he can hit the ball six hundred yards."

The golfer heard that comment, turned to the therapist and said, "Sixty-eight-year-old duffer? I'd like to drive that guy's head two hundred and fifty yards."

"Would you like to play softball with us?" asked Larry. "Our team is made up of prostate cancer patients. You could play for us. We're looking for some more players."

"I was planning to continue on with golf. I'm pretty good for my age," said the golfer.

"Bet you were great when you were younger," said Larry. "Anybody who can hit the ball as far as you can could sure help us. If you can't run real fast, we can use you as a designated hitter. When you get on base, we can use a courtesy runner for you around the bases. Are all your parts still working?"

"I try to keep in shape," said the golfer.

"We play softball here every afternoon. If you want to come join us, you're more than welcome. We'll furnish the gloves, the bats and the balls, too," said Larry.

"That's really very nice of you. I'm not sure that I'm up to it. I'll see you out here tomorrow. I try to get two or three hours of golf in every day," said the golfer.

"That's good," said Larry. "We have to practice that much to be good at softball. You'll have to spend that much time if you're going to amount to anything in golf. See you tomorrow." As Larry trotted off, he yelled, "You can keep the driver."

Larry trotted back to the ball field, as Leo finished explaining to the players and the officers, "I had our research and development team use the same structure from the golf clubs in the production of these new bats. They have never been tested. I would like you to take a swing to see how effective they are."

One officer said, "If you want it tested, let me test it for you."

The patients trotted to the outfield. Angelo pitched the first ball. There was a resounding smack. The ball took off like a comet and landed about four hundred feet away.

"Wow, said Larry. "Did you see that thing? It must have gone over the fence by a hundred feet."

"He hit that ball like a rocket," said Bill. "That cop's really good."

There were five more balls pitched, and the officer knocked all five over the fence. The second officer hit five pitches with equal success. The players had to stop practice and collect all the balls from behind the outfield fence.

"Wow," said Leo, "you officers really knocked the tar out of those balls."

Larry said, "Let's see how they'll work for us."

The first officer said, "We'll go in the outfield and shag some for you."

Angelo then pitched ten balls to each player. Larry hit the first three about fifteen feet in front of home plate. Everyone was disappointed.

Sarah said, "I guess it's not the bat; it's the players." On the fourth pitch, Larry connected and the ball hit the fence on the third bounce.

"Did you see that?" said Larry.

"I can't believe it," said Michael. "Hit two more."

Angelo pitched Larry two more. Larry hit two of them to the outfield fence.

"This bat is great," said Larry.

"Let me try it," said Leo. Leo hit all five into the outfield, and one of them went over the fence.

Allen then came up and hit five pitches. Two went into the dugout. One went over the fence. Bill hit five to the fence. Michael hit two deep balls.

They all raced back in. "Leo, I don't know what you've got here, but these bats are fantastic," said Larry.

The cop yelled, "Those bats are dynamite! Even you old guys with your cancer-riddled bodies are knocking them out to the fence."

"What do you mean by 'cancer-riddled bodies'?" asked Bill.

The officer's face turned red. "Sorry."

The patients were stunned by their ability to hit the ball. The wives were flabbergasted. The officers got a call and had to leave. The six ballplayers sat there.

Larry screamed, "We could really sneak up on somebody!"

"Yeah, but who'd play us?" asked Bill. "Besides, we only have six players. We need seven or eight more just to field a team. Where are we going to get seven more players with cancer who can hit?"

"What do you mean hit?" asked Bonnie. "You guys couldn't hit until you got my husband's bats."

Larry looked at Leo and asked, "What's the story on these bats?"

"About one year ago Leisure Enterprises was working on a new metal which is a composite of titanium, magnesium and depleted uranium," said Leo. "We developed an alloy that absorbs the initial shock and then bounces back like a trampoline. We tried it in golf clubs. The golf associations banned them. About a month ago I told Research and Development to make baseball and softball bats. You can't use them in the major leagues, but there's a good market from Little League on up. From what I've seen today, I'm not sure we wouldn't run into the same problem."

"We wouldn't have any problem," Larry said, "if nobody knew about it until after our team were the senior citizens champions."

"We'd still have to learn how to catch and throw," said Bill.

"And run," said Michael. "We've got a problem with that, too."

"Yeah, there's nothing like a little tenderness in the groin to slow down your running," said Bill.

Bobby spoke up. "I can help out."

"How's that, Bobby?" said Leo.

"I understand I can't play with you. I've got some friends who were pretty good ballplayers, and three of them are cancer survivors. They might be willing to play with us, especially with that new bat."

"Bobby, we know you've got baseball savvy. You had a few months in the majors. You could be of invaluable assistance," said Allen.

"That's right," Bobby said, "but that was many years ago. That's behind me. It's still fun to get out on the diamond."

"Yes," said Leo, "it's fun to feel like you're thirteen again. Nothing to worry about but your parents, school teachers and baseball. Women and business weren't even a part of my life."

"I hear that," said Bill.

"Okay, but we need a plan. We need an active coach. No offense, Bobby," said Larry.

"No offense taken. I'll be glad to help out," said Bobby.

"We need a couple more good ballplayers. And we've got to come up with a team name," said Leo.

"Since we all have cancer, why don't we call ourselves the Cancer Club," said Michael.

"No way," said Allen. "If we tell anybody that we have cancer, they won't even play us."

"Yeah," said Bill, "they'll come up with something like insurance regulations and prohibit us from playing, or some doctor will say we're not physically fit to play."

"We need a name that means we have cancer, even if the rest of the world doesn't know," said Leo.

"I've got no problem with that," said Larry.

"Try this," said Michael. "We'll spell cancer backwards."

"What the hell is cancer spelled backwards?" said Larry.

"It's recnac, r-e-c-n-a-c," said Michael.

"RECNAC," said Leo. "That ought to confuse people."

"R-e-c sounds like recreation. They call them rec departments," said Allen.

"What would the 'nac' be?"

"How about the Navajo American Club?"

"We don't have any Navajos on this team," said Allen. "It could stand for the Negro American Club."

"What negroes do we have on this team?" said Leo.

Allen looked at Leo. Leo said, "You don't count. You have cancer just like us."

Allen held up both hands as if asking God for a little help. Bill whispered to Larry, "Did you hear what Leo said to Allen?"

"I did," said Larry. "One hundred and twenty years of elitism changed in sixty days."

"Who visited him, the Ghost of Christmas Past?" whispered Bill.

"Anyway, let's call our team RECNAC," said Leo. "On the top line we'll have r-e-c like it's recreation, and the bottom line will be nac, n-a-c. Our wives can come up with a logo."

"We'll come back tomorrow. We have to take our wives shopping for being good sports about this," said Larry.

"Yeah," said Bill.

"I don't have a wife to take with me," said Michael.

"Come along with us," said Larry.

Leo snapped, "That's no problem for you. You take your wife shopping, it costs you fifty dollars. I take Bonnie shopping, she costs me five thousand dollars."

"Hey," said Allen, "you're making lots of money. You've got to take the good with the bad."

As they were leaving, Angelo asked, "I've got a friend who has cancer. Can he come out?"

"Sure," said Larry. "If he's got cancer and is over fifty-five, he can play for RECNAC. Bring him out."

The next day all five were there, plus Angelo and his friend Pablo. Leo said, "We've already got seven players. Bobby, where are the guys you were going to furnish?"

"Hold on, they'll be here in a minute," said Bobby. Sure enough, in about three minutes, up pulled a Hummer and sitting in it were three men. All of them stepped out with characteristic military posture and assertiveness. The one in the lead was about six-foot three and weighed about two hundred and fifty pounds.

"Gentlemen, let me introduce you to my good friend and competitor and a person who's volunteered to be your player-coach. This is retired Col. Norman Blitzkrieg," said Bobby. Norman shook hands very firmly, looking each one in the eye. "I also want to introduce two other players, Carl Timm and John Vogue."

Immediately, Coach Blitzkrieg launched into a speech. "Gentlemen, I appreciate your coming here today. I understand each and every one of you has suffered the debilitating effects of prostate cancer, and you are in the process of rehabilitation. Our mission here today is to prepare a softball team, a winning softball team, with dedication, drive, enthusiasm and never-say-die spirit, building together a feeling of camaraderie, congeniality, and team attitude, that when put together will lead us to success on the softball diamond. From now on, it's not necessary that you call me Norman. You can call me by my proper title, Coach. Here's the situation. We're going to line up the players. We're going to see who can play the outfield and who can play the infield."

He continued even more vehemently. "We're gonna hit the field. We're gonna hit the field hard. We're gonna hit the field determined. We're gonna hit the field with a strong attitude. It's not the size of the dog in the fight, it's the size of the fight in the dog. Remember, whenever we have a ball game and when the going gets tough, the tough get going. We're going to go out there, we're going to fight, and we're going to win. I don't like losing anytime, anywhere. I don't like to lose anything. I get mad when we lose. We're going to go out there, and we're going to be winners. Right?"

Angelo and Pablo stood wide-eyed. Angelo said, "Sí Señor, Sí Señor." Michael nodded his head. "Yeah, sure coach, right." The first thing Coach did was make them all run a lap around the whole field.

"The whole field?" said Leo.

"That's right. Everybody works around here," said Coach.

Leo, for a change, was awed and took his first lap around the field.

"Holy cow, Larry," said Allen. "What have we got ourselves in for here?"

"I don't know, but it looks like we're going to have a halfway decent coach," said Larry.

"I don't know if the players are going to be alive after running the field," said Leo.

As the players trotted around the field and headed toward home plate, Coach Blitzkrieg encouraged them to run faster. "Pick up your feet," he yelled, "you lousy, double-clutching, chicken-pluckin, damn lazy asses. You are the sorriest players I've ever seen."

The players dutifully touched home plate, and then Allen turned to Larry. "We've got to tone down his language."

"I agree," said Larry, and he walked over to the coach and took his hat off.

"What's your problem?" demanded Coach Blitzkrieg.

Larry said, "It's your language, Coach."

"What the hell is the matter with my damn language?" asked Coach.

Allen walked up. "I'm a Baptist minister."

"We got a chaplain on the team?" asked Coach Blitzkrieg.

"Yes," said Allen, "and we have a profanity-obscenity problem."

"Oh," said a suddenly subdued coach. "You're not holding a few colorful expletives for demonstrative purposes against me, are you?"

"Yes," said Allen.

"What words?" demanded the coach.

"No 'F' words or 'C' words are permitted," said Larry.

"Of course the 'N' word can't be used," said Allen.

"Goes without saying," said Michael.

"And no 'H' word either," said Leo.

"No problem," said Allen.

"And no 'G' word or 'J' word is okay anymore," said Bill.

"In short," said Rev. Allen, "no obscenity, profanity, or other comments are permitted."

"Shit, hellfire and damn! How am I supposed to kick ass on this team and get 'em in shape if I can't encourage them?" said Coach Blitzkrieg.

"You've used your entire ration of vulgarities for the day in one sentence," said Larry.

"What?" yelled Coach Blitzkrieg, "no swearing?"

"No cussin' either," said Bill.

"Our grandchildren could be watching us," said Larry. "What would they think?"

"Ahhh rats," said Coach Blitzkrieg.

"That's very good," said Rev. Allen, "you're learning."

"What's the 'H' word?" said Pablo.

"We're not allowed to tell you," said Larry.

"How will I know what it is, if you don't tell me?" said Angelo.

"Anyway, you can say whatever you want in Spanish because nobody here understands you," said Larry.

"Sí, Senor," said Pablo, smiling and giving a wink to Angelo.

They began practice. The two cops whom they had met the day before pulled up again and stepped out with gloves. "Can we take some batting practice and use those bats?" The cops hit the ball just as hard as yesterday. Coach Blitzkrieg knocked the ball almost as far as the police officers. Carl and John were good players and knocked the ball over the fence almost half the time. The rest of the team began to pick up. At the end of practice they all agreed: they were beginning to come together.

Coach Blitzkrieg said, "Before we enter any tournaments with teams our age, we need to have some skirmishes with other teams." The coach looked at the police officers. "Do the police athletic leagues have any teams?"

The officer replied, "Yes sir, but they're all young players. I don't think it would be fair."

Coach asked, "Average age about twenty-five?"

The officer said, "Yes sir. Wait a minute, we have a team you could play. It might be competitive."

"Okay," said the coach, "could we have a game with them about two days from now?"

The officer said, "No problem. The day after tomorrow at six o'clock."

The coach said, "Good, six o'clock will fit. Okay, we'll see you all then."

Coach Blitzkrieg turned to them. "All right, every one of us, before we can play, should get the doctor's okay. See the good doctor right now to get approval. We'll practice at two o'clock tomorrow and five o'clock game day."

All the team members jumped into their respective cars, drove to the Mayo Clinic and trooped into the receptionist's office. "We've got to see Dr. Gee," said Leo.

"What's this all about?" she said. When no one responded, she said,

"I'll put you in the conference room."

The entire team—all eleven players—walked into the conference room. Dr. Gee walked in and said, "What's the problem?"

They explained to the doctor that they'd put a team together. They had eleven players and they had a game. The doctor said, "Okay, we have to do the normal check. Let me get two or three doctors to help." Two other doctors came in, and the players were told, "All right, assume the position."

They all stepped back about two feet and dropped their trousers and shorts down to the ankles, and the doctors proceeded with the normal digital examination. The doctors also checked their hearts. "Okay, all of you can play except Bobby," said Dr. Gee.

"We know Bobby can't play," said Allen, "but is he okay to coach?"

"Sure, he's okay to coach. I don't think that's going to be too strenuous, but I think he shouldn't do it by himself."

"That's okay," said Coach Blitzkrieg. "I'm really the coach. He's the third base coach. He's in charge of the lineups and things like that."

"I don't think that would be any problem," said Dr. Gee. "When are you playing?"

"Six o'clock, day after tomorrow," said Larry.

"Angelo, are you playing as well?"

"Sí, senor."

"Okay guys, I'll come watch the game," said Dr. Gee. "Make me proud!"

The players were impressed by Dr. Gee's supportive attitude and apparent enthusiasm.

CHAPTER 10

AT FIVE O'CLOCK RECNAC was on the diamond. Coach Blitzkrieg was at his organizational best. The outfielders were catching fungoes hit by John. Coach was drilling the infielders on double plays. Allen said, "We'll probably be dead by game time."

After a half hour of warm-up practice, they went to the dugout. "Where's the other team?" said Allen.

"Don't worry, they'll be here," said Coach.

"Time to get dressed," said Leo.

"Dressed how?" said Bill.

"I've got shirts and hats for the team." Leo dumped a box on the bench. "Grab a number and snag a hat."

They put on the cheap yellow shirts and high-rise polyester green hats. Wearing identical hats and shirts, they did look somewhat like a softball team even though they wore different color shorts.

As the wives watched the pre-game preparations, Bonnie said to Sylvia, "They really don't look half bad."

"Looks aren't everything. They look like twelve old coaches, not players."

"Being on the team sure has invigorated Allen," said Lisa.

"How do you mean?" Bonnie asked.

"Ever since he got involved in softball, he's acting like a fifteen year old," said Lisa.

Larry came in yesterday and started helping me change my underwear," said Sarah.

"Yes," said Sylvia. "Bill's made a tremendous recovery. When they're all alone, they're depressed. When they get together, they're full of life, and with us."

Sarah said, "I couldn't get Larry to go anyplace. Yesterday he took me to the mall, and to a movie. Of course, he wanted his payback."

"Payback?" asked Joan.

"You know," snickered Bonnie.

"Ohhh yeah," laughed Lisa.

A yellow school bus pulled up to the field and out trotted their opponents. The RECNAC team stared as their opposition got off. They were women, dressed head-to-toe in fancy uniforms, hauling tons of equipment, with an entourage of off-duty police officers. They jogged over to the third base dugout.

"They're all women," said Michael.

"They're not bad looking," said Leo.

"I'll see about this," said Coach. He strode aggressively across the pitcher's mound to the third base dugout.

"See here," he said, "which one of you is the manager?"

"I am," came a sweet voice from a forty-year-old, attractive, five-foot eight ballplayer.

Coach was surprised. "You're the manager? We're the RECNAC team. We're expecting to play someone here today. Why are you on this field?"

"We're going to play you and probably beat you. We are a police women team. You have any problem playing women?" asked the women's coach.

"Well, no," said the Coach, "we might as well play. Frankly you're just so much younger than we are."

"We tried to get some competition for you. You couldn't play with the men, so you're going to play with the young women. Hopefully, it'll equal out. It ought to be a competitive game," said the women's coach.

She stuck her hand out and Coach Blitzkrieg shook it firmly. Her grip was as strong as his. "Okay, let's turn in the lineups," said Coach Blitzkrieg.

The coach returned to the dugout, laid out a lineup board and reviewed with the team. The umpires appeared and called both managers for the coin toss.

"Hey coach, we want to win the coin toss so we can be the home team," said Michael.

Coach Blitzkrieg and the female coach talked to the umpire, who covered the ground rules and pointed to first base where there was a white bag for the first baseman and a red bag for the runner. "Remember," he said, "we don't want injuries. The runner uses the red bag. There's sliding at second and third. At home there are two plates six feet apart. The catcher stands on the regular plate, and the runner crosses home at this other plate. If the catcher has the ball before the runner crosses his plate, he's out. Just like first. That way there'll be no collisions. We're trying to keep physical contact between players to an absolute minimum." The umpire paused to see if both managers understood. Both nodded their heads.

The umpire pointed to the on-deck circle for the next batter. "Keep it filled. No dragging up here. The next batter should be here in fifteen seconds. Just because you're old doesn't mean you can slow down the game, understand?"

Both managers nodded.

"I'm going to toss the coin, and the female coach gets to make the call."

The umpire threw the coin into the air. The female coach shouted, "Tails." The coin came up tails.

"You win," said the umpire.

"We'll be the home team," said the female coach.

The umpire turned to Coach Blitzkrieg. "You're the visiting team. Batter up."

Coach Blitzkrieg walked back. As he walked he got madder with every step. His face turned red, a maniacal look spreading over it. Allen asked, "Did we win the coin toss?"

"Like hell, we did. That damn umpire put a curve on that thing—it came up tails. That makes me mad." He kicked the water cooler over and the ice spilled on the ground. The players were astounded. "I hate losing," said Coach. "Let's win this game."

The first batter was Carl. He hit a hard ball right over second base. It looked like it was going to go through, but the shortstop made a great play, whirled, fired, and got Carl by one step. The next batter, John Vogue, hit a single. Coach Blitzkrieg came up and hit a ball deep.

It looked like it was going to go out. But with a great leaping stab, the left fielder caught the ball at the fence. Coach Blitzkrieg was at first base when the ball was caught.

"It's a good thing he didn't have the bat with him. He'd have broken it," said Allen.

"Yeah," said Leo, "we've only got three of them."

The next batter was Leo. Using his new special bat, he parked one over the fence. The next batter, Larry, grounded out weakly to the pitcher. RECNAC two, Women zero.

The women came up to bat; Angelo was pitching. The first three batters all hit singles. Their cleanup hitter was a six-foot two-inch, two hundred forty-pound behemoth of a woman.

Larry yelled to Allen in left center, "She may be coming your way. She looks like she can really hit the ball."

"Ah, she's just a woman," said Allen.

Angelo pitched the ball, and the cleanup hitter smashed it off the outfield fence. The base runners scampered like jack rabbits around the diamond. When Allen finally got the ball in, the behemoth was on third base. The women had three runs.

The next batters reverted to singles. After they hit three singles, their big catcher came up. She cleared the fence with a home run. At the end of the first inning, RECNAC was losing 9-2.

Coach Blitzkrieg marched over to the wives. "We need a scouting report on these players. Every time the outfielders come in, they hit it over our heads. When they play deep, they hit it in front. We need an intelligence report. I want three of you to go behind their dugout. I want a report on each player. We want to know where to position our people. I want to know everything there is to know about the cleanup hitter," he said pointing to the large woman on first base. "And their catcher. I want to know all the tendencies."

Bonnie stood up and gave him a mock salute. Sarah, Bobby and Lisa went with her to reconnoiter. The bottom of the RECNAC lineup came up. Bill scratched out a single to the third baseman. Michael hit a clean single. Angelo hit another single. The next batter hit into a double play with one run scoring. The last batter meekly popped out to the shortstop.

Allen said to Larry, "A lot of good these bats are doing us."

"Right," said Larry, "we've still got to hit the ball."

"Well, it's only 9-3."

The intelligence team returned with the scouting report. Bonnie walked up to Coach Blitzkrieg. "Here's the report on that big first baseman. Her name is Amy. She wears men's jeans, size thirty-eight, with a thirty-four-inch inseam. She does not belong to any civilized country club. She has no society background, was never a debutante, and never even went to a cotillion. Her lingerie is by Western Auto."

"What else," said Coach impatiently.

"She's a member of the SWAT team, isn't married and has no fiancée. Internal Affairs has had one complaint, of sexual harassment. It appears a male police lieutenant made an improper remark to her, upon which she promptly decked him." Bonnie gestured with her fist. "Isn't that a great report, Coach?" Bonnie smiled sweetly.

"What the hell kind of report is that?" fumed Coach Blitzkrieg. "I don't care what kind of underwear she wears. I want to know tendencies. How does she hit? Is she a good fielder? Can she throw the ball? I need to know about every player on the team."

"Coach," Sarah said, "Bobby and I did some scouting. Here's the report. The second baseman is three months pregnant, can't bend down to get ground balls. She is a liability in making a double play if the ball is hit too short."

"The third baseman normally wears glasses. She won't wear them when she plays before a bunch of men."

"She's looking for a husband," interjected Lisa. "You notice the last time we hit a ball down third, she dropped it."

"The first three batters in the order are spray hitters with no power," Bobby said. Play the outfielders in the gaps and get the throw in right away because they can run like deer. That big first baseman has a lot of power. Get Angelo to put a good arc on the ball. She'll make a two hundred-eighty-foot out. Don't let her extend her arms. Don't let her hit the ball below the waist. Their number eight hitter doesn't have quite the power, but she's still got to be played deep. Those are the only two power hitters on their team," concluded Bobby.

"Another thing, Coach," said Lisa. "That nice-looking manager who coaches third base for the women."

"Yes, yes," said Coach Blitzkrieg impatiently.

"She's had cancer, both breasts, radical mastectomy."

Bonnie said, "You mean...?"

Sarah said, "Chopped 'em both off."

"Ooooo!" said Joan.

"Not only that," said Lisa. "Her husband left her and married another woman. She hasn't had a date in three years."

"The old damaged goods syndrome," said Joan.

"Who the hell cares about that? Everybody on our team has had cancer," said Coach Blitzkrieg.

"I guess you are all playing with a handicap," said Sylvia.

"That's not true. We're back in good shape," said Coach.

Sarah noted, "That coach seems to be very effective at managing the players. They're scouting us just like we're scouting them."

"Oh, no," said Sylvia. "I told Bill not to put on those shorts with all the holes in them."

Bonnie punched her. "That's not what we mean. Why don't you have Michael play over there where that white pie plate is?"

"You mean third base?" asked Sarah.

"Yes," said Bonnie. "That way he could talk to her."

"What!" said Coach Blitzkrieg. "They're going to carry on a discussion while she's coaching third base and he's playing third base?"

"Hey, it's worth a try," said Bobby. "Distract her from what she's doing, mess up her concentration. Look at it this way, Coach. It'd give you an opportunity to out-manage her."

"Yeah," said Coach Blitzkrieg. "That's a good idea. If the team wins, the manager wins. Let's do it! Michael, you play third base," the coach said. He sent the third baseman to the outfield.

Bobby said, "Michael, all the time you're out there I want you to talk to the third base coach. She's the manager. Distract her, get her mind off anything."

"What'll I talk to her about?" said Michael.

"Talk to her about cancer," said Bobby.

"I thought we were keeping it a secret," said Michael.

"Talk about your problems," said Bobby.

"Hey, what if she's married?" said Michael.

"She's not," said Bobby.

"Are you sure? I don't want her husband to beat the crap out of me," said Michael.

"Get out there," Coach ordered, pointing to third base.

The women came up in the bottom half of the second inning. With a scouting report and a shifting of his defense, Coach Blitzkrieg showed a keen knowledge of defensive softball. Bobby kept up the statistics book. From time to time Coach would look in, and Bobby would give him hand signals. He would maneuver the players. It worked well, as the women scored only three runs in the second inning. The top of the third, the score was 12-3.

RECNAC had a second look at the pitcher. Carl and John both got on base and Coach Blitzkrieg hit a triple. Allen singled him in; Larry beat out a single to deep second. He was forced at second. By the end of that inning, RECNAC had scored seven runs and it was 12-10.

The women were playing well and the men were improving. At the top of the seventh, the score was RECNAC 17--Women 21. Angelo led off with a single to center, followed by Michael with a single, and Bill with a single, scoring Angelo. Allen hit a single leaving men on first and third.

Coach Bobby was jumping up and down on the third base line with unbridled enthusiasm. The tying run was on first and the go-ahead run was at bat. Pablo hit a ball to right center. Bobby had moved down from the third base coach line, halfway to home, windmilling his arms as fast as he could. As Bill went by, Bobby yelled at him, "Keep going, keep going!" Bobby got his legs tangled and fell down.

Bill didn't see him fall and scored. Allen, who had been on first and was circling third, thought Bobby had fallen down as a result of cancer and immediately stopped and asked, "Bobby, are you okay?"

Bobby screamed, "Get going!" Allen ran but was thrown out at home. RECNAC 20--Women 21. It was the end of the game. REC-NAC went out and shook the hands of the women, who were all very cordial. Sylvia asked Bobby, "Are you okay?"

"It's nothing to do with my condition. I just tripped over my clumsy feet," said Bobby.

They felt better and went back to the dugout. Coach Blitzkrieg was approaching. "Uh oh," said Larry. "We're in serious trouble now."

Coach Blitzkrieg stormed up to them. "Gentlemen. That was quite a display. There are two things in any maneuver—the accomplishment of your mission and the welfare of your men."

The players looked at each other. "What's he talking about?" said Allen.

"This was an exhibition game, and you didn't do too bad. Allen, it's okay you checked on Bobby. You did the right thing." The team looked at each other in amazement. "It's a lot of fun. I enjoyed coaching you. Maybe we'll meet again."

"This is it?" said Larry. "Just after we all got together, we're going to quit?"

"Yes," said Leo. "It was fun. Especially when everybody thinks we've got one foot in the grave."

"Me, too," said Michael. "Certainly a break from all the other things we've had to do."

"Right," said Angelo and Pablo. "Sure beats waiting around for another rectal exam." Pablo pulled his batting glove onto his hand as if it were a rubber glove.

"Don't do that," said Angelo. "You know that bothers all of us."

"Yes," said Bill. "I don't like to think about it."

Dr. Gee walked up. "Hey, Doctor," said Larry. "We got a team together finally. We got enough guys over fifty-five. They all had cancer. They can run the bases. We lost to that team today, but the umpire made some bad calls."

"Si," said Angelo. "He really blew some calls. He called strikes when they were balls, and out when we were safe. The umpire lost the game for us."

Dr. Gee smiled. "Okay. What is it you want to do?"

"Isn't there someone that we can play? You got a Mayo Clinic in some other town?" shouted an exuberant Larry.

"Yeah, they're in several cities, but there's no crew like you."

"Can you help us out on this?" said Larry.

Dr. Gee smiled. "Maybe I could arrange a game for you."

"They have to be over fifty-five; that would only be fair. They can be without cancer and we'll see who wins."

"Yeah," said Leo. "And no humpty dumps either. We want some guys who are pretty good."

"Si," said Pablo. "Like us."

Dr. Gee said, "You're sure that you want to play some fifty-five year olds who haven't had cancer?"

"Yeah," said Bill. "We don't care who they are. We just want to have at 'em."

Dr. Gee said again, "Are you sure you want to do this? There are a lot of good players over fifty-five."

"We're not afraid of them," said Leo. "Bring 'em on."

The doctor turned to Coach Blitzkrieg. "Are you in charge?" "Yes," said the coach.

"I'll see what I can do. Maybe we can arrange some type of exhibition on the Arizona State Fairgrounds." Dr. Gee walked over to his car phone and dialed a number. "Dr. Hinkley."

"Yes."

"You know how you always talked about demonstrating that cancer patients can lead normal lives?" said Dr. Gee.

"Yes," said Dr. Hinkley.

"I've got about eleven of them who play senior citizen softball," said Dr. Gee. "I saw them take on a good women's team and lose by just one run. You think the Cancer Society would put on an exhibition game, say at the fairgrounds? Use it as a money-raiser. Just say they're local people and have them play some celebrities. Hopefully, the game would be close. If my patients win, we'll reveal they have cancer."

"What kind of ballplayers should they be?" Dr. Hinkley asked

"Get some good ballplayers. These guys aren't bad. They've got a decent coach. Let me know what you can do. Call me back right away," said Dr. Gee.

About fifteen minutes later the doctor called back. "I talked to the Arizona Cancer Society. They love it. They're going to get all the celebrities they can," said Dr. Hinkley.

"This team claims they're in pretty good condition," said Dr. Gee.

"All right, we can't set it up next week. Give me two weeks," said Dr. Hinkley.

"Okay, I'll tell them." Dr. Gee walked back to the dugout. "Gentlemen, come back and see me the day after tomorrow. We'll see if we can set up a celebrity softball game. Good players, over fifty-five years old, on the other team. You can get anybody who's had cancer on your team. You've got time to do a little more recruiting."

"Maybe we can get a designated hitter for Larry," said Allen. "He really knocked the tar out of the last ball, got it to the pitcher on only one hop, instead of two."

"At least I didn't run the bases backward, said Larry. "I think you stopped off for a hamburger when you ran from first to third."

Dr. Gee said, "Don't forget. You've all got to come back and see me next week for our evaluation. If you're going to be playing, I want to keep a check on you. I don't want you to hurt yourselves."

Dr. Gee left. Larry turned to his teammates. "You know we talked two months ago about all our dreams. I just don't know how to say thank you."

"Ah," said Leo. "At least you're going to get your dream. I always dreamed of being an important CEO and having my picture on the front of *Fortune* magazine. Here I am."

"Yeah," said Bill. "I'm getting disability pay from that medical insurer. I ought to get some benefit for being a maintenance man and cutting grass."

"I don't know how I'm going to lead a civil rights march. I'm having more fun here than I would be sitting at home," said Allen. "What about you, Michael?"

Michael was grinning.

"I saw you talking to the manager of that team," Larry said. "She's a good-looking woman." Michael just smiled.

Leo said, "Michael, did Bonnie get you that coach's phone number?"

Michael's face turned red. Allen said, "Leave him alone."

"You going to call her?" said Bill.

Angelo said, "Hey, she's a nice-looking woman. I think you should call her."

"Leave him alone," ordered Coach. "Give him a little space."

Michael said, "Hey, guys, help me out here."

They grinned.

"You guys are all married," said Michael.

They all nodded.

"I'm not," said Michael.

"Okay," Bill said.

"Suppose I take this girl out," said Michael.

"Yeah," said Bill.

Larry said, "You're just taking her out for the first date. Go to a movie, go to McDonald's. Take her to a concert, watch Frank Sinatra or Lawrence Welk."

"He's not that old," said Allen. "There's plenty of Motown songs, and Beatles. How about that guy that sings, 'Hey coach, put me in, I'm ready to play center field.'"

"Yeah," said Leo. "Just take it easy."

"What if I really like her?" said Michael.

"You ain't gone out with her. You haven't even rung her up, have you?" asked Bill.

"Tell you what," said Leo. "It's always tough on a first date. Why don't you invite her to go with all of us. There'll be four other women there. She'll feel much more comfortable. I do that in business with difficult customers."

Michael said, "What if, I'm not saying this is going to happen, but what if I like her. I take her home and she invites me in?"

Angelo said, "Ahh, you old fox."

Allen said, "It's always the quiet ones you have to worry about."

"No, no," said Michael. "What if I get in there and it comes time to do something and because of this cancer and this procedure I'm, uh, I can't do it?" said Michael.

"Yeah," said Leo. "I've had it more times after the cancer than before."

Bill whispered to Larry. "Leo is full of more crap than a cattle auction stockyard."

Coach Blitzkrieg said, "Michael, there's no problem. When the time comes, and you're ready, and she is ready, and you're both agreeable, I'm sure you'll rise to the occasion and perform your duties. I'll be proud of you when you come back afterwards."

"Coach," said Michael, "this isn't a military operation."

"This whole conversation is a waste of time unless you call her," said Allen.

"Yeah," said Leo. "We just had a great ball game and we're all feeling good. I'll buy dinner. Be there at eight o'clock tomorrow night. Michael, we'll see you then."

The next evening they all arrived for dinner. Michael showed up with Theresa, the coach of the women's softball team. Bonnie had called Theresa and told her Michael was a widower. When she walked up, Bonnie introduced her to everyone.

The dinner passed happily. They drank beer and wine and were noisy. One of the waiters said to them, "You're disturbing the teenagers over here."

They all left after Coach Blitzkrieg reminded them that they had practice every day for the next sixteen days. The following Monday they'd have to be in for their weekly examinations. "Ohhh, no!" said Larry. "The finger and assume the position."

"Just remember the big game," said Coach.

Michael left with Theresa. The husbands and wives went their separate ways, returning on Monday. The week passed quickly. Coach kept them busy fungoing outfield balls and with infield practice and batting practice. In the evenings there was always an opportunity to go out together. Michael and Theresa seemed to be hitting it off.

Bonnie, the inquisitive one, approached Theresa. "How are you and Michael doing?"

Theresa smiled. "Thanks for giving Michael my phone number."

"Some of that was to distract you from your coaching duties," said Bonnie.

"Yes," Theresa said, "but Michael's a hunk. I'm glad you did that, and besides, we won the game."

Bonnie said, "How do you think our team is going to do?"

"Our women's team is not that great," said Theresa. "We beat them. They're going to be in trouble."

"Why is that?" asked Bonnie.

"I heard through the grapevine that they're going to bring in a loaded lineup," said Theresa. "Every good player that they can get."

"They're not going to beat our team bad, are they?" asked Bonnie.

Theresa said, "I'm afraid they are. Talk to Coach Blitzkrieg. Tell him he'd better do some recruiting. They're going to bring in some really good hitters."

"You don't think we have a chance?" asked Bonnie.

"Every game, there's a chance. But they're really stacking their lineup," said Theresa.

"What do you think we should do?" inquired Bonnie.

"Get a couple more chaplains to go with Allen," said Theresa.

Bonnie said, "That bad, huh?"

"They don't know how bad they're going to get beaten," said Theresa.

"What about the new bat that Leo's furnished?" asked Bonnie.

"What new bat?" asked Theresa.

"In the games they have special bats. They don't use them at practice," said Bonnie.

"What are you talking about?" Theresa asked.

"Leo's company has come up with this new metal, or something. Anyway, it makes the ball go a long way," said Bonnie.

"How come I haven't seen it?" asked Theresa.

"All the players don't get to use it. Some of them can't hit good enough," said Bonnie.

"You mean like Larry?" Theresa inquired.

"Yeah. The ball's got to make three hops just for him to get it to the pitcher," said Bonnie.

"He's good in the outfield," said Theresa, "catching, running, and throwing, but he can't hit."

"Leo doesn't let him use the bats because it doesn't do him any good," said Bonnie. "Leo, Angelo, Pablo, John and Carl can hit the ball over the fence using the new bat. They don't use them in practice. We don't want to break them."

Theresa asked, "When could I get to see the bats?"

"Come to practice. I'll ask Leo if he'll let you look at it," said Bonnie.

"Okay," said Theresa. "I'm curious about these bats."

With a big smile, Bonnie asked, "How are you and Michael doing?"

Theresa said, "I already told you. We're doing quite well."

"Have you told him you had cancer?" Bonnie asked.

"No, I haven't," said Theresa.

"Didn't he notice?" asked Bonnie.

"How would he notice?" Theresa wanted to know.

Bonnie looked back and said, "You mean you've had about five dates with him and you haven't...?"

Theresa shook her head and said, "No, Bonnie. We haven't. I don't want to answer any more questions." Theresa walked off.

The next practice Theresa approached Leo. "I understand that you've got some bats."

Leo replied, "Yeah, we've got some specially designed bats."

Theresa asked, "Can I see one?"

"Sure," said Leo, and handed one of the special bats to Theresa.

Theresa waited until the next batter was finished, stepped up to the plate and yelled at Angelo, "Come on, throw a couple to me."

Angelo laughed, "You didn't do so good against me the last time."

Theresa said, "I just want to see how this bat works."

Angelo threw her a pitch. The first one she fouled off. She stepped back from the plate. Angelo pitched the next one and she bounced it off the fence. He pitched another one, she hit it to the fence. He pitched another one and she put it over the fence.

The men watched in amazement. "Damn," said Larry. "She hits better than I do."

Allen turned. "Everybody hits better than you do."

"That's harsh," said Larry.

After Theresa finished hitting, she walked up to Coach and Bobby. "I understand they're really stacking up the other team. They're bringing in some ex-major leaguers."

"Are they over fifty-five?" said Coach.

"Sure. But they're some really good ball players," said Theresa.

"If they're going to stack their lineup, we'd better too," said Bobby, "Our team isn't bad. We have average people who have been working hard. If we run into some super athletes who have been working hard, we're going to get our butts kicked."

"We'll be back tomorrow and work on this," said Coach.

"Maybe Theresa can give some hitting lessons to Larry," said Bobby.

Coach Blitzkrieg said, "Yes, Larry, Bill, Michael and Allen."

"Good idea. I will be back tomorrow," said Theresa.

CHAPTER 11

THE RECNAC TEAM enjoyed the camaraderie of softball practices, which were free of the fear of making errors. After practice they would stop at a highway cafe for some snacks and beverages. Dressed in softball shoes, hats and shirts, and accompanied by their wives, the team stepped into the café and settled at four tables. They ordered Gatorade, Cokes, granola bars and cookies. They were bantering about the balls they had caught or dropped in practice.

In the background could be heard the heavy chugging of two old pickup trucks pulling into the parking lot of the café. As soon as they parked, five heavyset, hard-hatted construction workers sauntered in and sneered at the RECNAC crew. Two of them winked at Bonnie. She looked away. The five workmen walked over to the beverage cooler, picked out a twenty-four pack of beer and sat down at a table about ten feet away from the senior citizens.

Bonnie and Sylvia got up to go to the restroom. As Bonnie walked by, a six foot, two hundred forty-pound workman reached up and grabbed her arm. Bonnie immediately withdrew her arm.

"What's the matter, honey? Can't you take a real man?" asked the bearded, bald-headed workman.

Larry, who had been watching, told Leo, whose back was to the bikers' table, "They just grabbed Bonnie's arm."

Leo didn't even turn around. "Bonnie can take care of herself."

"No," warned Bill, "I think they're going to give her a hard time."

"Are they big guys?" asked Leo.

"They're pretty big," said Allen, "but they're not that young. Three of them have gray hair."

One of the workmen grabbed Bonnie again. Bonnie yelled loudly, "Keep your hands off me!"

Bill got up, walked over to the table and put his hand on the worker's shoulder. "Friend, these are our wives."

"I don't care and I ain't your friend," snarled the workman.

"Wait a minute," said Leo, turning around in his chair. "We're not looking for any trouble." Leo's face was totally white. "Aren't you a little old to be acting like Marlon Brando?"

"Shove it," said the second workman who sported a "HATE" tattoo, as he pushed Bill back and made a lunge for Sylvia.

Larry jumped right in his face. "Please don't do that."

The workman pushed Larry backward about five feet. "Get out of my way or I'll beat your ass."

Surprising everyone, Larry leaped forward and punched him right in the nose. Blood gushed into the workman's mustache. Larry stepped back and shook his hand, as if he'd hurt his knuckle.

The workman picked Larry up by the shoulders and threw him about ten feet. He landed on a dining table, fell over and bounced on the floor. Unhurt, Larry got up. Sarah yelled, "Are you having a fight?"

"Hell, yes," said Larry, "and I'm not doing too well."

"Take off your glasses," screamed Sarah.

"I can't see who I'm hitting if I take off my glasses," said Larry.

"I'll wipe off the glasses," said Sarah, as she put water on his spectacles and dried them off with a tissue.

"Thanks," said Larry.

"You ought to consider LASIK surgery," said Sarah.

Larry lunged at the workman, screaming an incomprehensible "Damn that Board of Education" as his past docility erupted in red hot fury.

Leo and Bill jumped on one workman, as Leo yelled, "Screw you, QRX!"

Allen turned another workman around and laid a strong heavy fist full in his face yelling, "Take that you Baptist Board bully!"

Michael, the quietest one of them all, hit another workman, yelling, "You've screwed your last accountant!"

The construction workers were surprised by the savage response from the senior citizens. The proprietor of the café called 911 as soon as Larry hit the deck for the second time.

Bonnie yelled, "Theresa, can't you do something about this? Aren't you a police person?" Bonnie was crying as the bald workman had just punched Leo in the solar plexus and he was slowly sinking to the floor.

"Yes," said Theresa, "but I'm supposed to stop fights."

"We've got two bats here," said Bonnie

"You know how to swing them?" asked Theresa.

"No, but I play tennis," said Bonnie.

"Take the bat," said Theresa.

"What do I do?" asked Bonnie.

"See that guy with his back to us?" asked Theresa.

"Yes," said Bonnie.

"Hit him in the back of the head," said Theresa.

"With the bat?" asked Bonnie.

"Hit him," shouted Theresa.

Bonnie swung the bat and hit him lightly in the back of the head. The blow stunned him and he turned around. As he turned, Theresa showed her softball experience and swung as hard as she could on an upward stroke to nail him right in the groin. He froze for an instant and then crumpled to the floor.

"Is that how you do it?" asked Bonnie.

"Right," said Theresa. "Let's get the next one."

Bonnie walked over to the bald-headed workman who had just finished punching Leo in the stomach and the head, and then knocked him to the floor. Theresa hit him in the head. It didn't hurt him. He just turned around. Bonnie swung the bat and nailed him right in the groin. He crumpled to the floor.

Bonnie high-fived Theresa. "Not bad, two for two. Now there are five of us and three of them."

Suddenly Larry was thrown between the two of them, hit a table, overturned it and bounced right back up. "How're you doing, Larry?" asked Theresa.

"I'm not doing too well," yelled Larry. "Those guys are very strong. I'm just keeping them busy." He looked behind him. "Looks like Leo and Bill are doing okay. I see they knocked out these two guys. I'll try to keep this one busy. Where is Coach when you need him?"

"Just run over toward the door," said Bonnie, pointing to the worker with "HATE" on his forehead. "So he has his back to us, and we'll handle it from there."

Larry ran back to help out, screaming at the top of his lungs about the Board of Education, turned the tattooed workman around and punched him in the head. The workman again punched Larry, who careened off nearby tables. As the workman hit Larry, Bonnie swung again and hit him lightly in the back of the head. He turned around quickly and knocked the bat from Theresa's hand.

"I'm getting tired of getting kneed by broads like you," he said as he grabbed Theresa by the throat.

Theresa looked scared. Bonnie swung the softball bat as hard as she could and hit the workman right between the eyes. He dropped to his knees.

"Thanks, Bonnie," said Theresa, "that guy was really mean."

"I didn't intend to hit you that hard," apologized Bonnie as she bent over the prostrate worker.

"Anything less and he'd still be choking me," commented Theresa.

The wail of a police siren could be heard in the distance. The two workmen standing saw their three buddies on the floor, and ran out to their pickup truck. As the driver got in, he turned to the other one, "What was the matter with that nerdy guy with glasses? He kept yelling about school administrators. He sure was pissed at me. I never went to no school."

The other worker agreed: "That black guy kept yelling at me I was a 'Baptist bully' and tried to knock my block off. He did get a few licks in." He rubbed his jaw. "I ain't no Baptist. Hell, I don't even go to church."

The driver said, "Let's get outta here. Who would think those old guys would get so damn mad just because you were messing with their women?" He shook his head and let out the clutch, and a cloud of gravel spewed out as he screeched onto the highway as the police cars were a quarter mile away.

As the deputy sheriffs pulled into the parking lot, Allen rushed up. "Those two guys in that pickup truck just started a fight and left."

Bonnie rushed up. "Can't you catch them?"

"We sure will," and the deputies drove off in hot pursuit.

"Quick," said Allen, "while they're chasing that pickup truck in that direction, let's go this way."

"Shouldn't we stay around to be witnesses?" asked Lisa.

"No way," said Sylvia. "Let's get out of here."

"Let's get out of here before those three guys in there wake up," said Theresa.

"I'm for that," said Leo.

The RECNAC team drove home from the brawl. Leo enthusiastically turned to Bonnie. "That was really a great fight back there."

"You sound like you're happy about being in it," said Bonnie.

"I haven't been in a winning fight my entire life. I have always lost," said Leo.

"You did fine," said Bonnie. "Larry surprised me."

"How's that?" said Leo.

"He started the fight. He was mad down deep and he just let it out. He was taking out the frustration of his illness on that poor workman."

"Poor workman," shouted Leo, "he was trying to provoke a fight!"

"I know," said Bonnie, "but three months ago all of you would have groveled your way out of there. Those workers never expected you to protest, let alone fight. They were even more surprised when they knocked you down and you got back up. They hit Larry about five times."

"Are you serious?" asked a shocked Leo.

"They kept knocking him down and throwing him over the tables. He never seemed to get hurt. He came back and kept harassing them," said Bonnie.

"Yes," said Leo. "He must be a pretty good fighter because I don't remember tangling with those three on the floor. I had my hands full with the one I had."

"I don't think Larry hit them," said Bonnie.

"If it wasn't Larry, maybe it was Allen or Michael. Bill and I were fighting with the same two. Anyway, one of those three has got one hell of a punch. They were really knocked out cold. Our team did great!" said Leo.

"I know," said Bonnie smiling exuberantly. "I never had anyone fight over me before."

The following day, they showed up for practice and bragged about the fight. Coach Blitzkrieg had been recruiting. He brought out two new players. One of them was about six-foot four and weighed about two hundred and fifty pounds. Allen said, "He looks just like that guy who played in the movie *Rooster something-or-other*."

"Yes," said Larry. "He's the spitting image of." He stopped, "But I thought he was dead."

"No, he made three movies after he had cancer," said Bill. "But I think he's going to have to take that vest off."

The big recruit walked over to Coach Blitzkrieg. "Where do you want me?"

Allen, Larry, Michael and Bill walked over to Coach Blitzkrieg. "He really can hit," said Larry.

Coach said, "Yeah, can't he though. He'll knock it a country mile."

Coach Blitzkrieg looked at Larry, Bill and Allen. "What are you doing here? Get over there and take batting practice," he said, pointing to the ball diamond. "Theresa has come here to coach you in hitting. You better get your ass out there." Coach caught himself just as he was going to obscenely chastise Allen.

As they started trotting out to take some swings, up walked another recruit. He's was about five-foot eleven and looked fairly athletic but had a deformed right hand.

"Nice to see you here, Bob." Coach said.

Allen looked at Angelo. "Don't I know that guy?"

Angelo said, "He looks like a politician."

"He's got only one good arm. He probably can't hit for shit," said Larry.

Allen looked at Larry. "You got two good arms and you can't hit for shit."

"That's harsh," said Larry.

Theresa yelled, "Come on over for batting practice." Allen went first. Theresa coached him. "Get your hips level. Shift your weight from your back foot to the front foot." In another few swings, Allen started placing the balls. She then worked with Bill. Left-handed Larry stepped up. He was tense. "Ease up," said Theresa. "Your arms are long enough. You ought to get good extension on the ball. You should be able to knock it easily." Larry took three swings. They were all grounders. Theresa said to him, "Relax. Just follow through."

"I always try to give one hundred ten percent when I'm batting," Larry said.

Theresa responded, "When you play the outfield you're very relaxed. You're a good outfielder. Now, just relax at the plate." Larry swung again and hit another grounder to second base.

Theresa watched him. Just as the ball was about to be pitched, she asked, "Did you get 'any' from Sarah this morning?" Larry had a smile on his face. His body relaxed. He made solid contact with the ball and knocked it about two hundred sixty feet into right field, to the surprise of everyone.

"See," said Theresa. "You've got to relax. Keep your eye on the ball and don't worry about hitting it. You're too tight," she said. "Step up there again." Just as Angelo was going to pitch, she said, "Which do you like best—topless or bottomless dancers?" A smile came to Larry's face and he hit the ball again about three hundred feet. Allen, who had been playing in, saw the ball go over his head."

Allen turned to Bill, "I don't know what Theresa is telling him, but Larry hasn't hit like that this year."

"I'll bet he ain't hit like that his whole life," Bill said.

As Angelo threw another pitch, Theresa asked, "Does Sarah wear white or black panties?" Larry smiled and stroked the ball almost to the fence this time.

"Unbelievable," said Larry.

Coach sent Bob and the big guy up to the plate. Surprisingly, Bob hit very strong line drives.

The big recruit came up and just pounded the ball. Every one was deep in the outfield. The balls that didn't go to the fence, or over it, were rocket shots that bounced off the fence. Coach Blitzkrieg watched him. "We've really got a chance."

Theresa walked over to the coach. "These guys will help, but I still think we're seriously out-personnelled."

"We've got to play a whole game, or else it's not going to prove that cancer patients can fully recover," said Coach.

"Were trying to show we're good in spite of cancer. We definitely don't want to be embarrassed," said Bobby.

The coach called them in. "Listen up. We've got some lineup changes. Larry, you're going to be batting last, in the eleventh position. Bob's going to bat sixth."

"That's okay," Larry said, "I just want to play in the championship. If I start in the outfield, I'm making a contribution."

The coach went over the starting lineup, gave them the positions and told them, "Be ready for tomorrow."

Leo walked up with some new, flashy uniforms. He also brought out eight new bats. "We're going to be using these tomorrow."

"I want one of these bats. I want to take it home and work on it for Larry," Theresa said.

Coach Blitzkrieg looked quizzically at her. "Okay." He gave her a bat as the team left the diamond.

Sylvia, Sarah and Bonnie approached Theresa. "How are you doing?" said Bonnie.

"Fine," said Theresa. "It's fun being out here."

"I bet you it's more fun because Michael's here," said Bonnie.

"Yes, it is. In fact, I'm leaving with him. He's taking me out tonight. We're meeting my brother and sister for dinner," said Theresa.

"He's meeting your family?" asked Sarah.

"He's not scared off?" asked Bonnie.

"No," said Theresa, "as a matter of fact, he's been looking forward to meeting my brother and sister. They live in Tucson and they're here to watch the game tomorrow."

"We always see you out here for softball practice. Do you coach softball full time?" asked Sarah.

"No," laughed Theresa, "I was a regular road deputy for Maricopa County. After my cancer diagnosis, I was transferred to the records division. I played competitively up until I had cancer. I'm forty years old. I'm a little old to play."

"Only forty?" questioned Lisa. "And you're too old to play? You're twenty years younger than the rest of us."

"Speak for yourself," said Bonnie.

"What happened that you're not married anymore?" asked Sylvia.

"When I developed breast cancer and told Frank, he couldn't handle it. He stayed with me for four months and left after my hair fell out from the chemotherapy. We got divorced. He remarried and moved to Denver. I haven't seen him in two years."

A sympathetic silence descended upon the questioners. Sylvia asked, "Do you have any kids?"

"No, wish I did. The doctors tell me that I can have them, but I'm forty years old. I'm not sure my biological clock is ticking, I believe it stopped," said Theresa.

"Good luck tonight with Michael and your relatives. I hope they hit it off."

"Thanks," said Theresa, "I really appreciate your support."

Bonnie, with a lecherous smile, said, "Are you going to do it tonight?"

Theresa got red-faced. "That's none of your business."

"Yes, it is," said Sylvia. "We're very interested in Michael and you."

"Michael is a little hesitant because he's not sure whether he can perform or not," said Sylvia. "You're probably a little bit concerned because of your mastectomies."

"Dammit," said Theresa, "I don't need to be reminded of that."

"It's okay," said Sylvia. "Look at most of these models. They don't have breasts like oranges or lemons. They're like two eggs."

"Yeah," said bosomy Bonnie, "fried eggs."

They all laughed. Theresa said, "Yeah, I am a little concerned."

"Well, ply him with a few drinks," said Lisa.

"No, no," said Sarah. "Tomorrow is game day. One, max."

She walked off, and Michael put his arm around her. Bonnie said, "Ah, young love. We'll see if she has any stories to tell tomorrow."

Lisa looked at Bonnie. "And you'll be hanging on every tantalizing detail, won't you?"

"What's the matter with that?" said Bonnie. "We'd all better get our husbands home and rub ointment on their aching muscles. It's going to be over tomorrow. I don't know what's going to happen to all of us after the game."

"I've been around this for years. There's always going to be next year," Sarah said.

Lisa, Bonnie and Sylvia looked at her. "Are you really sure there's going to be a next year?"

"Yes," said Sarah. "There is going to be a next year. This isn't the end. I don't even think you should be thinking about it."

"You're right," said Sylvia.

They all nodded.

"We've got to get home and massage their aching bodies," said Lisa. "We're supposed to be there about five o'clock tomorrow. I just hope they don't get humiliated."

As always, they had to go to the doctor's office. He was waiting there with a group of his colleagues. The ball players all went into the conference room and assumed the position. The doctor and his staff performed the digital examinations.

Leo chimed, "What kind of dreams do you guys have at night?" The doctors laughed and chuckled and continued changing the gloves.

"We're also going to do a PSA blood test as well."

"Thank God. I know when the nurses come in we're going to be treated properly. Why are there no female prostate doctors?" asked Bill.

"No self-respecting woman would want to hang around with scurvy scum like you," said Dr. Gee.

There was quiet for about ten seconds. Then, Allen said, "Real nice bedside manner, Doc."

Dr. Gee said, "Several of my colleagues, some staff members and I are going to the game tomorrow. We'll be in the stands. If anything happens to you, we'll be right there."

Bill turned around. "What do you mean if anything happens to us?"

"Not from the cancer," said Dr. Gee. "But you're probably going to pull a hamstring or two. If any one of you hits a triple, we'll probably have to bring out the oxygen."

"Nice comment. Next time you play golf, do you mind if we come out and heckle you?" asked Larry.

Dr. Gee turned to Larry. "On a golf course, you're only allowed to whisper."

"Why is that?" asked Leo. "We're swinging at a moving ball. Both teams are yelling. You go to a golf course, and the ball is lying there, and no one is allowed to talk."

The doctor pulled himself up and said, "That's because golf is for gentlemen, and softball..."

Angelo said, "Is for cancer-ridden vermin like us."

"That's harsh," said Dr. Gee. "You're all in good shape. We'll see you tomorrow. Gentlemen, I appreciate the opportunity to treat you and wish you good luck tomorrow." After they left Dr. Gee commented to his colleagues, "There goes the most unusual combination of men I have ever met."

CHAPTER 12

THE RECNAC TEAM showed up at the Arizona Fairgrounds at five o'clock, resplendent in their new yellow and green uniforms. "They really look cute, don't they? With those uniforms, some of them have young looking tushes," said Sylvia.

"Who's got a young-looking tush?" asked Bonnie. "I haven't seen any."

"Look at those three right there. Those pants must have a built-in girdle in them," commented Lisa.

Bonnie said, "Those are the special compression shorts that Leo had made."

"Has anybody here seen Michael? Or Theresa?" asked Lisa.

"No," said Sylvia, "and I'm dying to find out about last night. Oh look, here they come."

Michael and Theresa walked up. Bonnie immediately yelled, "Theresa, come here, come here." Theresa walked over, wearing a RECNAC uniform.

"What happened last night? Did you and Michael get together?" asked Bonnie.

"He took me home. He said he had to go meet with the guys," said Theresa.

"Tough being a batting coach and girlfriend at the same time," said Lisa.

"That's right. All five of them were over watching a ball game on television, telling lies and spreading liniment on themselves," said Sarah.

"That's normal," said Lisa. "Allen went to bed and slept like a log. He got up early. He's been nervous all day."

"What's that picture on the bat?" asked Bonnie.

"Oh," said Theresa, "I found out Larry's batting problem."

"Yesterday in batting practice he was hitting really well," said Sylvia.

"He had to relax. I would make a suggestive comment on every pitch. The trick is," she continued, "you've got to keep him relaxed. I took this bat home and put a decal of a blond pinup on it. Every ballplayer always looks at his bat. If he'll look at it, smile, and relax, he'll be able to hit."

"Are you kidding?" Sarah asked. "That will make him a better hitter?"

"Worked yesterday," said Theresa.

They all stood up as the crowd cheered. The RECNAC team watched as the opposing team took the field. Bill said, "Holy cow! Do you know who that is?"

"No," said Rooster.

"That guy in left field, that's Hank Ostrafski. In left center, that's George McKie."

"Fine," said Larry. "Why don't they bring Babe Ruth out here, too."

Just then a roar went up from the crowd and Coach Blitzkrieg said, "Don't worry. It ain't Babe Ruth."

Theresa came over. "Coach, I told you they had a good team. They really loaded up."

"Why are they bringing out these people to play us?" Coach asked.

"They think that you've got a pretty good team, and they don't want cancer patients beating healthy people," said Theresa.

"Who else do they have?" Coach asked.

"They've got three that played minor league ball and a couple of guys that played for Cleveland," said Bobby.

"I thought they were going to be celebrities like movie stars, sportscasters, and maybe a couple of weather men," said Larry.

"They are movie stars and weather men who just happen to be great ball players," said Theresa. "These people came to play, and we're going to have our hands full."

"Look at that lineup," said Leo. "Ken Johnson is their designated hitter, Dave Whitcomb is at first base, and Lewis Boyer is the short-stop."

"Charles Strong? He played AAA ball for the Los Angeles Stars," said Allen.

"Yeah, and in the infield you've got Rene Cormier at second base, and Wayne Sutton at third."

"Yeah," said Allen, "and the catcher for the Cleveland Indians."

"Ed Davis is relief pitcher. D. Valle is pitching."

"Don't worry about the pitcher," said Rooster. "Seems like I've met him before."

There was a crash in the dugout. Everyone turned to watch Larry throw his bat, bag and other equipment on the concrete floor of the dugout. Two of his prized bats bounced off the fence fabric and hit the dugout bench. Larry was trying to pick up the water cooler and smash it to the floor when Coach and Allen grabbed him.

"Hold on, Larry!" yelled Coach. "What's the matter?"

"Look at those S.O.B.s up there," said Larry, pointing at the crowd. "They're waiting for us to lose this game."

"They can root for whoever they want to," said Allen, "it's a free country."

"Screw them!" shouted Larry. "Those people would root against the kids in the special Olympics."

"What the hell's the matter with you!" exclaimed Coach. "I've never seen you get mad."

"We're supposed to come here and play a softball game for charity. I expected a fair game with competitive personnel. They've recruited the best players within five hundred miles to play us," said Larry.

"Why the hell do they want us to lose?" asked Bill.

"Hold on," said Leo. "They don't want us to lose. They just want a good game. The celebrities increase the gate receipts. Remember, we're playing for cancer research and treatment."

"You got what you asked for, Larry," said Coach.

"No!" said Larry. "They want to beat us bad. They brought these players out here for one reason. They want to be sure that someone with cancer doesn't have a chance to win."

"Sí," said Angelo and Pablo, both nodding.

"I don't know why they want us to lose. They sure aren't giving us any breaks. Screw 'em all," screamed Larry, "I'm tired of being a damned loser. I'm tired of being downsized, terminated and early re-tired."

"You got that right," said Bill. "The damn insurance company says I can't be a carpenter anymore. Now I walk around mowing yards at half the pay."

"Who the hell gets to make these decisions?" said Larry.

"It's not the players over there. Somebody just paid 'em to show up," said Leo.

"I thought they might send people out to lose to us so we would look better," said Allen.

"That ain't the way it's going to be today," said Bobby. "We're going to have to win this game."

"Those fans could be our brothers and sisters up there, even our kids. They're out here after our blood, the bastards," yelled Larry.

"Larry, will you calm down?" asked Coach as he grabbed both of Larry's shoulders with his big, meaty hands.

Larry, who was on the edge of tears, nodded. The veins in his neck still stood out.

"Take it easy," said Allen. "Let's go outside and form a circle. I'll lead a prayer."

Larry calmed down. They formed up around the on-deck circle. They each knelt down on one knee and put their hands in the center. Allen led a prayer: "Lord, thank you for this opportunity to play in friendly competition," Allen looked right at Larry. "We thank you for giving us the opportunity to gather in fellowship and prayer. We ask that none of the players on either team sustain injuries and that all demonstrate good sportsmanship." With a slight wink at Larry, Allen lifted his eyes sky-ward. "God, we know you are very busy but we would really appreciate it if you would send down some angels to help us stomp their celebrity asses! Amen!"

"AMEN!" roared the entire team. They broke up and high-fived each other.

The umpire came over. "Coach, get your team on the field." REC-NAC stormed onto the diamond.

As they ran out to the field, Bill turned to Leo and said, "What kind of bats do they have?"

Leo grinned. "The other team is used to playing with wooden bats. I gave them the best wood bats that I could find."

"Wow," said Larry. "They're going to be using wood bats and we get metal bats?"

"Yes," said Leo. "Even you might get a hit."

"I don't know about that," said Larry. "But I'll be able to catch them."

Theresa and Bobby stayed in the dugout and looked at the celebrities. Theresa said, "Those guys are mighty old."

"They are old," said Bobby. "Nobody on our team is a teenager either. We average fifty-eight years and nine months. The first guy up is McKie. Let's see if Angelo can get the old bloop ball on him."

Angelo pitched to McKie and he smashed it. Larry had been playing deep; fading back all the way to the fence, he leaped up and caught the ball over the top of the fence.

Allen rushed over to him. "Great catch! How did you do that?"

Larry looked at the eight-foot high fence. "How did I do that?" asked a perplexed Larry.

"I don't know." Allen gently reached over and took the ball out of Larry's glove and threw it in.

"How did I catch that ball?" muttered Larry.

Joe Natural came up to the plate, and he lined a hit behind the shortstop, John. Rachel came up and smashed a single. With two men on and one out, James Wiley came up to bat and Angelo pitched a couple of pitches outside.

Rooster yelled at Angelo, "Throw it in. Let him hit it."

Angelo pitched it in, and Wiley parked the ball over the left field fence.

Allen and Larry both watched the ball. Larry said, "He's pretty good, isn't he?"

"Good thing he had a wooden bat. If he had been using our bat, it would probably still be in the air," said Allen.

Johnson came up next and grounded out to short, and Whitcomb hit a liner to third base that Michael snagged with a really fine play. Sylvia jumped up. "Way to go, Michael. Good play." Celebrities 3--REC-

NAC 0.

RECNAC went up to bat. "Come on John, get hold of one," yelled Theresa. John punched a ball through the infield. Coach nailed a pitch, but McKie went back to the fence and caught it.

Rooster was up next. The catcher for the Celebrities was giving him a hard time, trying to distract him. "That pitcher's got your number," said the catcher.

"Yeah," said Rooster. "It's written on my back."

"You're not going to touch him," said the catcher. The first pitch was a ball. "The next one's going to be right over the plate." Rooster didn't say anything. The next pitch was a called strike.

"You'd better watch out, old man," said the catcher. "You're gonna strike out." The next two pitches were balls.

Rooster glared at the pitcher. "If you throw me another ball, I'll walk. If you throw a strike, I'll knock it over the fence. Which will it be?"

The pitcher laughed at Rooster. "I'd call that bold talk for a one-eyed fat man."

Rooster's face turned red. He got all of the next pitch. The moment he hit that ball, there was no doubt. The ball cleared the left field fence by forty feet. Rooster trotted around the bases.

Leo came up and lined to Wiley in right center. Allen grounded meekly to Charles Strong at shortstop. End of the first inning, score 3-2. In the top of the second, the celebrities got two runs before Larry made a diving catch to retire the side.

Bob led off as the designated hitter and got a single. Angelo got another single, and Michael got a single. Bases loaded. Bill got a single, scoring Bob and Angelo. Pablo lined to Wiley, and the throw came in so fast that no one could score. Larry stepped out of the on-deck circle. The umpire said, "Batter, what's on that bat? You can't have a nude woman on your bat."

"It's for medicinal purposes," said Larry.

"You're one of these tight hitters," said the catcher. "You put that decal on the barrel of the bat."

"It's illegal," said the umpire.

The umpire sent Larry back to the dugout to get a new bat. Theresa, who was coaching third, walked over to Sarah. "That was a gimmick

I used so he wouldn't stay so tight. If he's worried about his batting, all he does is ground to the pitcher."

Bonnie watched Larry come back to the plate with a new bat.

"You can do it," yelled Bonnie.

"Yeah, sock it," said Lisa.

The pitch came in, and Larry swung. It was a miserable two-bouncer to the pitcher, who converted into a double-play. At the end of two innings, Celebrities 5--RECNAC 4.

Theresa came back to the dugout. "We're not doing so bad."

"I'm surprised too," Bobby said. "The team has started to come together. If they don't make any horrendous errors, at least there won't be any mercy killing."

"You think we can hold this team?" said Theresa.

"That's their lead-off man up again. He is not going to be surprised this time, and I think Angelo's got a better idea of how to pitch to their batters, too," said Bobby.

Bobby shook his head. "I don't know how these guys can play competitively. These Celebrities are really a stacked team."

The Celebrities got three runs in the top of the third inning. Larry nailed the runner at home when he tried to score on an outfield fly. RECNAC got two runs in the bottom of the third. The Celebrities jumped on the RECNAC team and scored six runs in the fourth inning on two errors. In the bottom of the fourth, RECNAC scored three runs, but Larry hit into another double play to kill the rally. At the end of four innings, the score was 14-9.

The Celebrities did not score in the fifth inning, on sparkling plays by Michael at third base, Coach at first base, and Larry in left field. In the bottom of the fifth inning, RECNAC scored two more runs, but Larry again hit into a double play to end the rally. Score, 14-11.

In the sixth inning, the Celebrities scored three more runs. At the top of the seventh inning, the score was Celebrities 17, RECNAC 14. Theresa paced in the dugout. "They're really playin' them a game."

"Yes," said Bobby. "I didn't think it would be this close. We've got to hold them this inning, and then we need four runs. We've got the bottom of the batting order coming up. Larry's hit into three double plays."

"We'll worry about that later. Maybe they'll walk him," Theresa said.

"Why would anybody walk a guy who's hit into three double plays? We've got to hold them," said Bobby.

"They're playing against a team with three Hall of Famers, three other professionals, and some good natural athletes," said Theresa.

"No matter what happens here," Bobby said, "I'm proud to have been a part of it. Two months ago when these five guys pulled up to the Mayo Clinic for cancer treatment, they had probably just finished writing their wills. Now they've done something together with the other six that would have been unbelievable."

"Let's see if we can get through this inning," said Theresa.

The Celebrities looked at the scoreboard. They had the bottom of their batting order up. Charles Strong led off with a double, but Sutton hit to the shortstop and was thrown out at first, leaving Strong unable to advance. Cormier, the designated hitter, slapped a single into left field. Larry was all over it, and his throw to John at shortstop held men on first and third with one out. Strong wasn't able to score. Their catcher lined to short, but it was speared by John. Eicher was walked on a close call, but D. Valle popped to Pablo at second base.

"Way to go, guys," shouted Allen. "We've held them. Now, let's get four runs and we're out of here."

"Okay," yelled Coach. "Bob, you're up first." Bob ripped another screeching single between first and second. Angelo followed with a bloop single over the shortstop's head, putting men on first and second. Michael hit a double, scoring Bob and advancing Angelo to third. The score was 17-15. Bill popped out, with the catcher for the Celebrities making an excellent play. Pablo hit a wicked liner over second base that was speared by the shortstop. Larry was on deck.

"Oh," groaned Theresa, from the third base coaching position. "Tying run on second, two outs, and up comes Larry. I can see he's as tight as can be." Larry walked up to the plate. The entire outfield played shallow.

"Time," yelled Coach Blitzkrieg. The coach walked up to Larry, "Now be calm, relax up there."

"I'm tight as I can be. There are fifteen thousand people in the stands watching. I'm really nervous. You got a pinch hitter for me?" said Larry.

"I don't have a pinch hitter," said Coach. "You're all we've got. They're playing you shallow. I want you to relax and just lift the ball."

"What?" asked Larry, pointing out to Wiley in center field. "You think I'm going to be able to hit a ball over his head?"

At that, McKie yelled, "Looks like he's coming your way. He may try to hit it over your head."

Wiley looked over at McKie, "Yeah, him and Vic Wertz."

"It looks like he's going towards center. Let's shade away from the foul lines," said Wiley.

Coach said, "I don't want you to hit the ball to center field," pointing toward center field. "Pull the ball toward the right field foul line."

Meanwhile, Theresa walked over to the wives. "You know they made him throw his bat out."

"Yes," said Sarah. "What was that about?"

"When he gets up to the plate, you have to distract him," said Theresa. "I put a decal of a pinup on his bat. It seemed to take his mind off the situation. The umpire won't let him use it. So I need your help."

"Anything," said Sarah. "Tell me what you want."

Theresa looked at her. "Unbutton your blouse, unhook your bra, and flash him."

"What!" exclaimed Sarah.

"Just before he goes in to the plate, call his name. When he looks over here, flash him. That'll take his mind off the ball a little bit. Just distract him so he's not so tight."

"Is that all it's going to take to win this game?" screamed the voluptuous Bonnie. "I'll do it."

"No," yelled Theresa, "you'll blow his fuse. You three take out your cameras. Put on the flash attachments. Just as Larry hits the ball, point the cameras at the outfielder and shoot. Make the cameras flash as fast and bright as you can. Sarah, you do it before the ball is pitched. Okay?" Theresa walked away muttering, "What a way to play softball."

"They do it in the bigs," commented Bobby.

Larry walked up to the plate. Sarah yelled at him. Larry was the only one who turned around. She opened her blouse and flashed her husband. He'd seen her naked, but he'd never seen her breasts in front of so many people. He shook his head in disbelief. A smile came to his face. He stepped into the batter's box and waited for the pitch. It was a ball and he didn't swing.

After the pitch, Larry stepped away from the plate. Sarah yelled and threw him a kiss. He began to laugh. He stepped back into the plate. You could see that he was relaxed. The ball came over the plate, Larry swung, THWACK, and the ball rocketed along the right field line.

"Yo," said the second baseman, "right field." The right fielder, blinded by camera flashes, lost the ball. He heard the thud as the ball hit and started skipping along the right field line. He managed to get his glove on it and deflect the ball. Angelo scored. Michael ,scampering at the crack of the bat, scored, and Larry was rounding second going into third.

As he approached third, Theresa held her hands down. "Slide, slide!" screamed Theresa.

The throw from right field came in hard, but high. "Safe!" signaled the umpire. "He's under the tag!"

"I thought I was going to hit a home run to win the game," said Larry as he dusted himself off.

"Nice hit! Home runs only happen in movies. Two outs. Crack of the bat, you're gone," yelled Theresa.

"Gotcha," said Larry.

John lined the first pitch to left center for a single, Larry scored, and the game was over. The RECNAC team jumped on each other. They pounded each other on the back. They congratulated John for getting the winning hit, and high-fived Larry for hitting a triple in the clutch.

Coach said, "Larry, nice hit. You made one helluva contribution. You scored the winning run."

Larry ran over to Sarah. "We won! We won! Thanks for the help." He gave her a lecherous smile, a big hug and a sweaty, salty kiss.

"Yes, nice triple," she said. "You need a bath!"

"I love you, Sarah." He hugged her some more. "Hey, Theresa, I really appreciate your working with me," he said as he jogged over to her.

"Nice hit. All you have to do is relax," said Theresa.

"That's what Coach told me. Wow, I guess he does know what he's doing," said Larry.

All the women looked at each other, as the men trotted off to the dugout to collect their equipment.

"Theresa," said Bonnie, "that whole thing was your idea. Sarah flashing Larry to make him relax. Us flashing the cameras to distract the outfielders. How can those men be so dumb?"

"That's probably why we love thcm," Lisa said.

"Yes, and that's why we punish them by making them buy us fifty thousand dollar automobiles, or two-carat diamond rings. It's kind of a marriage fine for stupidity," said Bonnie. All the women laughed.

"Look," said Sylvia, "there are television crews here, with camera equipment."

"Coach Blitzkrieg," said the attractive brunette TV reporter, "what is the purpose of this game?"

"To prove to the patients, the players and their families that they can lead normal lives. They can get back in the game."

"Can they lead normal lives?" asked the reporter?

"You saw them play. What do you think?" said Coach Blitzkrieg. "They beat a good, healthy team. We also raised funds for cancer research, thanks to your station's publicity."

"Theresa came with us to say good-bye," said Sarah.

"Good-bye," said Michael, "why?"

"The ball game is over," said Theresa. "You will all be going back home. I had a great time. I wish you all the best."

"You can't leave now. What about Michael?" said Bonnie.

Theresa walked over to Michael and shook his hand. "I wish you the best; you can be a good softball player."

Bonnie hugged Theresa. "With all the things that happened, I forgot about your problems."

Michael heard Bonnie's statement and asked Sylvia, "What's Theresa's problem?"

"Theresa had breast cancer," said Sylvia. "Didn't you know?"

"How the hell would I know that?" asked Michael. "If you knew, why didn't you tell me?"

"We didn't think any of the men had a right to know," said Sylvia.

"I would have liked to know. I didn't want to put my problems on Theresa. My ex-fiancée sent the ring back when I became ill, and Theresa may feel the same way."

"She doesn't," said Sylvia. "She really likes you." They watched Theresa pick up her equipment bag as she started to walk to the parking lot.

"Michael," said Bill, "don't let that prize-winning heifer get away. Go carry Theresa's bag. I'll carry yours. You've only got two minutes to tell her how you feel."

Michael ran after Theresa. "Wait up," he said, "I'll carry your bag."

"You don't have to. I can manage," said Theresa as she held on to her equipment bag. There were tears in her eyes. One had run down her sweaty, dusty cheek leaving a clean path.

"Why are you crying?" asked Michael. "Does your cancer cause you pain?"

"It's none of your business. My cancer doesn't cause any pain and who told you?" Theresa asked him.

"Sylvia did, just now," said Michael. "How's the cancer?"

"It's just like yours; it's in remission," said Theresa.

"You knew I had it. Why didn't you tell me your problems?" said Michael.

"I thought if you found out I had cancer you wouldn't want to have anything more to do with me. Besides, you never even tried to kiss me," said Theresa.

My last girlfriend, fiancée actually, mailed back the engagement ring after I told her I had cancer," said Michael.

"So, you're still carrying a torch for her, I guess," said Theresa.

"Not any more," said Michael.

"For who then?" asked Theresa.

Michael said nothing. He just reached over and pulled her to him as tightly as he could. The sudden movement surprised Theresa. She hugged him back.

"Don't you try to kiss me, I'm sure I have bad breath, and I'm stinky and wet with perspiration," said Theresa.

"Do you think a shower and a toothbrush would help?" asked Michael.

"Couldn't hurt," said Theresa. "I have a great big shower." Michael picked up her bag with his right arm and pulled her to him with his left arm, and they walked to the parking lot.

Bonnie watched Theresa and Michael walk away. "There they go," said Bonnie, "I have to worry about Leo and that pair, too."

"Where are they going?" asked Sarah.

"They're going to her home, I bet," said Bonnie.

"Do you think they will be successful?" Sylvia asked with a mischievous smile.

"Theresa and Michael are going home together. You done good, Bill," said Sarah.

Larry walked over. "Well," said Larry, "you think they're going to be able to do it?"

"That's why we're concerned," said Lisa. "Theresa's concerned that she won't be sexually attractive to Michael. Michael's not sure he's sexually potent. Even if he's partially potent, we're afraid that Theresa's not going to be able to turn him on."

"What the hell can we do about that?" asked a tired and exasperated Bill.

"Maybe we should pray," said Allen.

"You mean we stand around and pray that they can screw? Ouch!" said Bill as Sylvia elbowed him in the ribs. "Sylvia, why did you do that?"

"Bill, sometimes I think you're so damned dumb," said Sylvia.

"At times like this, I think we ought to all join hands and pray," said Allen.

"It don't seem right," said Bill. "We're going to ask God to help people screw?" Sylvia elbowed him in the ribs again. "Ouch! Sylvia, quit doing that."

"Bill, you say one more dumb thing and I'll knock a knot on your head," warned Sylvia.

"What the hell's the problem?" asked Bonnie. "You act like it's unusual for people to join hands and pray for two people to screw."

"Not screw, sleep together," said Lisa.

Rev. Allen said, "We want our friends who know Theresa and Michael to hold hands. They have gone off into the evening and hopefully will be able to have sexual relations with each other. If they are successful in this endeavor, they will probably be married. We are asking for divine guidance and assistance in this undertaking."

The entire RECNAC team joined hands in a circle.

Rev. Allen continued, "Oh Lord, we request your assistance for thy servants Michael and Theresa, who have been medically afflicted with a partial sexual dysfunction that could prohibit them from consummating a marriage union. We are praying here with their friends that with your help and intercession, both parties will be successful in their endeavors through thy mighty power. Amen."

The entire RECNAC team shouted, "AMEN!" Bonnie went out and high-fived Sylvia, Sara and Lisa. Allen and Larry shook hands.

Bill turned to Larry. "Did we do a fornication prayer?"

"That's right!" said Larry jubilantly.

"I tried that when I was seventeen." Bill said, "God never answered."

"What next, Coach?" asked the reporter.

"All of us are going back to our careers with renewed emphasis on our families," said Coach Blitzkrieg.

The men were cleaning out the dugout, taking congratulations from the other team and from each other. They were whooping and hollering, and behaving like fifty-nine-year-old teenagers.

The wives watched as three cars pulled up. Six men wearing dark-blue suits, white shirts, dark ties and sunglasses approached the REC-NAC team.

The television crew had finished talking with Coach Blitzkrieg. As the players in uniform walked out of the dugout, the six men yelled, "F.B.I.!"

The F.B.I. agent in charge asked, "Which one of you is Leo Able?"

"I'm Leo Able. What's the problem?"

"We have a warrant for your arrest," said the agent.

"What for?" Leo asked.

"Violation of the Securities and Exchange Commission regulations relating to insider trading with the QRX Corporation," said the agent.

"I have no idea what you're talking about," said Leo.

"You're under arrest," said the agent as he placed his hand on Leo's shoulder.

Bonnie asked, "What do you mean he's under arrest? He hasn't even been there for the last three months."

"Ma'am, that's not our job. Our job is just to arrest him," said the agent.

"We only want Leo Able. The rest of you are free to go."

The F.B.I. escorted a handcuffed Leo Able to their car. Bonnie walked along, but she couldn't go with Leo. She came back and asked, "Larry, isn't your brother an attorney?"

"Yes, I'll call my brother right now. Can I use your phone?" asked Larry.

"Sure," said Bonnie, and Larry followed her to the car.

Bill, Larry, Allen and Michael watched Leo leave in the F.B.I. sedan. Allen observed with the experienced eye of a minister who had seen members of his congregation go off in a black and white. He told Bill and Michael, "At least it's the F.B.I. They observe the Miranda Rules. He's a white executive charged with a white-collar crime. He'll be out on bond in twenty-four hours."

"How do you know that?" asked Bill.

"Experience in dealing with police in my neighborhood," said Allen. "The F.B.I. guys don't know why they arrested him. Leo will keep his mouth shut. By the time the real investigators get here, Leo will have a hearing, and they can't talk to him without a lawyer."

"Wow," said Michael, "you sound like a lawyer."

"Every inner-city minister is kind of a lawyer," said Allen.

Larry, Lisa, Sylvia, Sarah, Bonnie and Theresa joined the men. Bonnie showed great composure as she said, "Larry's brother will be at the Federal Courthouse at ten a.m. tomorrow for Leo's hearing."

"What's Leo done?" asked Bill.

"He ain't done nothing," said Sylvia as she stepped on Bill's foot.

CHAPTER 13

THE U.S. District Courthouse in Phoenix sits at a busy intersection. It is a Greek Revival granite bastion of solemnity, which excludes all visitors. The Constitution of the United States says that courts should be open to the public. Yet signs on the door warn: "Enter On Official Business Only."

The arraignment in the case of United States vs. Leo Able was scheduled for ten o'clock. Wendell Nedil put his briefcase on the X-ray scanner, where it was reviewed for any dangerous implements. After it was determined he had only papers, including copies of the indictment and pens, which were definitely not more powerful than the sword, and had showed his bar identification card, his driver's license, and two other types of identification, he was permitted to enter the courthouse. All the members of the RECNAC team had to drop their wallets, purses and keys, and walk through a metal detector. Then a marshal ran a hand-held detector up and down their bodies to see if they had any metal implements. After this search, the members of the RECNAC team and their wives were permitted to enter the courtroom.

Wendell and Leo were seated in the area restricted to the bar. The members of the RECNAC team sat two rows behind. They had no idea what Leo was charged with. Before the judge came out, Bill handed Wendell a "get out of jail free" letter from the Mayo Clinic.

Wendell went over to the U.S. District Attorney and the Assistant District Attorney, shook their hands and exchanged a business card. Several newspaper reporters entered and sat down to watch the hearing.

The bailiff stamped his foot and said, "Hear ye, hear ye. The United States District Court for the southern district of Arizona is now in session, Judge Merkle presiding." Judge Merkle, age 75, entered, sat down, looked sternly toward the defense table where Leo was sitting and then smiled at the prosecutors.

Wendell stood up to get a clarification. Judge Merkle said to him, "Sit down. I'll hear from you later." The judge turned to the district attorney. "Mr. District Attorney, are you prepared to go forward?"

"Yes sir," said the district attorney.

"Have you met the defense counsel in this case?" asked the Judge.

"Yes, we have, your honor," said the district attorney.

At that time the judge turned to Wendell. "Please hand two business cards to the clerk."

"Your honor, I am Mr. Pierce, assistant federal district attorney. We are here on an arraignment in the case of the United States vs. Leo Able, who is charged with a violation of 47 U.S.C. §127. To wit, that during the period of June first of last year through October first of this year, he did engage in insider trading of stock of the QRX corporation of which he was a division president."

"Continue please," said the Judge.

"In a period of three months, shares of QRX corporation dropped twenty points. He sold his stock short on June first of last year, and covered it in October, netting a profit of approximately one million dollars. We are requesting disgorgement of one million dollars, criminal penalties of five hundred thousand dollars and twenty years in jail."

"Mr. Pierce, present your case!" said Judge Merkle.

"The defendant had inside information that QRX stock was going to go down. He knew that a news release would reveal he had cancer and he was being relieved of his job. The stock market would react to such an announcement. He sold 50,000 shares short. The stock plummeted twenty points. He covered the stock and made a million dollar profit."

"All right, defense counsel, do you have any exhibits to offer?" Wendell handed a letter to the Judge.

"Defense Counsel, have you shown this exhibit to the prosecutor?" asked the Judge.

The judge said, "This is a letter from the Mayo Clinic. It states that the defendant, Leo Able, has a serious cancer condition."

Bonnie whispered, "Nobody told me about that."

"Shhh," said Michael. "Bill typed in Leo's name on Bobby's 'Get out of jail free' letter."

"Wow," said Sylvia. "You think we'll get away with that?"

"I don't know. Let's see what the judge is going to say," said Sarah.

"Mr. Prosecutor, have you seen this exhibit that has been handed to me by the defense counsel?" asked the Judge. "The defendant is suffering from cancer. It doesn't appear that he has a long life expectancy. Mr. Pierce...?"

"No, your honor, we weren't aware of this.." said Mr. Pierce.

"Let's go off the record. Side bar," said the Judge.

"Mr. Pierce, this letter indicates that the defendant hasn't got a long to live. What is the prosecution's position?" asked the Judge.

"We think that Mr. Able is only peripherally involved. He may have sold his stock because the company shunted him out to pasture," said Mr. Pierce.

The judge looked at Wendell. "Is that right?" When Wendell started to talk, the judge cut him off. "You don't have to say anything. The prosecution has to make their case."

"Our procedure was to scare him with twenty years in prison. Offer him immunity, and see if he would testify against the company executives," said Mr. Pierce.

"You're threatening him with twenty years. The doctor says he's got three months," said the Judge.

"He might want to be a government witness," said Mr. Pierce.

"If he becomes a government witness, would he have to give up the million dollars?" the Judge demanded to know.

"Yes, he would," said Mr. Pierce.

"He might have sold his stock because he was dying of cancer and trying to get his estate in order," said the Judge.

Wendell tried to say something, but the judge said, "Now hold on. It's not your turn yet. Mr. Prosecutor, can you guarantee him he'd live for twenty years?"

"No sir," said Mr. Pierce.

"You can't guarantee he's going to live for three months," said the

Judge.

"Your honor, the prosecution does not want to drop its case."

"If he sold his stock because he was trying to get his probate in order, doesn't that ruin your case?" asked Judge Merkle.

"That would be a fact that would have to go to the jury," said Mr. Pierce.

"I'm sure defense counsel would raise that issue. You're looking at a defendant who has three months to live. The government can't offer him immunity," said Judge Merkle.

"We weren't aware of this medical condition," said Mr. Pierce.

"He was playing on a team of cancer patients," said Judge Merkle.

"Just because a person has cancer doesn't mean he's going to die," said Mr. Pierce.

"Okay, Madam Clerk, get the Mayo Clinic on the speaker phone. Here's a defendant who's probably going to die before we can set a trial date. Now that's enough, defense counsel," the judge cautioned Wendell when he tried to speak again. "You don't have to make any statements until the government presents its side of the case."

"Madam Clerk, have you completed that call?"

"Yes."

"Do you have the doctor on the line?"

"Yes, I do."

"Hello, this is Judge Merkle in federal court. I'm making this call from a speaker phone in a courtroom. In attendance, besides myself, is Mr. Pierce, the assistant federal district attorney; Leo Able, who is a defendant; and his defense counsel."

"Is the lawyer Larry Nedil's brother?" asked Dr. Gee.

"Yes," said Leo.

The judge warned Mr. Able, saying, "You're not allowed to speak until you're spoken to. Do you understand me?"

"Yes sir," said Leo, meekly.

"All right, doctor, I have a letter from the Mayo Clinic, concerning one Leo Able."

"Yes sir," said the doctor.

"Are you presently treating Leo Able?" the Judge asked.

"Yes," said Dr. Gee.

"Can you tell me what his condition is?" inquired the Judge.

"Yes," said the doctor. "Leo Able has prostate cancer. It's two plus three on the Gleason scale, with slight capsular involvement."

Leo was really starting to sweat. He had seen the letter. He knew his name was typed in. The judge looked up, "Mr. Able, are you okay? You'd better go sit down. I understand that this cancer has spread, is that correct, doctor?"

"Yes, it has," said the doctor.

"Is it possible that he could die within three months?" asked the judge.

"It's possible," said Dr. Gee, "but three months sounds awfully, awfully short."

Mr. Pierce interjected, "Could he live as long as six months?"

"Oh yes," said the doctor. "I think he'll live a lot longer than that."

"But he does have cancer?" asked the Judge.

"Yes," said Dr. Gee, "no doubt about that."

"Mr. Pierce, any more questions?" inquired the Judge.

"I have no questions," said Mr. Pierce.

"Judge," said Dr. Gee, "I don't think his cancer prognosis is that unfavorable."

"Thank you very much for your considered medical opinion, doctor." Judge Merkle, disconnected the phone. "What do you think, Mr. Pierce?"

"I heard the same thing you did, judge. Those doctors are all optimistic," said Mr. Pierce.

"I agree with you," said the judge. "Doctors told me my wife would live for fifteen years. Before I walked out of the hospital, I got a call to make funeral arrangements."

"In light of the letter submitted by the Mayo Clinic, it would appear that it would be a waste of the government's resources to prosecute this case," said Mr. Pierce.

"All right, based upon the government's recommendation, it's the decision of this court that this case is dismissed."

The newspaper reporters ran to submit their stories. Everybody crowded around Leo. Bonnie gave him a big hug and a kiss, and hugged Wendell. The team walked out together.

Lisa turned to Sylvia and said, "Larry's brother is a good lawyer."

Sylvia said, "Isn't he though?"

"He don't waste his time doing a lot of talking either," Bill said.

"Yes," said Michael. "I've seen lawyers spend more time clearing their throat than Larry's brother does on a whole case."

They all walked outside the courtroom. Leo exclaimed, "Let's go out tonight. I'll buy dinner for everybody."

"I guess you should," said Bonnie. "You made a million dollars. You never told me a thing about it."

"I was just hiding it. I was afraid my ex-wife would find out about it."

"Oh," said Bonnie. "Does that ogre get a share of that, too? I'd like to punch her in the mouth."

"Don't you ever hit her," said Leo. "She would blame me and hire some lawyer to sue me for more money."

"Okay, okay," said Bonnie.

CHAPTER 14

AT EIGHT O'CLOCK the RECNAC team walked into the Australian Steak House's private dining room. Leo and Bonnie welcomed them effusively. All smiles, Angelo and Pablo came in. Angelo brought his wife, who had cleared through immigration that morning. Pablo was resplendent in a pink suit with a red velvet collar. Pablo was mistaken as a server and requested to fill the water glasses of other restaurant patrons. He declined.

They were all in great spirits. Since Leo was buying, everyone had drinks. Leo tapped his water glass for attention and everyone stopped talking.

"I want to thank you for helping me yesterday. None of my old friends offered any assistance," said Leo.

"We thank you for this dinner," Sylvia said. Michael and Theresa nodded in agreement.

"You don't know what a relief it was to leave court this morning without worrying about going to jail." Leo said, turning to Larry. "Your brother Wendell is a good lawyer, doesn't talk a lot." Everyone nodded.

"I hope I can get even with those QRX executives. They set me up. It would have worked if not for all of you. You provided me inspiration, determination, and a fantastic defense."

"We were concerned because we figured you were guilty," said Bill.

"Someone in any congregation is always having run ins with the police. Routine work for a minister," said Allen.

Leo smiled. "You SOBs. You thought I was guilty and still you came to help. I'm amazed."

"Watch the language!" yelled Allen.

Leo just looked at them all for a minute.

"Do you get to keep the million dollars?" asked Angelo as the room exploded in laughter.

Leo and Bonnie doubled over in laughter. "Yes," said Bonnie.

"Eez as good as a lottery ticket," said Pablo.

"Yes, but it's tough being put out to pasture. They start calling for the undertaker," said Leo.

The men nodded.

Larry stood up. "Wait a minute. I owe you men. One of my dreams was to play in a championship softball tournament and contribute."

"You sure did that," said Coach. "A triple with two men on, two men out, bottom of the last inning. That's a contribution! You tied the game up."

"Way to go, Larry," said Bill, and he high-fived him.

"It gave me something to do. None of us have any jobs, except you, Leo," added Larry.

"I don't think I have a job anymore," said Leo. "They are not giving me my old job back. As a matter of fact, the most fitting justice that old son-of-a..." Leo was interrupted.

"Don't you say it," said Rev. Allen.

Leo raised his hands, "All right, that's right. Made an agreement. No 'F' word, 'G' word, no 'N' word..."

"No 'H' word," said Allen.

Pablo turned to Angelo, "What's the 'H' word? What's the 'H' word?"

"We're not allowed to say the 'H' word," said Angelo.

"If I don't know what it is, how do I know I don't say it?" said Pablo.

"If you say it, I'll let you know," said Angelo.

"Maybe you can help me," said Allen as he stood up.

"What can we do?" asked Bill.

"Sure," said Michael, "let us know."

"I've always wanted to lead an important civil rights march," said Allen.

"So?" said Larry.

"I've tried four times. The most I ever got to show up was about fifty people."

"Allen," said Lisa, "it was only twenty-two people and fourteen of those were your relatives."

"Yes, whatever," said Allen.

"What kind of a civil rights march can you have? And especially with us?" asked Michael.

"Yeah," said Leo. "I'm not a Negro."

"And I'm not black," Bill said.

"I'm not African-American. No matter what the current phrase is," Michael said.

"I don't think that we would be a help in such a situation," said Sarah.

"Remember when Leo said to me that I wasn't black. I had prostate cancer just like you?" asked Allen.

"Yeah, I remember that. Leo learned himself a hundred years of compassion and understanding in sixty-two days," said Bill.

"That's what I'm talking about," said Allen.

Bill looked at Allen. "Go ahead." He raised his hands in wonderment.

Allen continued, "Every one of us learned that as soon as our employers discovered we had cancer, having access to our medical records, or rumors, we were out of our jobs. Nobody even cares about us."

"Yes," said Michael. "After the diagnosis I was excess to their needs. Kids in their thirties think when you get close to sixty you've lived long enough—get out of the way."

"Leo and I haven't always been in agreement," said Allen.

"That's putting it mildly," said Michael.

Allen raised his hand. "What's the difference between being fired by a white Board of Directors or a black Board of Elders?"

"The Board of Elders didn't try to put you in jail," said Leo.

"I wasn't as arrogant as you were, Leo," said Allen.

"Me, arrogant, just because I'm a great executive?" asked Leo.

"Easy, Leo," said Bonnie as she gently put her hand on his arm. "We are working things out here."

"But there are good reasons a person with cancer may not be able to do his job," said Leo.

"Yes," said Larry, "if the cancer hasn't been stopped, in a year or two we may look like walking ghosts. We may not be physically able to do our jobs."

"Wait a minute. That is not what you and I have been told by the doctors," said Sarah. "They've all told you that it's in remission and you'll have an average life span."

"That better be true," said Theresa, as she looked at Michael.

"What are you proposing?" asked Sylvia.

"Why don't we have a march? Get people who have had cancer and been fired from their jobs," said Allen.

"You think anybody would be interested?" asked Leo.

"Do you think anybody cares?" asked Angelo.

"We could find out," said Rev. Allen.

"That's right," said Lisa. "With the number of people already in the room, and relatives, we've already got thirty-five people. That's an improvement over anything we've ever done before."

"How would we do it?" asked Bill.

"We'd have to do it in Chicago. We'd have to get some time on television," Allen said. "We'd have to tell them that you can't discriminate against a person just because he has cancer."

"That's good," said Leo. "If we get people to appreciate that principle, I'm going to sue my company for back pay. I'm going to talk to Wendell and see if he'd represent me."

"I've never done anything like this before," said Bill.

"Yes," said Sylvia, "how do you start a march?"

"We're not too good about it ourselves. But cancer is an equal opportunity disease, so I don't think we're going to have much opposition," said Lisa.

"What we need is a plan," said Larry.

"When it comes to plans, that's my field," said Coach Blitzkrieg. "Allen talked to me ahead of time, and I brought a chart. My plan is a triple envelopment."

"A triple WHAT?" said Bill.

Coach Blitzkrieg stood up. "Here's a map of Chicago." He hung it on the wall. "This is Grant Park."

"You're going to hold this at Grant Park?" asked Leo.

"Yes," said the coach, "and we'll have a triple envelopment. First of all, we'll start at Northwestern University in Evanston."

"I went to Northwestern University," Leo said.

"Do they win any football games there?" asked Coach.

"Hey," said Leo. "I went in 1962. We beat Notre Dame, Miami and Ohio State that year."

"Great!" Coach said to Leo. "You know something about Northwestern. We'll use college students and residents from Evanston coming down from the north side."

"On the south side there ought to be help from the University of Chicago, marching north to Grant Park. Then we'll get people coming in from the west, the Elmhurst area. Have them come down the Eisenhower Expressway. We'll have to provide staging areas and port-o-lets. Hopefully we can have fifteen to twenty thousand people in Grant Park," he said, pointing to a green spot on the map.

"In Grant Park?" asked Leo.

"Yes," said the coach, "I'll assign positions just like on the softball team. Larry, you work with the teachers in the Cook County area; Allen you work with the ministers; Bill, you work with the building trades; Michael, you work with the accountants; Angelo and Pablo, work with the Hispanic community."

Pablo looked at Angelo and spoke to him in Spanish. "They talk about losing jobs because of cancer? We can't even get jobs when we don't have cancer."

"Cut 'em some slack," said Angelo.

"Wait a minute," said Larry. "Where are we going to stay while we organize this march? How long will it take?"

"It probably could be done in about thirty days. I'll get members of my congregation to put you up," said Allen.

Lisa noticed immediately that the team was concerned. "Allen," she said, "who in our congregation is going to provide living arrangements for our white friends, assuming that they'd be willing to accept?"

"I don't know," whispered Allen.

The coach interrupted. "Accommodations will have to be worked out with people in the community."

Bonnie looked at Leo. "Do you realize since you've had cancer you've been fired, you got into a café brawl, you've been arrested and jailed, you've been playing softball for a month, and now you're going to participate in a civil rights march? Not to mention we're going to live in the ghetto?"

"Let's see what happens," said Leo. "We can always run off."

"You told me your life would be interesting. I'm not sure I want it to be this adventuresome," Bonnie said.

Three days later, they all landed at O'Hare Airport. About thirty of Allen's church congregation showed up. A couple from the church was paired off with each team couple. Leo and Bonnie were paired off with a mid-level executive who worked for Sears.

Larry and Sarah were paired off with an assistant principal from the Cook County Board of Education. Bill Kibler and Sylvia were paired off with a carpenter, and Michael and Theresa with an accountant. Pablo was provided accommodations by the Catholic Social Services. Angelo and his wife, Marguerita, were paired up with a school nurse from the Board of Education. The next evening they met at Allen's church to discuss march coordination.

Leo and Bonnie rented a Lincoln Towncar and drove to the church and greeted Allen.

"How do you like your accommodations?" asked Allen.

"They're very nice. Our hosts are extraordinary. He's more Republican than I am," said Leo.

"They have a very nice house," said Bonnie.

Larry and Sarah showed up with their hosts, as did Bill, Michael, Pablo and Angelo. Rev. Kilpatrick reviewed with them their different assignments. Allen told them, "I want you to come back in a week. Larry, you'll have to work with the teachers. Every one of you go out, contact the groups and see if you can get some radio assistance."

"I'll contact these Yankee carpenters," said Bill.

The next day, Leo visited an executive of a large manufacturing corporation that had supplied his old division with various components. When he walked in, the executive stood up. "Hey, Leo. It's good to see you. Sorry to hear about your health problem."

"How did you know about that?" asked Leo.

"I read the newspaper trade articles. The S.E.C. tried to indict you for insider trading. Your illness provided you with a perfect alibi. You're a lucky man."

"Thanks, I think," said Leo. "We're trying to get some support for cancer patients."

"No problem. I can certainly direct a large contribution. Would you like a check for twenty-five thousand dollars to, what do you call it, the Prostate Cancer Society?"

"No," said Leo. "I'm not here for money."

"Oh," the executive said, looking a bit guarded. "You know, of course, that we won't be able to hire you because of your health condition."

"We're trying to get a pledge from executives in corporations that an individual won't be fired if he receives a diagnosis of cancer," said Leo.

"Are you crazy? There's no corporation that's going to make a pledge like that. We have laws that tell us we can't discriminate on account of age, race, sex. Now you want to hamstring us with older people who have cancer?"

"Like me?" said Leo.

"Nobody will touch you with a ten-foot pole. If we hire an executive, it takes a year to get his feet on the ground. At your age, you could be dead before we recoup our investment in you. Besides," the executive continued, "cancer is the one reason that you can fire people. You don't have to worry about their race, age, sex, or anything like that. It gets rid of people that you'd have to fire anyway. We'll be glad to give you twenty-five thousand dollars. We won't sign any pledge. One year ago would you have signed a pledge like this?"

Leo thought a moment. "No, I wouldn't."

"Okay," said the executive, "so now you've got cancer. You want the rules changed for your benefit. We all know as workers get over the age of sixty, they're often not as productive. The law makes us keep them for another five years."

"Until they can collect social security," said Leo.

"Would you want a regulation on a professional baseball team that says you've got to have five players over the age of thirty-five? You wouldn't have a very good baseball team. We don't want older workers. The fact that they have cancer gives us an excuse to get rid of them. We'll be glad to give you twenty-five thousand," said the executive again.

"Is that the best you can do?" asked Leo.

"You want the twenty-five thousand?" asked the executive.

"Sure thing," said Leo.

"Tell me the name of the charity," said the executive.

"Mount Moriah Baptist Church," said Leo.

"This is a normal church, right? We want our income tax deduction," said the executive.

"No problem. Just mark it 'Cancer Support Group,'" said Leo.

"Okay," said the executive, and he stuck out his hand. "If you'll go to the third door on the left, there'll be a check for you in about five minutes. Leo, I'm sorry to hear about the cancer. It could happen to any one of us."

"Yes," said Leo, "it could even happen to you."

Leo walked down to the accounting office. Sure enough, there was a check for twenty-five thousand dollars.

Larry donned his best blue suit. Sarah had personally picked out a subdued maroon tie to complement it. The assistant principal took him to the headquarters of the Illinois Teachers Association and introduced him to the vice president. Larry began his presentation. "I appreciate your meeting with me today."

"I'm sorry to hear that you have cancer. How can I help you?" asked the vice president.

"When the school board learned I had cancer," said Larry, "they canceled my teaching contract, offered me sick leave for two years, and retired me. The school board treated me like a leper. We need assistance from you to dramatize our plight. Give us some marchers and financial help."

The vice president said, "We'll give you financial assistance, and maybe some marchers. But we fought long and hard to get sick leave. We don't want teachers who qualify for sick leave because they have cancer continuing to teach. Young teachers come into the education system every year. If we kept old teachers, there would be fewer jobs. Once a teacher, always a teacher. They've got sick leave—that's what we fought for."

"But," said Larry, "everyone who is a victim of cancer over the age of fifty-five is going to be automatically retired."

"They're not really losing their jobs," said the vice president. "They're just making places for younger people coming up."

"But what if I feel that I can do the job?" asked Larry.

"It is predominantly an older person's disease. It doesn't have appeal to the public. Twenty-five years ago, you were probably teaching five classes of thirty students each. Now, you teach four classes of twenty students each. Twenty-five years from now, we may even have it down to where you teach three classes of fifteen students, one semester a year. You can teach for the Cook County Board of Education in the fall term, and you can teach up in Waukegan in the spring term. Or you can get the same pay and only teach five months a year."

"What about the students?" asked Larry. "What'll they be learning?"

"Whoa," said the vice president. "Learning belongs to the Board of Education. We're the Illinois Teacher's Union. Our job is to maximize working conditions and financial remuneration for our members."

"What about the ones who have cancer?" asked Larry.

"We give them sick leave, and early retirement," said the vice president.

"Do you think that we could get some marchers?" inquired Larry.

"We'll send out our monthly newsletter. Give me your name and address. I'll ask them to contact you," said the vice president.

"How about some financial assistance?" Larry asked boldly.

"Would five thousand dollars help?" said the vice president.

"Sure," said Larry. "That would be a good start."

"Where do you want us to send the check?" asked the Vice President.

"Send it to Mount Moriah Baptist Church," said Larry.

"In south Chicago?" asked the vice president.

"Rev. Allen Kilpatrick is heading the project," said Larry.

"Larry, what kind of cancer do you have?" asked the Vice President.

"Prostate cancer."

"Oh," said the vice president, "how many more months do you have?"

"Well," said Larry, "from what they tell me, I've got ten to fifteen—"

"Months? That's too bad." He put out his hand. "Best of luck to you, Larry. We'll mail a check to the church within the week. Always glad to hear from a teacher."

"Thanks," said Larry. As he walked out he turned to his host. "They don't seem to be concerned about teachers with cancer."

"That's the least of their worries. A lot of the teachers who are over fifty-five are suffering burnout. They don't want to go to school every day. Sometimes I wonder if we should have a truant officer for teachers," said his host.

Larry walked along thoughtfully. "That bad, huh?"

"Yeah," said the assistant principal, "hardly anyone over fifty is in it for the teaching anymore. They're just putting in their hours until pension time."

"At least I got five thousand dollars," said Larry.

"Yeah," said his host. "Frankly, I was surprised."

Bill Kibler got a ride to the local union hall of the Carpenters, Joiners, and Cabinet Makers of America. It was an old building with church pews for the monthly meetings. He was introduced by the carpenters' business agent to the local president.

"Hello," said Bill. "I'm a carpenter from Tennessee. I'm up here to ask your help in dramatizing the problems of carpenters over age fifty-five with cancer."

"That's a serious problem," said the president, dressed casually in a red flannel shirt. "My mother died of cancer. What can we do to help?"

"I was diagnosed with cancer. It's now in remission, but no employer or insurance company will touch me with a ten-foot pole. I can't get a job. I've been reduced to being a maintenance man. If it weren't for some disability insurance I had, I'd be on food stamps."

"So," said the president, "don't you have disability insurance through your local?"

"Yeah, but it lasts only six weeks," said Bill.

"Can you take an early retirement?" asked the president.

"Sure," said Bill. "I can take an early retirement and mow my yard, and rake the garden. I'm able to work."

"What do you want us to do?" asked the president.

"We're asking employers not to fire people because they get cancer. We'd like you to support us," said Bill.

"We will do anything to help people get jobs. You're talking about people who are fifty-five years of age? How long do you expect to live?" asked the President.

"I'd kind of like to live to be seventy-five and not have people put me on the shelf because I'm going to fall apart," said Bill.

"When you're fifty-five or sixty, it's mighty tough in the building trades," said the president. "Our union has problems with older men keeping up with the younger workers. We've got non-union building contractors, and if we're not wage competitive, we're going to lose the jobs to those contractors. We've got forty percent of our people employed at twenty four dollars an hour, and the other sixty percent not working at all. We can't keep young people who don't have cancer employed."

"I didn't know that," said Bill.

"We can give you some financial support, but we're not involved in this battle. If I go to an employer and said, 'We've got people with cancer who don't have jobs,' the employer will say, 'There are a lot of people without cancer that don't have jobs. I want able-bodied people working for me.'"

"Hold it," said Bill. "I saw where you donated fifty thousand dollars for people with AIDS in the Chicago area."

"That's right," said the president. "We're mighty proud of that donation."

"Fifty times more people die of cancer than of AIDS. How about $50,000?" asked Bill.

"Look, Bill, I understand you have cancer. Everybody in the union is sympathetic. But we're not asking building contractors to sign a pledge to hire old people."

"What about getting some marchers?" Bill asked.

"We'll get you two hundred marchers at the drop of a hat. You have our moral support, and you have five thousand dollars of our financial support. I'll give you the name of our coordinator for the marchers."

"I guess getting four or five thousand carpenters is not realistic," said Bill.

"Four or five thousand," said the president, "no way. Most of our carpenters are young people. They've got wives, kids, soccer games, T-ball games, Cubs, White Sox and Bears. Take the check. We'll get you two hundred marchers. That's the best we can do."

"I 'preciate it. Thank you very much," said Bill.

Michael pulled up to the headquarters of the Illinois Association of Certified Public Accountants. He had an appointment with the executive secretary. Theresa and his host accompanied him. They were ushered into his office immediately. The executive director was six foot tall, gray hair, a public relations master. He shook Michael's hand cordially and complimented Theresa on her suit.

"I know what you're here for. Michael, you have prostate cancer, and Theresa, you've had breast cancer. You're both in remission It's anticipated that you're going to stay that way. You're more likely to die in an automobile crash than you are from cancer."

"We came up on the Dan Ryan Expressway. I was not sure that we would get here alive," said Michael.

"There's nothing like a Chicago freeway to give you the exhilaration of your life. I understand that you're part of an organization that's planning a march in about three weeks," said the executive secretary.

"We'd like the Illinois CPA Association to ask employers to pledge not to discharge or early retire employees who have developed cancer," said Michael.

"Have you had problems getting jobs since you were diagnosed with cancer?" said the executive director.

"Yes," said Michael. "My employer laid me off. Whenever you go to apply for another position, you're told to take a medical exam. You don't pass the physical and therefore you can't get a job."

"Is that right?" asked the executive director. "What can we do?"

"We'd like you to lobby with the big accounting firms. See if they'll change their policy. "

"You want the Association of Certified Public Accountants to take a public stance on cancer?" he asked.

"Yes," said Michael.

"What if we're auditing a New York Stock Exchange company and one of the key executives has cancer. Isn't our job to alert the stockholders and bankers to these problems?" asked the executive secretary.

"Leo Able was the president of a multi-billion dollar division; when they found out that he had cancer, they removed him," said Michael.

"What were the auditors supposed to do—conceal this information? The CPA firm would be sued for not divulging information. Look what happened at ENRON!" said the executive secretary.

"Do you mean," Michael asked, "the fact that a person has cancer is going to affect how investors and bankers would look at a corporation?"

"Michael, don't be naive. If people are going to invest in five- or ten-year bonds, and the key officer of the corporation has only a two-year life span, there's an exposure," said the executive secretary.

"So what?" asked Michael.

"How about getting a life insurance company to take the bet that you're going to live?" said the executive secretary.

"I don't know. I haven't applied," said Michael.

"I have," said Theresa. "I had breast cancer, and I can't get a life insurance policy."

"Exactly. You can't beat the odds," said the executive secretary.

"But," Michael said, "I've talked to my doctors. I'm in remission."

"Michael, I know what the doctors tell you. Maybe they're just building up a false hope," said the executive secretary.

Michael looked at Theresa. Theresa said, "I don't believe that."

"Neither do I," said Michael. I guess you're not going to be able to help us at all in this."

"Oh, no," said the executive director. "Cancer research and cancer assistance—we think that's great. If we learned there were key officers of a corporation that had cancer, we'd have to expose that to the SEC and the shareholders. We're not hostile to people with cancer. We'll give you a ten thousand dollar donation. My mother died of cancer." He stood up and stuck out his hand. "Appreciate your coming by."

He turned to Theresa. "You're a woman of courage to have suffered with breast cancer. I will tell my wife what a remarkable, courageous woman you are. It's couples like you who do America proud." The director shook the hand of their escort and motioned toward the door. His secretary came in and led them to the elevator.

CHAPTER 15

ONE WEEK LATER, the march organizers met back at Mount Moriah Baptist Church. The Elder's room wasn't set up to accommodate women, but an exception was made. At the front of the room was a table for the men. In the back of the room there was a table for the women. Along the side wall was a long table filled with sandwich meats, fried chicken, coleslaw, okra, greens and hush puppies. Theresa had bought a two-and-a-half gallon cardboard container of white wine. Bonnie was delighted. Drinking wine in a Baptist Church made it seem wicked and tastier.

The women busied themselves making small talk, preparing the food and listening to the men. Allen tapped on the table to bring the meeting to order. Leo, Larry, Allen, Bill, Michael, Pablo, Angelo and Coach Blitzkrieg were present. Allen started, "I appreciate your coming here. Each of you please give me a report on how much money you've raised and how many marchers you think that you can furnish."

Leo jumped in. "Allen, as far as raising money goes, I've had no problems. I've got checks that amount to almost fifty-five thousand dollars."

"Whewwww," said Coach Blitzkrieg. "Leo, that's a helluva lot of money. Did you take a gun with you?"

"No," said Leo. "It's very easy to raise money for cancer. Every place I went they threw money at me. They acted like I was a leper and threw me out the door. Here's fifty-five thousand, but I don't have one marcher," said Leo.

"Well," said Larry, "I've got five thousand dollars."

"Way to go," said Bill. "Where'd you get that?"

"I got it from the teachers. They said they'd give me two hundred marchers."

"That's a mite better than I've ever done," said Allen.

In the back of the room Lisa added, "Who's he kidding? That's five times as good as he's ever done."

"I've got fifteen thousand dollars from the Building Trades Council," said Bill, "but they're not interested in having employers hire people with cancer. I got five thousand dollars from the Carpenters, the same from the Plumbers and Steam Fitters. The Electricians and the Drywall people each gave me twenty-five hundred. The Carpenters said they'd furnish me two hundred marchers who had cancer. They're not sure how far they could walk."

"You did better than I did," said Michael. "I went to the CPAs and they gave me twenty-five thousand. They said it was their job to blow the whistle if they found any key officers with cancer."

Allen was absolutely amazed. "Do you realize that you have raised over a hundred thousand dollars?"

"Sure," said Leo. "We've raised it but we're lepers. They wouldn't even hand me one check. They mailed it. I guess they feel cancer is contagious."

"How many marchers?"

"Hopefully," said Leo, "we could maybe get a thousand. Let's see what Angelo, Pablo and the coach have to say."

Angelo said, "I went into the Hispanic community to several churches, and I've got about eight hundred dollars. If you'll give me some money, I can pay people to march. There's a lot of people unemployed in the Hispanic community, and for fifteen dollars they'll come out on a Saturday morning for three hours and march. If they have to carry a sign, they want five dollars extra."

"Sí," said Pablo, "they're not worried about dying of cancer at age fifty-five. They're not sure they're going to live that long. But if we raise one hundred twenty thousand dollars and then spend it on five thousand hired marchers, we have nothing to contribute for cancer," as Angelo translated.

"I went out to Fifth Army Headquarters," said Coach Blitzkrieg.

"They weren't too interested. Retired personnel with cancer take up beds in Army hospitals that they want to use for active duty personnel. They want veterans with cancer in civilian hospitals so that the Army doesn't have to pay for their care out of the defense budget."

"What are we going to do?" asked Leo.

"Call off the march. Contact the Cancer Society and present them a check for one hundred thousand dollars. That ought to get us a little public relations," said Larry.

"No," said Bill. "We got the money. Let's have a march, small as it is. If we can donate one hundred thousand dollars, at least it'll mean something. Maybe the media will cover this for us."

I'm bothered that you could raise money easier than you could get individual commitment to march for three hours," said Bill.

"I checked with our churches, and we can probably get a thousand marchers. It looks like two thousand people will show up. We can present somebody from the Cancer Society a check for one hundred thousand dollars—that's about it. There are two other marches on the same Saturday," said Allen.

"Really?" said Michael. "Who else is marching?"

"There's a national ecology group, and they're out to save a particular type of octopus. I've heard they'll have one hundred thousand marchers."

"Save the octopus?" said Michael. "What is that?"

"I don't know," said Allen, "but there's some type of octopus that's an endangered species and its demise could upset the ecological balance. We're liable to be ignored."

"One hundred thousand people marching to save the octopus, and we can't get but two thousand people to save humans from cancer?" asked Michael.

Allen looked at him. "Thou hast said it."

"Unbelievable," said Bill.

"That's only part of it," said Allen. "There's going to be a demonstration by the Mary Magdalene Society of Cook County."

"Mary Magdalene Society?" queried Leo.

"Prostitutes," said Rev. Allen. "They are protesting offensive language when they're being apprehended, lack of respect by the public in general, and the Johns in particular."

Leo and Coach sat there transfixed by Allen's comments.

"How many marchers will the Mary Magdalene Society have?" asked Bill.

"They'll probably have about two thousand marchers and twenty thousand leering onlookers. This demonstration by the Mary Magdalene Society will be two blocks from ours."

"I knew we shouldn't have picked Grant Park," said Leo. "Can't we change it?"

"No," said Allen. "That's what we've got the permit for. They're going to run them all at the same time."

"I can't believe this," said Coach.

"I can," said Angelo. "There's a whole bunch of people to watch the Mary Magdalenes."

They all stopped talking. Bonnie, Sarah, Lisa, Sylvia and Theresa had been listening and began to comment among themselves. Sarah said, "I can't believe that they didn't realize that people are not interested in cancer. Which one of us cared a lick about it one year ago?"

"Yes," said Bonnie, "but that's because we were ignorant. Lisa, what's the problem that we can't get more marchers?"

"Nobody cares. They've got families to raise. No one wants to think about it. Everybody thinks if you've got cancer you're going to die," said Sylvia.

"We've got to get this thing on track," said Lisa.

"Look," Bonnie said, "here's what we can do." The women huddled around their table.

Theresa said, "You're going to do WHAT?"

Early the next morning, Sylvia and Sarah went to the Chicago Police Department to coordinate the locations of the various marchers. Capt. O'Hallahan, of the traffic division, was happy to meet with them. "We have a copy of your parade permit. It's been approved by Mayor Daly's office. You're going to have some marchers that are going to be coming from three different locations. They're coming from Northwestern University, they're coming from the University of Chicago campus, and they're going to be coming in from the west," he explained.

"We can expect a maximum of three thousand marchers. We have allocated the northern portion of Grant Park for the Cancer Rally by Rev. Allen Kilpatrick. Frankly, I appreciate what you're doing. My mother died of cancer. We appreciate your efforts. There are two other marches scheduled for that day, but they won't concern you."

"You expect the Mary Magdalene Society to have about twenty-five thousand, and the Save the Octopus Society over one hundred thousand?" asked Sarah.

"That's right. Parades, marches, gatherings—they've got to be fun. People don't come out to march in some serious parade. The Save the Octopus convention is a bunch of young people. The girls will be chasing the boys; the boys will be chasing the girls. Do you think one hundred thousand people would come out to Save the Octopus if the Mary Magdalene Society weren't having a parade at the same time? You could attract one hundred fifty thousand people with ten kegs of beer."

"With just beer?" asked Sylvia.

"When they have serious fund-raisers in Chicago, they charge a thousand dollars. They have a dinner. They meet with celebrities. They auction off some mementos. Two hundred dollars of the ticket goes for wine and food, and the other eight hundred dollars goes to the charity. Rev. Kilpatrick is going to be one charismatic individual to get five thousand people to show up for this." Capt. O'Hallahan stopped for a moment. His comments had depressed Sarah and Sylvia.

"Let me show you what your routes should be, where I suggest that you hold your rally. Don't get involved with the congestion from the octopus people, or the Mary Magdalene Society. Do you have any bands?" the Captain asked.

"Bands?" asked Sylvia. "What do you need bands for?"

"If you're going to have a march, you've got to have some music. You can talk all you want about cancer, but you need entertainment and refreshments. Do you have any celebrities on board?"

"No," said Sylvia. "We don't."

"You've got a good cause and a quiet march. It's no problem to assist you. I'm really worried about this Mary Magdalene Society. We're going to have marchers and anti-marchers who don't like the prostitutes. We're going to have the octopus people. We'll probably have some counter-marches against them. We'll have heckling." The Captain outlined their march route.

Sylvia and Sarah left the precinct headquarters and met with Bonnie, Lisa and Theresa. They outlined what they had learned, Theresa said, "Let's huddle."

The night before the march, the Reverend's crew and their wives all met at the church. Rev. Allen was chairing the meeting, asking for reports from different members. Leo had collected another twenty-five thousand dollars. He couldn't get help from the medical associations. It was a holiday, and the Illinois Medical Association was meeting in Miami.

Larry announced he had secured additional financial backing, and that two hundred fifty teachers would be meeting on the Chicago campus of Northwestern University. Bill figured that he would have three hundred retired journeymen from the building trades.

Allen said his people had been working hard. He anticipated a thousand people would meet at the University of Chicago campus, then go to the northern portion of Grant Park.

Michael reported the accountants had been tight with money, but they had contacts in the news media. He expected coverage from three television stations, four radio stations and the local newspapers. Most of the news coverage would be on the two other parades. "It's too bad that we couldn't capture these people to help us. We could march around Grant Park, march back to our assembly point and have a rally there."

The wives looked at each other and smiled. Bonnie raised her hand. "Has anyone made any arrangements for bands?"

"No," said Leo, "we haven't."

Bonnie requested fifteen thousand dollars from the treasury, in cash, for the purpose of rescuing any members who might be arrested, helping to coordinate bands and other purposes.

"Bonnie, fifteen thousand dollars!" exclaimed Leo. "That's a lot of money."

"I will account for every penny. If we don't use the money, I'll just give it back," said Bonnie.

"How much money do we have?" Allen asked.

"I've turned in a good bit to Michael, our accountant," said Leo.

"We've got about one hundred thirty-five thousand dollars," said Michael. If Bonnie wants to be the purser, she's as good as anyone."

"I'll trust her with the money—that's not the problem. I'm just curious as to where it's going to go," said Leo.

"I'll be right there," said Bonnie, "and Lisa and Sylvia and Theresa will be there to help out."

At nine a.m., Leo was at the Northwestern campus. He had about three hundred fifty marchers. The University of Chicago campus had about twelve hundred marchers, which was the biggest turnout Rev. Kilpatrick had ever had. They boarded buses and went to Grant Park. Bill Kibler was coming in from the west.

About ten o'clock they assembled at Grant Park. Bonnie looked at Lisa. "We've got about twenty five hundred people here."

Lisa said, "That's the best Allen has ever done. I know it's not big, but it's still a lot of people. When you consider the amount of money that we raised, it's significant for a small pastor on the south side."

Sarah walked up to Lisa. "It's time for us to get this thing going."

"What do you mean?" said Lisa.

"We're going to steal all these people. You start Allen on a march around the park. We're going to steal all the marchers from these other groups to be in his parade."

"How're you going to do that?"

"Just have Allen get all his people together as if they're going to march. Make him think that they're just going to march around this perimeter for about a half a mile. We'll get this organized," said Bonnie.

A bus drove up loaded with a high school band. Sylvia flagged it down. She looked at the sign on the side of the bus and walked around to the front. "Is this the South High School band?" she asked.

"Yeah, who wants to know?" asked the business driver.

"I'm with the march committee," said Sylvia.

"I thought we were supposed to go down about two miles," said the driver.

"There's been a change in plans. We want you to start right here," said Sylvia.

"Okay," said the band director. "We were informed that if we were in this parade we would get compensation for our Boosters Club."

"That's correct," said Sylvia, "and our treasurer's right here to take care of the problem. How much were you promised?"

"The standard rate is six hundred dollars."

"Ordinarily it is six hundred dollars but," said Bonnie, "it's eight hundred today. What songs are you going to play?"

"We'll play some rock and roll, and we'll play our marching

songs."

"And," Bonnie said, "we want you to start out with 'Onward Christian Soldiers.' Just put your band on the side of the street and have them start warming up. We'll give you the go sign in about ten minutes."

As soon as that band got off the bus, another one drove up. Sylvia worked the same gambit with that band.

"What I'll do," said Sylvia, "is I'll have this first band start off the march; we'll have about a thousand of our people come behind. Then we'll throw a second band in."

"All right," said Lisa, "but we're going to have bands left over."

"Don't worry about that. Things are starting to pick up. Look, I see some television reporters."

Sylvia noticed that two Budweiser beer trucks were coming down the street. Sylvia turned to Bonnie. "Stop those trucks."

Bonnie looked at Sylvia. "How am I supposed to stop those trucks?"

"Oh," said Bonnie, "anything for the cause." She ran out into the street and raised her hand. There was an immediate screeching of brakes, and a smell of burnt rubber as the trucks came to a screeching halt.

Meanwhile, the driver's helper's head had smashed the windshield in the first truck. He was sitting there holding his forehead. He looked over at Bonnie and asked the driver, "Is that one of the prostitutes?"

"No," said the driver cynically, "that's Mother Theresa."

He got out of his truck and walked over to Bonnie. "I guess you were trying to get my attention," said the driver.

"Yes," said Sylvia, "we were. We noticed that you were driving by. This is the rally point. We'd like you to pull over. We're going to have a band in front; then we'll have about two thousand marchers, followed by another band. We want your trucks to follow the second band, drive around the perimeter, then come back to this field. You're loaded with draft beer, right?" asked Sylvia.

"Yes, Ma'am."

"Do you have plenty of cups?"

"We've got plenty of cups. We've also got ecologically recyclable containers and trash cans."

"Good. Do you understand that you're supposed to follow along and then come back here?"

"Okay," said the driver. "But, this is a cash deal."

"I understand," said Bonnie. "Could I see your invoice please?"

"Sure," said the driver, as he reached into his truck. "That's eight thousand four hundred eighty-five dollars."

"I have cash," said Bonnie.

"That's all right. We still take cash," said the driver.

"How many trucks do I get for this?" inquired Bonnie.

"You get these two trucks, and if you run short, we'll send over another truck."

"Okay," said Bonnie. "Go ahead and send the third truck. Now remember, I've paid you. You've been paid by us. You're going to drive on the outskirts of Grant Park behind the bands and you're going to come back here and set up afterward."

"No problem, ma'am," said the driver, tipping his hat. "The person who pays me gets the beer."

"Make sure your other driver knows it," said Bonnie.

"No problem. He's walking up right now," said the first truck driver.

The other driver walked up and looked at the voluptuous Bonnie. "Way to stop a beer truck, babe!"

"You watch your mouth," said Lisa.

"Don't get so huffy," said the second driver.

"Just follow where I place you," ordered Bonnie. "Pull your trucks over to the side so we can get this parade started."

Theresa and Sylvia walked by with some paper signs. Bonnie looked around. "We're ready to start. We haven't got anything but a whole lot of gall and some money."

Lisa walked over to Allen, who was delivering a prayer to the two thousand people of the cancer rally. "Start the march. I've got a band that's ready to go."

"Where did you get a band?" Allen asked.

"Bonnie arranged it somehow. I don't know," said Lisa impatiently.

Allen finished his prayer. "We're going to start on a march to demonstrate our support for cancer research and cancer victims and to demonstrate to employers that you can't fire people because they have cancer. We'll see a day that people of all colors—black, white and red—and all nationalities and all creeds understand the common scourge.

March to show our support."

Allen walked off for the first hundred yards. He got to the street, expecting to turn on the grass. Bonnie signaled to the band to start playing. "Onward Christian Soldiers." Bonnie yelled at Allen, "Follow that band." The band marched off. As the band marched off, and one thousand marchers had passed, Sylvia raised her hand and the second band marched into place with the song "Amazing Grace." Behind them came the second half of the marchers for cancer. Bonnie waited until the marchers had passed. She signaled the first Budweiser beer truck to follow behind the last of the cancer marchers. On the back of the beer truck, Theresa had placed a large sign which said:

FREE THE OCTOPUS
FREE THE WORLD OF CANCER
FREE BEER

The noise of the first two bands and the host of marchers, had attracted the attention of the TV cameras. Three thousand people were waiting for the octopus rally. As the beer truck drove by with the free beer sign, the very youthful audience immediately fell in behind.

Sylvia, who was the last marshal, started in the fourth band. As soon as the onlookers saw that the parade was in progress, they fell in behind. There were approximately twenty thousand people following the four bands and the three beer trucks.

Theresa rode by and yelled at Lisa, "I hope we don't get thrown in jail. Keep an eye on Bonnie—she's really getting into this flashing thing. She's going to flash the mayor, the chief of police and the archbishop."

Lisa shouted, "They'll think she's a member of the Mary Magdalene Society. I hope our husbands don't see us. Make sure you pull the sweater over your head. It hides your face."

Just then Bonnie raised her sweater over her head in front of the Mayor and the Chief of Police.

"Can't you stop her?" asked the Mayor.

"It's not so bad," said the leering police chief. "Besides, if we tried to stop it, we'd turn the march into a riot."

"It's not topless dancing," said the fascinated mayor's assistant.

"What is it?" asked the Mayor.

"She might be demonstrating a self-examination technique for breast cancer," volunteered the wide-eyed aide.

"My ass!" said the Mayor.

As Allen walked in front of the parade, he looked back. He was astounded to see approximately two thousand of his marchers, and behind them a long string of bands, more marchers and Budweiser trucks.

Leo commented, "Allen, you've got at least fifteen thousand people following behind you. It looks like we're going to have twice that many behind the trucks. We're going to have to walk around the entire circumference of Grant Park. That's a five mile walk."

"Yeah," said Allen, "the marchers have really turned out."

"It's a great turnout," exclaimed Leo.

"I always wanted to lead a civil rights march," said Allen.

"You're doing it now," shouted Leo.

"This is not a civil rights march. Who ever heard of a beer truck in a civil rights march?" said Michael.

"Beer truck?" asked Allen. "What beer truck?"

"Right back there," said Leo pointing. "I guess they had to make a delivery somewhere, got caught up and are having to follow along."

"What would the elders of the church say?" asked Allen.

"Beer drinkers get cancer, too," yelled Leo.

Bill and Michael walked up. "Way to go, Allen," said Michael. "You really know how to organize a parade. I don't know how you did it. You pulled them from all walks of life. There must be thirty-five thousand people following you. You've done a fantastic job."

On the first Budweiser truck, Bonnie was becoming frightened. The men seemed too interested in leering at her. She climbed down the side of the truck, asked the helper to slide over, and got into the cab.

"What's the matter?" asked the driver.

"I was getting scared. Those men looked like they were frothing at the mouth," said Bonnie.

"That'll happen," said the driver. "Made you feel a little uncomfortable?"

"Yes," said Bonnie.

"Just stay in here and rest for a while. Look, there's a Mary Magdalene contingent with some signs," said the driver.

Bonnie urged, "Slow down, and let them get in front of us." About fifty prostitutes from the Mary Magdalene Society got in front of the truck. Bonnie got out and talked to them. "If you want to attract attention, you can climb on top of those trucks."

A Mary Magdalener said, "Where did you learn that?"

Bonnie replied. "There's another beer truck back there. You can use that one, too." Bonnie walked back with the Mary Magdaleners and told Theresa, "Come on down."

Three of the Mary Magdaleners approached Theresa. "C'mon honey, come on down. We're here to replace you."

"Really?" said Theresa.

"You've been up there for twenty minutes. You need a break. We're professional toplessers."

"I don't do that," said Theresa.

"Why not?" asked a Mary Magdalener.

"I've had radical mastectomies" said Theresa.

"Too bad, sister. That's an occupational hazard," said a prostitute.

"Remember that girl who worked at that Stud Bar? One day she's making a hundred thousand dollars a year. The next day she's got breast cancer and her career is over," said another Mary Magdalene.

The woman looked at Theresa, "I know that hurt your career some. Maybe there's something else in this world you can do."

"I don't do this full-time," said Theresa.

The second Mary Magdalener spoke up. "Sure honey. We're just waiting for our acting careers to take off. Run along."

Theresa walked back to see Bonnie and Sylvia, as the Mary Magdaleners climbed up on the beer trucks.

Bonnie turned to Sarah and Sylvia. "Let's pick up Lisa and Theresa. Our husbands won't even miss us. We'll just tell them we stayed at the start point."

"We'd better get back to the start point. With all the bands and the beer, it's liable to be noisy. We want to make sure that none of our people get hurt," said Lisa.

"Good idea," said Sarah. "They won't know what we did here today."

"Hopefully, our children will never find out either," said Sylvia.

At the original assembly area, Bonnie, Sarah, Lisa, Sylvia and Theresa were standing by the speakers' podium as the head of the parade returned. In front were Rev. Allen Kilpatrick, local church ministers, Leo, Larry, Bill and Michael.

As they walked around the corner and saw the podium, Leo commented, "There are our wives, just standing around in the speakers' area. You'd figure they at least could have marched a little bit. All they did was just sit there."

"We really had a big turnout—about ten times as many people from the building trades as I expected," said Bill.

"Right," said Larry. "I wonder how much better it would have been if our wives had really gotten behind us and helped us."

CHAPTER 16

AS THE RECNAC team approached the microphone, they hugged and congratulated each other on the success of the march. The first beer truck pulled over to the side to set up and began to pour beer.

Allen asked Leo, "Where did those beer trucks come from? Are they giving water to these thirsty marchers?"

"Why would a beer truck be handing out water?" asked Larry.

"Our marchers are going over there to get something for their thirst," said Leo.

"Hope they don't run out," said Michael.

"What do you mean?" asked Leo.

"When the beer runs out, the marchers go home. I remember that from my college days," said Michael.

"What have we got to keep them entertained until the end of the parade comes in?" asked Leo.

Bonnie walked over. "No problem. We've got bands in the parade. They're going to provide entertainment."

"How good are the bands?" asked Rev. Allen.

Bonnie ordered, "Just step away from the speakers so the band can come up here."

Bonnie ushered Allen and the rest of his entourage off the stage and put on a heavy metal band.

At Grant Park the Chief of Police was reviewing the patrol division's handling of the crowd. "I don't know exactly how we're going to work this out," he said. "It appears that we've got all the parades together. They're listening to Rev. Kilpatrick on his cancer crusade. I didn't think he'd get ten thousand people to come out for his march, but somehow he put the beer trucks there. Putting the go-go girls on top of the beer trucks was classic. It doesn't seem to go with the religious background of this crusade. Maybe I'm just getting old."

"Traffic control and the patrol division are certainly going to have their hands full," said the traffic lieutenant. "We expected to have maybe a hundred and fifty thousand marchers, it appears, because of the weather and the free beer."

"Free beer. What free beer?" said the Mayor.

"Are they selling it?" the chief asked.

"No," said the lieutenant. "I believe they're giving it away."

"Three trucks of beer?" inquired the Mayor.

"Yes," said the lieutenant.

"How many port-o-lets do we have?" the Mayor wanted to know.

"Port-o-lets?" said the lieutenant. "That's not my job. I'm in traffic control."

"You better call in for two hundred port-o-lets. Otherwise, we're going to have all kinds of indecent exposure arrests. Where did these beer trucks come from?" asked the chief.

"I think they were supposed to be with the Mary Magdaleners but somehow they got mixed up with this cancer crowd. Of course, the rock band will play for anybody that gives them an audience. They've got a huge audience so they're having a good time," said the lieutenant.

The rock band took a break. The crowd assembled and Rev. Kilpatrick went up and outlined the problems. He started off,

"We have got to stand;
We are marching into the battle
With a two-edged sword
In our hand.
The promise that God,
Gave to Joshua is ours today.
Every piece of ground that our feet shall walk on
That ground is ours to take."

There was resounding applause to Rev. Allen's opening speech. Allen looked at Lisa. "Thank you."

Lisa turned to Bonnie and Sylvia. "I picked that out."

Theresa said to Sarah and Bonnie, "I hope nobody recognizes us."

"They won't," said Sylvia. "You made sure that you had your sweater over your head, didn't you?"

"No," said Theresa. "Sylvia told me to take my skirt off."

"That's not so bad."

Rev. Kilpatrick finished up his oratory, ending with the line, "All of us may be subject to different vicissitudes of life, but you have to play the cards that God deals you. Thank you."

There was resounding applause. Congratulations had come in from over one hundred community leaders. The news media converged around Allen. He gave credit to Leo, Michael, Bill and Larry, "who have assisted me," he said. In an offhanded manner, he added, "And, of course, to our wives."

Bonnie was outraged. "We're the ones who stole the damn people and put them in this parade."

"Easy, Bonnie," said Theresa. "We did a little embellishment of Allen's idea, but it probably took God to help us."

"Very nicely put," said Lisa. "I hope Allen doesn't get too big an ego."

"I'm sure he won't," said Sarah.

"It will be my job to bring him back to earth if he gets too big a head," said Lisa.

"Listen, we're all going to meet at the church on Monday. Let's go out for a celebration dinner," said Bonnie.

"Good idea," said Lisa. "We'll have everybody there."

Mount Moriah Church was packed on Monday. Allen was praised by the young minister. "I want to introduce Rev. Allen Kilpatrick who has led one of the most unusual civil rights movements seen in the city of Chicago. His charisma and dedication is outstanding. We're happy to have him as the assistant minister of this church."

Allen was becoming a little full of himself. Leaders in the community who had always treated him shabbily shook his hand and commented what a fine person he was. One of the Chicago aldermen said, "You would be a good candidate for political office."

"Really?" said Allen. "I'm just a small minister of a small church."

"No, the people love you. You have catapulted yourself into extraordinary fame," said the alderman.

Allen took a deep breath. "That's interesting."

As he was walking home from church with Lisa, Allen asked, "Did you know that they asked about me running for political office? They said I was a charismatic leader who had organized one of the greatest civil rights marches of our time."

Lisa said, "Allen, the alderman that said you would make a great politician doesn't want you to run against him. He'll probably encourage you to run against someone else."

"You're right. He suggested I run against another alderman," said Allen.

"Right," said Lisa. "By the time we get home, probably that alderman will be suggesting you run against this guy."

Sure enough, when he got home, there was a call from the other alderman. Allen had a great political future. Would he meet with him tomorrow?

Having been warned by Lisa, Allen showed up at the alderman's office. The man immediately stuck out his hand. "Rev. Kilpatrick, it is very good to see you. An absolutely outstanding march you organized last Saturday. You got almost no cooperation from any of the big political bases, power brokers or money brokers. In spite of that, you've appealed to everyone. I think it's fantastic that you've put together an organizational group. It means that many people agree with your ideas and concepts."

"Thank you," said Allen.

"You are a Democrat, aren't you? In any event, I want to tell you that you've made a lot of friends, and that if you'd like to run for office, say in the thirty-second district, I'd be more than glad to support you. The Cook County Democratic Party would be right behind you in any race."

"Frankly I was thinking that I'd run for your seat," said Allen.

"My job?" asked the alderman. "I wasn't asking you to run for my job."

"I heard that you were going to retire," said Allen.

"No way. I'm going to hold this job for life," the alderman said smiling. "Politics is a team sport. You've got to work with others."

"And against others," said Allen.

"That's right," said the alderman. "Besides, you couldn't beat me anyway."

"Why is that?" asked Allen.

"Everybody in the whole world knows you have cancer. I'm just going to come out and say, 'There's no sense voting for Allen Kilpatrick. He's a nice guy but he's dying of cancer—he'll never complete the term,'" said the alderman.

"If that's what would happen if I ran against you, if I ran against someone else, wouldn't they say the same thing?" Allen asked.

The alderman coughed. "That's possible they might do that, but I, I—"

"I have the picture," said Allen. "Every one of you thinks I might have political aspirations. If I do run, the fact that I have cancer is going to be the number one issue. It's just going to be a fear campaign of 'don't elect him, he might die.'"

"I appreciate your coming here today," said the alderman.

"It really reinforces, unfortunately, what I have thought-- that knowledge and truth have nothing to do with politics. Thank you." Allen left without even shaking his hand.

Monday night, at the restaurant, Rev. Allen Kilpatrick was picking up the tab. Allen tapped his water glass with a knife to get attention and turned to everyone. "I want to thank all of you here for your assistance on Saturday. I have underestimated the contribution of our wives. They have been more successful in the organization of this drive than I thought."

Bonnie, Theresa and Sarah looked at each other and then looked at Lisa. Lisa stared at them with no change of expression.

Bonnie leaned over to Sarah. "Do you think Lisa told Allen anything about what we did?"

"I don't think so," said Sarah. "I'm sure Lisa would have warned us ahead of time."

"Yeah," said Theresa. "I don't want Michael to find out. I hope there are no videotapes."

"Oh, there are," said Bonnie. "The television crews were at the finish line of the parade, filming the dancing on the trucks."

"I don't call what you did dancing," said Theresa. "What I did was dancing."

"I definitely got their attention," said Bonnie.

"You got the attention of a photographer from those grocery store tabloids too."

"What!" said Bonnie.

"There's a picture of you in those papers," said Sarah.

"Can you recognize me?" gasped Bonnie.

"No," said Sarah. "I know it's you, because of the skirt you were wearing on Saturday. I can tell by the belt buckle."

"Really? My face doesn't show?" asked Bonnie.

"No," said Sarah.

"What grocery store did you go to?" said Bonnie.

"Why?" said Sarah. "Do you want a copy?"

"Yeah," said Bonnie. "I'd like to see it."

"I thought you would," said Sarah, looking around furtively. "I've got a copy of it in my purse."

"Are there any pictures of me?" Theresa inquired.

"I don't know," said Sarah. "I just bought it to see if there was one of me."

"I think it's time for all of us to powder our noses."

"Good idea." The four of them got up, signaling to Lisa to come with them.

"What's up?" Lisa asked.

"You know there was newspaper and television coverage of the parade."

"Sure," said Lisa. "Everyone knows that."

"You know some of the embellishments?" asked Theresa.

"Yes," said Lisa.

"There were some pictures taken," said Bonnie.

"Where are they?" Lisa asked.

"Right here," said Sarah, as she handed the tabloid to Bonnie.

"Wow," said Bonnie. "I'm right on the front page—a nine by twelve inch picture. Good idea about raising the sweater over your head. It completely covers your face."

"Look on page five. That looks like Theresa."

"Yeah," said Sylvia, "and there you are, Sarah. Wow!"

"You can't recognize us. I heard Leo telling Bill and Larry that he thought the Mary Magdaleners on the beer truck were a huge attraction in getting the parade moving."

"Let's hope they never find out that they weren't Mary Magdalen-ers."

"Yeah," said Sarah, "even when you're fifty-seven years old you can attract attention."

Bonnie brought Sarah back to earth. "Hey, when you're dealing with twenty year olds drinking beer, anything looks good to them."

"Yeah," said Sylvia, "when you raise your arms above your head, you get good uplift."

"Okay," said Sarah. "I got your message."

"I would like to be a fly on the wall when our husbands are looking at those pictures. What will they say?" asked Bonnie.

"Why don't we try that," suggested Sylvia.

"What do you mean?" asked Lisa. "I'm a minister's wife."

"We've done everything to upset the minister. We ran beer into his parade, we flashed all the Save the Octopus Society and we danced in front of the Mary Magdaleners," said Bonnie.

"I'm kind of surprised at how good a response we got," said Sarah.

"We haven't been sex objects for thirty years," said Sylvia.

"Speak for yourself," said Bonnie.

"Cut us some slack," said Lisa. "Leo doesn't look like he's that virile."

"Oh, it shows, does it?" Bonnie asked.

"Yeah," said Lisa. "Allen's in there bragging about what a great civil rights leader he is. He doesn't know what we did to make it work."

"How can they be so dumb," said Theresa.

"That's why we love 'em," said Bonnie.

"Let's just drop this tabloid on the table and see what they say," said Sarah.

"What if they get mad?" asked Theresa.

"You just don't have a penchant for mischief," said Sarah.

"Yeah," said Sylvia. "I'm disappointed I didn't have a chance to get up on top of the beer truck."

"So am I," said Lisa. "But, I have a position to maintain." They all cackled, and then they walked out of the ladies room.

"Where have you been?" Allen asked. "We missed you."

"Yeah," said Angelo. "We're all bragging on each other for throwing one hell of a civil rights march."

"I wondered if any of you had seen this grocery store tabloid." Lisa put it on the table, and all six of the men immediately looked at it.

"Wow," said Larry. "Did you see the pictures of these two women standing on the beer truck?"

Theresa edged over to Larry, "Which ones, Larry?"

"This one right here," said Larry pointing. "She's really got nice legs."

Bill said, "Hey, look at this picture. Is that one of those Mary Magdaleners?" he asked pointing to Sarah's picture. "She looks mighty good."

"Funny," said Larry. "She reminds me of someone."

"We've got to bring this back to earth," said Allen. After all, this is a church meeting. However, we appreciate all the Mary Magdaleners who helped us in our parade."

"We probably couldn't have done it without them," said Michael.

"Yeah," said Lisa. "They were very instrumental in attracting the crowd."

"Allen, I've known that this is what you always wanted to do. I guess next Sunday you're going to be on the feature page, right?" asked Michael.

"Yes," said Allen, "People asked me about running for political office."

"You didn't tell me how that came out," Lisa said.

"I was contacted by three different politicians. Each one wanted to support me in running against one of the other two for office. So I asked one, 'Why don't I just run for your office?' And he said, 'If you ran for office I'd have to expose the fact that you had cancer and probably wouldn't live out the term.' When it comes to politics, what we tried to do hasn't even made a dent."

"I have a problem coming up. I need your help," said Leo.

"For what?" Larry asked.

"As you know, Larry's brother is representing me in my lawsuit against the QRX Corporation."

"You sued the QRX Corporation?" asked Bill.

"Fat chance of winning with all their lawyers," said Larry.

"The case is coming to court. Could we all meet tomorrow night?"

Leo inquired.

"Okay, we'll all come back tomorrow night," said Larry.

"Who's buying?" Angelo wanted to know.

"Since I'm asking you to help me out, you've got another free dinner tomorrow night," said Leo. "Seven o'clock sharp."

CHAPTER 17

TUESDAY EVENING THEY all met at Bonnie's favorite Chicago steak house restaurant. Leo had reserved a private room. Leo and Bonnie were dressed in business suits although the rest of the team was dressed casually. After dessert Leo stood up apprehensively.

"What's the matter, Leo? You look like you're off your feed," said Bill.

"After the way you and Bonnie helped me, just tell me what I can do," said Allen.

"Anything you want," echoed Larry and Sarah.

"As you know," said Leo, "after my termination by QRX Corporation, I consulted Larry's brother, Wendell. He agreed to represent me in a lawsuit against QRX."

"Good choice," said Larry.

"Next Monday, in federal court here in Chicago, there's a pre-trial conference. The judge meets with the attorneys and parties for both sides. That's me, and it'll probably be that S.O.B. Mr. Williams, along with Margaret Novak."

"Leo, watch your language," said Allen.

"What's this here suit all about?" asked Bill.

"I sued them for setting me up on the criminal stock manipulation charge. You verified that I couldn't have been involved in it," said Leo.

"No problem," said Michael. "It was the truth. That's easy to tell."

"I've also filed a lawsuit against QRX because they demoted me because of cancer," said Leo.

"Did you get fired?" asked Allen.

"Not really," said Leo. "I got demoted. After I was arrested, I got fired."

"I used to be the carpenter foreman, now I'm the janitor," said Bill. "My pay was cut in half. None of us here got canned—we just got..."

"Retired," interjected Larry.

"In any event, they're a large corporation and I'm suing them," said Leo.

"Sock it to those Angelinos," shouted Pablo, talking on his third margarita.

"Wait just a cotton pickin' minute," said Bill, "we're Angelinos."

"Sorry," said Pablo apologetically, "I forgot."

"Tell us how we can help," said Sylvia.

"Yeah," said Sarah, "I'm not sure we know anything about the law."

"Except winning softball games," said Larry.

"And staging one helluva civil rights march," said Lisa.

"Here's how you can help," said Leo. "We're going to have a pre-trial conference. The judge will determine how much time the case will take. They also talk settlement. Wendell will warn them that any jury in Cook County is going to be tough on large corporations who treat cancer patients badly."

"Too bad he couldn't take on the Board of Education," said Larry.

"I need Allen to show up. Wendell isn't sure how good a case we have. If QRX feels that the jurors in this county would be sympathetic to my position, it might help a settlement."

"Are you hoping to get some money?" asked Larry.

"How much?" demanded Theresa.

"I don't know. They didn't cut my pay. They transferred me to a dead-end job as president of the Leisure Services Division."

"What's the Leisure Services Division?" Sarah asked.

"It's a small division of the QRX Corporation. It does about one hundred million dollars in sales per year."

"You were the president of a company that does one hundred million dollars a year in sales?" questioned Angelo. "That's not too bad."

"Yes," said Leo, "but it loses money. The company makes sporting equipment."

"Like those super bats that you gave us for the softball games?"

"Yes," said Leo, "but we can't even market them."

"Hey," said Larry, "give those to me to market. I'll tell them that this bat made me a hitter."

"It's got to be a miracle bat for Larry to get a hit," said Michael. Everybody chuckled as Michael high-fived Angelo.

"The company is not interested in pursuing bat sales," said Leo. "The whole purpose of this division is to furnish golf memberships and outings for the corporate executives. The division is a tax write-off for the executives. They take a chartered plane from the corporate headquarters to some golf tournament and entertain customers of the automotive parts or trucking divisions."

"Maybe something can be done about that," said Larry.

"I don't know what we can get if we win," said Leo.

"Why did you file the lawsuit?" asked Lisa. "It doesn't appear that you've got anything to win."

"I was mad at them for trying to set me up with that criminal stuff. I insisted that Wendell push the suit. I'm afraid I got Wendell in a suit he can't prove."

"What do you want us to do?" Allen inquired.

"I'd like you to come to court and sit," said Leo. "Wendell will come up with some way of introducing Allen as the person who led the civil rights march on cancer. Make them think that a lot of people don't like the way that I've been treated!"

"Like me," said Larry.

"Yes," said Allen. "I got made a visiting minister."

"How are you going to convince this large corporation that jurors don't like it?" asked Michael.

"If I know Mr. Williams and Miss Novak, they don't want to pay any money," said Leo. "We have to make them think we have a better case than we do."

"It's like a two-hour side bar with a lot of bluffing," said Sarah.

"That's right," said Leo. "I don't think QRX wants a trial. I want them to think it would be better to settle the case than try it."

"No problem," said Allen. "Lisa and I will be there. Should I bring others with me?"

"Wendell said just you and your wife's presence would be enough," said Leo.

"Larry and I'll be there," said Sarah.

"Thanks," said Leo. "Larry, you know you got a lot of publicity from that triple you hit. One of the senior softball magazines has a picture of you in it."

"Really," said Larry, "a picture of me?"

"Anyway," said Leo, "you've got a following. The judge that's hearing the case plays senior softball. He knows you have cancer. He might be impressed."

"What will we do?" Michael asked.

"Coach Blitzkrieg, I want you to be there," said Leo. "You've had a good career, you might be recognized. Angelo, I want you to be there because you'd be representative of the Hispanic jurors. If nothing else, you'll be moral support."

"No problem," said Angelo.

"You have to be at federal court about nine," said Leo. "Pre-trial starts at ten. I want you to talk with Wendell ahead of time."

"He's a really good attorney," said Theresa.

"Yeah," said Lisa. "He doesn't babble on like the rest of them."

"He says a few words, and he's done," said Sylvia.

"I never heard him say a word," said Angelo. "Why is he so good?"

"Why is this case in Chicago?" asked Sarah.

"The case was filed in New York where QRX is headquartered," said Leo. "Their New York attorneys wrote a five hundred-page legal brief arguing it should be in Chicago. Wendell couldn't beat them. When QRX had it transferred to Chicago, no one knew there we would be a civil rights march for cancer patients one week before the pre-trial."

"Amen," said Allen.

"I've got work to do," said Leo. "Wendell will call you. Please show up on Monday morning to help me."

"Sure will. Count on it." They all left eager to help out.

RITZ-CARLTON HOTEL, CHICAGO—9 P.M.

"Frankly," said Mr. Williams, "I'd like to settle this case and get rid of another problem."

"What's the other problem?" asked Tom.

"How about getting rid of the Leisure Division and stopping the S.E.C. from breathing down our neck?" said Mr. Williams.

"As I've said before," Tom stated, "the Leisure Division of QRX is an absolute loss. Its chief utility to the corporation is that it provides recreational junkets for executives, customers, and congressmen. My recommendation is that we utilize this lawsuit to dump this division on Leo."

"What do you mean?" asked Margaret. "How could we do that?"

Tom continued, "If we tried to close this division down, we would have unemployment compensation payment, workers' compensation premiums, final income tax, separation pay and medical insurance. If we dump this division on Leo Able in exchange for settlement of this case, we'd come out ahead. We could write this off as a thirty million dollar lawsuit payment. We'd reduce our federal and state income taxes by twenty million dollars to QRX's bottom line."

"If we can sucker Leo into taking this division off our hands in a spin-off," said Mr. Williams, "we can eliminate these losses plus generate a twenty million dollar tax refund?"

"Tell our lawyers to plan a spin-off of the Leisure Division," ordered Mr. Williams.

"Right," said Tom. "For the dismissal of his lawsuit, we will spin-off to him one hundred percent ownership of the Leisure Division. He's always thought he was a great business talent. Let's take advantage of his ego..."

"And his stupidity," said Margaret.

At nine a.m. Leo, Bonnie, and Wendell arrived at the Federal Courthouse. Larry and Sarah, Allen and Lisa, Bill and Sylvia, Michael and Theresa, Angelo, Pablo and Col. Norman Blitzkrieg were already lined up in front of the courthouse waiting their turn to be searched. As Leo walked inside, the QRX executive and six corporate attorneys brushed them aside and marched in front.

"Nice to see you, Leo," said Mr. Williams.

Margaret commented, "It's so nice to see you, Leo."

Bonnie flicked Margaret the bird.

Margaret looked at Bonnie. "Really! Too bad that you have nothing to offer your husband but a great body and no mind." Bonnie lunged at Margaret, but Allen caught her. He cautioned her, "It is better to turn the other cheek."

After being screened and searched by the federal marshals, everyone sat down. Leo told Wendell that he'd gotten an encouraging call concerning the marketability of the graphite uranium composition for baseball and softball bats. Wendell nodded his head.

There was a shuffling of papers followed by the exchange of information and exhibits between the attorneys.

At precisely ten a.m., Judge Steve Simmons arrived at the bench.

Judge Simmons noted the six attorneys and three officers representing the QRX Corporation, Leo Able and his attorney, and about ten people in the courtroom.

"The court calls the case of Leo Able, plaintiff, vs. QRX Corporation, defendant. Are all the parties ready?"

"May it please the court," said the tall, gray-haired lead counsel for QRX Corporation, "I would like the opportunity to address the issues that are presented here today."

"Proceed, counselor," said Judge Simmons.

"Your Honor, this case is a flagrant, wilful and malicious disregard of the loyalty which an employee owes to a corporation. The corporation learned that Mr. Able had developed prostate cancer. In view of the medical complications, the Board of Directors decided that he should be given a less stressful job. He was transferred to the Leisure Services Division and paid the same salary," said lead counsel.

"Then why this lawsuit?" asked Judge Simmons.

"The plaintiff has slandered this corporation by saying that by transferring him, they terminated his opportunity for promotion and profit-sharing compensation," said lead counsel.

"Is there any truth in that allegation?" asked the judge.

"None whatsoever, your honor. As president of the Leisure Services Division, he had an opportunity to earn a bonus commensurate with his ability to operate this division profitably."

"Go on," said the judge.

"Leo Able was a well-paid corporate executive earning over four hundred fifty thousand dollars a year. His attorney should be charged with violations of ethical considerations Nos. 42, 45, 46 and 62. In short, the actions of plaintiff and his attorney in bringing this case are that of a back stabbing, cowardly cur!" yelled the attorney.

Sarah turned to Bonnie. "Leo's going to get some money."

"What do you mean?" whispered Bonnie.

"They've just accused Wendell and Leo of everything back to and including original sin."

"I know," said Sarah. "Wendell said if the attorney on the other side really cusses you out, he's just setting you up to take a settlement offer. If they're going to pay you something, they at least want to dump on your head in public."

"I hope Leo gets some money," said Bonnie. "On the way out of court, I might just punch Margaret Novak in the eye. I'm also itching to kick her attorney in the balls."

"No," said Lisa, very sweetly. "You're Leo's wife. That wouldn't look good. I'll kick him in the groin."

"Way to go," said Theresa, and high-fived Lisa.

The judge looked up rather sternly at the people behind the plaintiff's table.

The judge turned to the counsel for QRX. "You were discussing the horrendous, false, libelous and slanderous allegations in this lawsuit. The QRX defense is a veritable cacophony of violations highlighted by your vitriolic diatribe," said the judge.

"Judge, it's important that we be a zealous advocate of our client's position," said the lead counsel.

"Very well, counselor," the judge said. "You've had an opportunity to vent your individual spleen upon the head of the plaintiff. I've let you speak; now how about saying something?"

"Your honor, I appreciate your kindness and consideration in this matter," said lead counsel. "In the spirit of compromise, we would make the following offer to settle the case. In exchange for a complete dismissal of this slanderous and scurrilous lawsuit, and the release of any and all claims by the plaintiff, we are willing to spin off to the plaintiff the Leisure Division of QRX Corporation."

"That's an interesting offer. This company has one hundred million dollars in sales?" the judge asked.

"Yes, your honor," said the corporate attorney.

"That's quite an offer," said the judge. "He turned to the plaintiff's table. "What's your response to that, counselor?"

Leo jumped up. "I'll take it."

The judge turned to Wendell. "Your client has answered for you."

Wendell nodded.

"Okay," said Judge Simmons, "I want this agreement on my desk in five days. I expect the settlement to be implemented within thirty days after the agreement is filed with the court. Court's adjourned, gentlemen."

The judge walked back into his chamber.

"Wow," exclaimed Leo as he walked out of the courthouse, "I own this division. What a surprise. How did Wendell pull that off?" wondered Leo.

"I smell a rat," said Bonnie. "They wouldn't have given you the Leisure Division if they had thought it was worth anything."

"It's my job to make it worth something," said Leo emphatically.

"How ya gonna make this company any good?" asked Bill. "The golf clubs are illegal. The softball bats are experimental. You'd be better off racing a three-legged horse."

"That's going to be my job," said Leo. "Each one of you is going to be a salesman. We've got to make this work. If you think Coach Blitzkrieg is a tough boss, wait until you work for me. Let's have lunch. I'll tell you what we're going to do."

"Hey," said Pablo. "How about eating at a Mexican restaurant for a change? I'm tired of these Italian and Australian restaurants."

"Yeah," said Angelo, "how about something that we can sink our teeth into."

"Okay," said Bonnie.

"Sí, I know just the place," said Pablo, and he led them to a Tex-Mex restaurant in Chicago.

Everybody was in good spirits because they had won the lawsuit—they thought.

"The first thing," said Leo, "is we're going to change the name of this company."

"To what?" asked Michael.

"We're going to call it the Recreation of North America Corporation."

"The Recreation of North America Corporation?" said Allen.

"Yes," said Leo. "You know what the initials will be?"

"No," said Bill.

"Recreation of North America Corporation...RECNAC."

"YEAH!" said Larry.

"Way to go," said Allen. "RECNAC!"

Bonnie, Sarah, Lisa, Sylvia and Theresa looked on while the men high-fived each other.

"I'm not sure they graduated from grade school," Sarah said.

"I'm not even sure they graduated from kindergarten," Bonnie said.

"Are we going to help them sell this stuff?" asked Theresa.

"Yeah, but first," said Sylvia, "let's find out what this corporation sells, and then figure out a way to sell it."

After the men got through high-five-ing themselves, Sylvia asked, "Leo, what is RECNAC going to sell?"

"Can't sell our golf clubs because the PGA has banned them. We sell softball bats and gloves, and that would be Larry's job. Sarah, you help him. We sell lawn chairs, and frankly, I don't think they're any good," said Leo.

"What else?" said Bonnie.

"The last thing is our line of shoes," said Leo. "They have a new type of sponge polyester plastic composition that makes them comfortable and easy to walk on. Some of the senior citizens liked them."

"Have you sold very many?" asked Michael.

"Not yet," said Leo.

"My idea is to get rid of the golf clubs and stick to the softball and hardball bats, gloves and shoes. About ten million dollars each year was used to buy sponsorships for the World Series, the Super Bowl, golf tournaments and tickets. The division would buy the stuff and give it to all the corporate officers of QRX."

"Wait a minute," Michael said. "Do you have rights to these

items?"

"Yeah," said Leo, "we've got tickets for the World Series and Super Bowl for the next ten years. We've got rights at Las Vegas to buy fifty ringside tickets for ten years. We even sponsor a golf tournament."

"Are these things like options?" asked Michael.

"Yes," said Leo.

"Could we sell those things?" inquired Michael.

"I don't know. You might be able to exchange them or lease them," said Leo.

"Wow," said Michael, "let me take a look at these options and see what I can do."

"No problem," said Leo. "Be glad to have you do that."

Angelo and Pablo asked what they could do.

"Everyone will get the rate of pay that they had before they got fired because of cancer. Now you've got to produce," said Leo.

Pablo started talking in Spanish. Angelo had a tough time keeping up with him.

"Angelo," said Leo, "what's the problem with Pablo?"

"Pablo's upset," said Angelo.

"I can see he's upset," said Leo. "What's he upset about?"

"He says everybody else is getting the pay they had before they had cancer," said Angelo.

"That's right," said Leo.

"Pablo was making two dollars and twenty-five cents an hour," said Angelo.

"Who pays two dollars and twenty-five cents an hour?" asked Leo.

"If you don't have a green card, the gringos pay that. If you complain, they turn you in to the immigration officials," said Angelo.

"You mean Pablo doesn't have a card to work in America?" Bonnie asked.

"That's right," said Angelo.

"I'll have Wendell check on that. We have a job for him. He's like everybody else, a salesman on commission," said Leo.

"Pablo's going to be a salesman?" Angelo asked.

"That's right. We're going to put people on a straight commission, but I'll give you a draw. You've got to sell shoes or ball bats," said Leo.

"Who are we going to sell these shoes to?" Sylvia asked.

Bill suggested, "You'll probably have to sell the shoes to shoe stores. Wouldn't make much sense going door-to-door."

"What kind of shoes do we sell?" asked Sarah.

"Where's your headquarters or factory?" asked Larry.

"Our headquarters used to be in New York. Since they are kicking us out, the headquarters can be anywhere," said Leo.

"Where's the factory? It might be a good idea to put the headquarters near the factory," said Michael.

"Leisure Services didn't have any factories," said Leo. "All we have is corporate research and development. We buy everything from Korea, Thailand, Taiwan, Argentina and Puerto Rico."

"Who makes the bat?" asked Larry.

"Nobody makes the bats," said Leo.

"Where did they come from?" asked Larry.

"We did it in research and development," said Leo.

"Where's research and development?" Michael inquired.

"It's about fifteen miles from Atlanta," said Leo.

"Okay," said Sylvia, "that's where we'll locate. I know as much about shoes as anybody else here."

"What do you know about shoes?" asked Bonnie.

"I wear them," said Sylvia.

"That's your expertise in shoes?" Theresa asked.

"Sure. I wear lots of them," said Sylvia with a wink.

CHAPTER 18

TWO WEEKS LATER RECNAC held its first employee meeting in an old warehouse in Atlanta. Leo had leased an abandoned QRX facility that had been vacated because of a leaky roof. The rent was cheap. He had installed some "instant" dry wall office partitions. The director's table was a plywood panel on sawhorses. The fluorescent lights flickered occasionally. Seats were wooden two by ten planks on concrete blocks.

"Okay," said Leo, bringing the meeting to order. "Let's take stock of this corporation. All our employees are involved in sales, distribution, warehousing and shipping. We devise the products and have companies manufacture and ship them to us. We have to create a demand for these products. The only asset we had was that we were part of QRX Corporation. Now we're going to be known as RECNAC. What can we sell?"

"One thing we can't do is get into the youth market," said Larry. "We don't have the money for high-priced basketball player endorsements."

"That's right," said Sarah. "We can sell what we know. We can sell shoes for people who are over forty. If the young people want 'No pain, no gain,' that's fine, but our slogan will be 'Have fun and still gun at fifty.' Do we have any money?"

"Let me take care of that," said Michael. "I'll be the treasurer. I'll sell those golf sponsorships, tickets and badges. We won't use those tournaments to get business. We'll sell our leases to other corporations. If we get back what RECNAC has spent, we'll have two or three million dollars."

"I'd always thought of them as a liability," said Leo.

"Let me work with the Research and Development people and contact some bat manufacturers. I'll handle sales for softball bats and gloves," said Larry.

"Before you start selling anything, you check with Michael and me. I don't want you selling softball bats for less than what it costs us to produce them," cautioned Leo.

"Let me design a line of sports clothing for women who have figure deficits," said Theresa.

"What does that mean?" asked Leo.

"It means we would provide artificial enhancement. Kind of like mascara for the eyes," said Bonnie.

"Sounds interesting. I understand there's a lot of money in cosmetics," said Leo.

"I'll explain it to you later," said Bonnie, shaking her head.

Bill, Allen, Angelo, Pablo and Col. Blitzkrieg asked what their jobs would be.

"It appears," said Leo, "you will sell shoes. We've got to advertise the RECNAC name. You've got to develop a sales campaign that is going to make people buy. Contact stores that could purchase from RECNAC and see what they will buy. We lost our sales department. Margaret Novak called all of our sales people. She said I would fire them so they got new jobs with competitors. We need someone to call on all these past accounts."

"Señor Leo, how can I call on these corporate accounts?" said Pablo.

"We'll assign everyone to an area with which he's familiar. Pablo, you're going to deal with the southwest—Los Angeles, Albuquerque, Santa Fe, Nogales, Phoenix."

"You mean I'll only sell shoes to Hispanics?" asked Pablo.

"Just at first until you get the hang of it. Angelo, you'll be handling Texas. Col. Blitzkrieg, your job will be to see if the Armed Forces would be interested in shoes. Find out what they need and see if we can make something for them. Bill, see if you can design work boots that would be comfortable."

"Right," said Bill.

"Our lawn equipment and folding tables are gone. The manufacturer learned of the spinoff and won't ship unless it's C.O.D."

"Michael has discovered the Leisure Division sold sixty million dollars of lawn furniture last year," said Lisa.

"I can explain that," said Michael. "Mr. Williams set up a dummy export-import company. His import company bought the lawn furniture for forty million dollars and sold it to QRX for sixty million dollars. Since he was the boss, no purchasing officer could complain. Margaret Novak was the president of the import company. If we cancel our purchases, their scheme goes down the drain. They will have twenty million dollars of lawn chairs on their hands."

"Okay," said Leo grimacing. "We'll all be back here in four weeks. Every one of you has to call on these stores, or the Pentagon, to find out what they need. Michael will give you the information. We don't have much money, so nobody get fancy. Everybody flies coach class or cheaper. If you have to rent a car, get a cheap one."

"No problem," said Angelo. "I'd love to rent any cheap car."

One week later, the following article appeared on page ninety-seven of *Fortune* magazine:

QRX CORPORATION SPINS OFF
LEISURE DIVISION

QRX financial spokesman Tom Warehouse announced today that the spinoff of the Leisure Division from QRX had been accomplished. The spinoff was instigated by a disenchanted former president of the Radio and Computer Division, Leo Able, in response to a lawsuit over age and health discrimination, filed by Able.

Wall Street insiders speculate that the spinoff of the Leisure Division to Leo Able is akin to a naval officer asking to take command of the *Titanic*.

Allen, dressed in a dark blue business suit and wearing white REC-NAC shoes, went to a Chicago sporting goods store. He was directed upstairs to the purchasing agent, who instantly recognized him. "Aren't you Rev. Kilpatrick who led that cancer march about a month ago?"

"Yes," said Allen, shaking his hand. "I am he. I'm here on behalf of RECNAC Corporation to talk with you about buying our shoes."

"You're a salesman?" asked the purchasing agent.

"Yes," said Allen. "I've never done this before, I'm here to ask you to purchase and stock RECNAC shoes."

"Do you have a pair?" asked the agent.

"Yes," said Allen. "They're great for walking. I wouldn't dream of leading a march without them."

"How much do they cost?" inquired the agent.

"You could retail them for about forty dollars," said Allen.

"How come they're so cheap?" asked the agent.

"All shoes are made in the Pacific rim," said Allen. "The shoes probably don't cost ten dollars, but a pair of those one hundred dollar shoes are endorsed by sports athletes. Ten dollars of that hundred goes to pay the athlete's endorsement. Twenty dollars goes to television. Another fifteen dollars goes to pay for the newspaper ads. The rest is corporate markup. The shoes are really all the same."

"I know that," said the agent. "We buy them for sixty dollars, sell them for one hundred dollars, and that's a fantastic markup."

"Yes, but how many would you sell for forty dollars?" asked Allen.

"Who's going to buy a forty dollar pair of shoes?" the purchasing agent asked. "Only old people are going to pay forty dollars."

"That's my point," said Allen. "These shoes are designed for the forty-and-older crowd."

"Do you know how many people forty and older come into this store?" said the agent. "They're stingy with their money. The only thing they buy would be shoes for their grandchildren. You might want to try Wal-Mart or K-Mart. They sell to older people."

"I really think you should stock these," said Allen.

"I'll tell you what I'll do," said the agent. "I respect you. As an accommodation, I'll order two hundred pairs of shoes—one hundred men's, one hundred women's. If they don't sell within sixty days, I'm going to send them back to you. I'll give you shelf space. Fair enough?"

"Fair enough," said Allen. "I don't have all my forms in my salesman's kit. I'll have to go back and check."

"No problem. I'll be here," said the agent. "Reverend, I really appreciate what you've done. My father passed away from cancer and I think your march was great. Thank you very much." Allen walked out.

Rev. Allen Kilpatrick went to fifteen other stores. He was courteously received. He managed to get consignment orders for a minimum of one hundred and a maximum of five hundred pairs of shoes at each location. He was absolutely ecstatic.

Meanwhile Angelo, dressed in khaki pants and a white shirt and tie, stopped in El Paso, Texas, to do his selling. He walked into a sporting goods store and was directed to their corporate headquarters about four miles away. He went to see the purchasing agent about shoes.

The buyer looked. "Angelo, the shoes you've got are too high priced. Most of our customers have large families. They need something in the area of twenty dollars. You're going to have to sell us a pair of shoes that's as good a quality as these, for fifteen, that we can mark up to twenty."

"Thanks, señor," said Angelo. "I will contact my boss and work out pricing policies favorable to you!"

Col. Blitzkrieg was pounding on military doors. He went to the footwear testing department of the exterior clothes division of the battle dress unit and talked to the assistant quartermaster in Natick, Massachusetts. As he started making his pitch, he was interrupted.

"It's nice to see you here," said the major. "What are you doing here peddling footwear?"

Colonel gave his pitch about the RECNAC shoes and was interrupted.

"Colonel, you're coming to the wrong place. These shoes are something that the individual soldier purchases on his own—probably nine times out of ten, from a discount store or at an army PX. Why don't you try the Army-Air Force exchange headquarters in Dallas?"

"Thank you," said Colonel. He left immediately, realizing that he was knocking on the wrong door. He knew that the advice he'd received from his friend was correct. "What do I know about jogging shoes?" muttered Coach. "I've got this design for a hunting vest. I'll go to a seamstress with my idea and get one to fit me."

Coach Blitzkrieg located a seamstress near the Georgetown area of Washington and told her that he wanted a shooting vest. He described what he wanted and furnished a picture from an old Sears Roebuck catalog. He told the seamstress, "I want it in camouflage, green in front and brown in the back."

The seamstress told him, "Come back tomorrow morning. I'll have it laid out for you."

"Don't forget the pockets," said Coach Blitzkrieg.

The next day Coach picked up the vest. He called to talk to Leo, but he wasn't in the office. Bonnie answered. "Hey, this is Coach Blitzkrieg."

"Yes, Coach," said Bonnie.

"I'm no good selling shoes," said Coach. "I've been to Natick, Massachusetts, and to the military. There's no market there for our shoes. But I've come up with an idea for an outdoor vest. I'd like to show it to Leo."

"You should show it to Theresa," said Bonnie. "She's in charge of clothing."

"No problem," said Coach. "I'm used to dealing with bureaucracies. Could I show it to her tomorrow?"

"Fine," said Bonnie. "Come about two o'clock. You know where our office is?"

"I'll find it," said the Coach.

"Bring the vest with you," said Bonnie.

As soon as the Coach hung up, Bonnie called Theresa.

"Theresa," said Bonnie. "Coach just called. He isn't a shoe salesman. He's designed a hunting vest and wants RECNAC to sponsor it. I told him we'd meet with him tomorrow at two o'clock. Let's boost his morale and take a look at his vest. He knows a lot about outdoor clothing. Maybe it could be profitable with a great markup."

"Since when do you know anything about markups?" asked Theresa. "I thought you were a cocktail waitress when Leo met you."

"I was a cocktail waitress when Leo met me," said Bonnie, with a touch of pique in her voice. "That doesn't mean I'm uneducated. I was just waiting tables until I got a chance to open in an off-Broadway play. I have a bachelor's degree, magna cum laude from John Carroll University. I majored in theater and minored in business. I'm in charge of doing all the personal income tax for Leo. I'm no dumb blonde."

"I didn't know, and I'm sorry," said Theresa.

"No problem," said Bonnie. "I still think we ought to take a look at Coach's vest."

The next day, Coach walked into the so-called office and met with Bonnie and Theresa. He showed the vest and pointed out its utility. "Sizes aren't going to be a problem since it doesn't have sleeves. It's got pockets on the outside and on the inside. You can put shotgun shells on the front and your cigarettes on the inside, and it's even got a little game bag in the back."

"For the person who's got a little bit of a stomach, like me, you have these Velcro loops over the front. That way, you can loosen it. I put four of them on the front. If a guy has a stomach, it still fits. If a guy is trim, he can just use the zipper."

"That's good, Coach. How many do you think that you could sell?" asked Theresa.

"There's not a huge market for shooting vests," said Coach. "We could manufacture them for ten dollars and sell them for twenty, and the sporting goods stores would sell them for thirty dollars. If we're lucky we could probably sell twenty-five or thirty-five thousand of these."

"Would you be interested in selling vests, Coach?" asked Theresa.

"Yes, I would," said Coach. "I don't belong in running shoes. I'd like to sell outdoor vests, outdoor boots, work boots, probably with Bill. I know what I'm doing, since I've worn boots all my life."

"Coach, I'm going to talk to Leo and see if you can work in the outdoors division with Bill," said Bonnie. "I think this vest has potential."

"It's going to be a great idea," said Theresa.

"What should I do?" asked the Coach.

"You check in with Bill. We'll get some preliminary quotes. Get a hundred made and see what other people think."

"Thanks," said Coach. "So many times I've had ideas and they've just fallen on deaf ears."

"You've got a very good idea here," said Theresa. "I think we can sell this."

After he left, Bonnie turned to Theresa. "What do you mean, he's got a great idea here? He might be able to sell twenty-five or thirty thousand, but you seem to think that this is really going to take off."

"Yes, I do," said Theresa. "I think the vest is great. I think we can probably make it for eight dollars in the small and extra small sizes."

"Small and extra small! Those would fit a one hundred ten pound man. How many men are that size?" Bonnie wanted to know.

"I'm not going to sell it to men," said Theresa. "I'm going to sell it to the fashion-conscious young woman. Look, a woman who is trim in the waist, she uses the zipper. Where she's a little fuller at the top, she can't use the zipper, she uses the tabs." Bonnie examined the vest and nodded. "In addition, look at the pockets on this vest, especially on the inside. Where he put shotgun shells, you could easily put lipstick. You could put your credit cards on the inside. You don't have to worry about carrying a purse and having it stolen all the time. It doesn't look bulgy like when you see a woman put a wallet in her jeans."

"A man can wear jeans and stick his wallet in the back pocket," said Bonnie. "A woman does that and it's terrible."

"We're not going to fight fashion," said Theresa. "We're just going to go with the flow. I think that we can sell one hundred to one hundred and fifty thousand of these."

"You're dreaming," said Bonnie.

"No way," said Theresa. "I think we can capture the fashion market with this idea."

"Women aren't going to go into a men's outdoors store," said Bonnie.

"Why not? All your sporting goods stores sell women's clothing. Besides, we'll put labels on the inside of the smalls and extra smalls, that say Lady RECNAC," said Theresa.

"You have a hell of an idea there," said Bonnie.

"Our only problem is going to be dealing with Coach's morale," said Theresa. "He just left thinking that he has designed a great vest for outdoorsmen. He doesn't realize that his design is going to be used by every young urban woman in America."

"You're right. I think he'll be proud of the design anyway," said Bonnie.

One month later they all returned to the old warehouse for a sales meeting.

"Leo," said Allen, "I have probably got orders for about eight thousand pairs of RECNAC shoes, but they're all on consignment. They'll give us the shelf space and they'll display the shoes, but if they don't sell in sixty days, we're going to have to take them back."

"That's a start, but I don't know where we're going to get the money to pay for the shoes. What bank would back RECNAC? This really is a gamble," said a grim Leo.

"I've raised ten million dollars," said Michael.

"You've WHAT?" yelled Leo.

"Way to go," said Larry. "How did you do that?"

"Yeah," said Pablo, "did you blackmail somebody?"

"Hey," Coach said, "I'm not getting involved in any kind of drug deals here. I've got my pension to think about."

"No," said Michael. "It's all perfectly legitimate. I sold the sports rights that the Leisure Division owned. RECNAC has options, and some of them are held in perpetuity. As long as we buy them every year, we keep them. I sold the corporate sponsorship, tenting rights, tickets and limousine service at the US Open to a Japanese automobile company for a half million dollars for this year."

"Way to go, Michael," said Bill.

"We got ten million dollars this year for the tickets that we've purchased," said Michael. "In addition, pre-paid corporate planes were leased. I sold the leases as well. We should receive ten million dollars within the next ninety days. Some of these rights are going to be worthless in the future, but with inflation, some may be worth more."

"It's good to know we've got an influx of capital," said Leo. "We've got no inventory to sell except what we're going to buy. The question is, where are we going to buy the shoes, how many should we order, and how much can we spend? Any suggestions?"

"We ought to spend five million on shoes, but hold back some in case the saw mill breaks," said Bill.

"Bill, what do you know about five million dollars?" asked Sylvia.

"How many pair of RECNAC shoes would five million dollars buy?" asked Leo.

"It depends," said Michael, "if we're going to get the good quality shoe, or the best quality shoe."

"We ought to get at least one million dollars worth of the good quality shoes," Angelo said. "I can sell them if we can get them out."

"Okay, let's do this, Michael. Forty percent good quality shoes, sixty percent the best quality shoe. Have a small design change so you can tell them apart," said Leo.

"Leo," said Larry, "I think we could sell a hundred thousand softball bats. We have to get players to try them. To manufacture the first ten thousand bats takes seven hundred and fifty thousand dollars."

"My idea for a body enhancing bra would need about a half a million dollars to get off the ground," said Theresa.

"Coach Blitzkrieg has come up with a new idea for an outdoor vest," Bonnie said. "He feels that we could manufacture that vest for ten dollars. We've done some preliminary research and we think we could make it for an average of eight dollars." Bonnie passed a prototype vest around.

"Eight dollars?" Coach Blitzkrieg asked.

"Yes," said Bonnie. "All the vests wouldn't be extra extra large size like yours. Some of them would take less material."

"Right," said Theresa. "I think there's a good profit margin as well. It wouldn't cost as much money as our body enhancement clothing, and we could probably tie it into the 'Lady RECNAC' line."

"Lady RECNAC!" exploded Coach. "These are men's outdoor vests."

"Oh yes," said Bonnie soothingly. "They're a very utilitarian vest. If we make them for both men and women, we can sell a lot more of them. It goes along with the outdoor line."

"Oh," said Colonel, "I hadn't thought about that. I just hadn't thought about women being able to use it."

"I think it's going to be a great seller for both men and women," said Theresa.

"Hold on," yelled a standing Rev. Allen. The room quieted. "You sound like drunken sailors. Michael's efforts have miraculously raised ten million dollars."

"And about five million each succeeding year," interrupted Larry.

"Exactly. This is a Godsend," said Allen. "We could close RECNAC down, go out of business, and live off the future sport rents. Isn't that right, Michael?"

A silence fell over the room. Allen made sense.

"Quit RECNAC just when it's getting started?" sputtered Bonnie. She looked at Leo.

"Let's hear him out," said Leo. "Go ahead, Allen."

"Leo, I know you were a corporate executive who had a half million dollar a year salary, but ten million dollars is a lot of money. A tithe to a church would be one million dollars. Michael has discovered a hidden pot of gold. Now you are thinking of gambling it on shoes, bats, and vests that none of us know anything about." He pounded the table with his fist.

"Leo, are you going to say anything?" pleaded Bonnie. Leo sat silently. Finally Michael stood up.

"If we followed Allen's suggestion we would spend four million dollars in unemployment compensation, medical insurance close outs, state and federal taxes. We could clear six million dollars this year and four to five million dollars for the next three to four years. But there would be nothing for us to do."

"Why would anybody hire us to do nothing?" asked Bill.

"He is not hiring us to give us jobs. He is paying us back for what we did for him. We got QRX to give him RECNAC," said Allen.

"Wait a minute," said Lisa, "I helped him. I didn't do it for money."

"Yes, but he made money, lots of it. He wants to gamble it away," snapped Allen. "Part of it belongs to us."

"Allen," said Lisa as she put her arm on his shoulder, "when were you ever concerned about money?"

"Ever since the Board of Elders fired me. They still haven't offered me a full-time ministry," roared Allen. "I want some financial security. I don't want to rot of cancer in some Medicaid-funded extended-care home." Allen burst into tears. Lisa hugged him.

The rest of the group watched uneasily and looked down at the floor. "Allen, this is not like you," said Lisa as she hugged him. "You have never been afraid before."

"I am now. I just can't see squandering this money when we all could use it for retirement," said Allen.

"It's not our money. It's Leo's. He has his dreams, too. He wants to get back in the game," said Lisa. Allen sat down. Tears streamed down his face. Sylvia put her hand on Allen's shoulder.

"Allen has made a solid financial analysis, said Leo. "I think we should hear from everyone. Floor is open."

"Senor Leo," said Angelo, "me and Pablo would like to work for you. We have done nothing to have a part of this lawsuit money. *Ora et labora*. Work gives a man dignity."

"It's a real gamble," said Michael. "As an accountant, I would agree with Allen. As a cancer patient without medical insurance, I would agree with Allen. I have insurance and I'm not afraid. I understand his fear. I'm fifty-seven years of age and I'm not getting another chance. I'll comptroller this corporation. What the hell do I have to lose?"

"Yeah, Michael," said Theresa quietly.

"Leo fought this battle with QRX without me," said Bill. "He didn't have to ask me to work. He could have hired young college graduates. I'm too good a carpenter to rake lawns. I'll do my best on selling shoes and that's all I can say."

"I'll go with you," said Coach. "I got cancer. I didn't make General. I want to prove them wrong."

"Watch your language," warned Allen, looking up.

"Glad to have you back," shouted Coach as he patted Allen on the back.

"I apologize to everyone," said Allen. "I'm ashamed. I didn't want to show fear. I'm sorry."

"Everyone has fear," said Coach. "Courage is the physical and mental control of fear."

"Thanks," said Allen.

Lisa smiled at Coach.

"Thank you for your candid comments," said Leo. "But as far as I'm concerned, we started as a softball team, and we will finish as a team. We will win or lose together."

The team members looked at each other. They had made a decision to spend ten million dollars. The ecstatic thrill of spending was tempered by a potential loss. There was a grim determination to succeed.

"We've spent all the money we've got," said Leo. Everybody has got to go out and sell. Sarah, we're going to wait for your advertising campaign."

All the RECNAC employees shook hands and hugged Rev. Allen. Angelo said, "Let's go get something to eat. I'm buying."

"You're buying?" Larry asked.

"Yes," said Angelo.

"Oh no, not another Taco Bell dinner again?" asked Bonnie.

"No, señora," said Pablo. "Let's do some good barbecue—ribs, chicken and all that. I am equal opportunity—how you say—chow hound."

As they trooped out, Leo said, "Michael, please stay a minute. I want to talk with you."

CHAPTER 19

LEO WALKED BACK to his "executive desk," a plywood panel on sawhorses. Leo was upset. "Damn it, Michael, why didn't you tell me you'd raised ten million dollars before the meeting began? It really created a lot of problems for our team."

"It was a lot more money than I anticipated," said Michael. "I just wanted to be appreciated for it."

"You did a super job!" said Leo. "But you should have told me ahead of time. You saw the problems when our team discussed spending money."

"I didn't think it was going to cause the dissension it did," said Michael.

"Rev. Allen was really upset about the ten million dollars," declared Leo. "He certainly caused me, and himself, a lot of pain."

"I'm sorry," said Michael. "I worked at large corporations where my boss always took the credit. I wanted to get the appreciation for this."

"Did you think that I was going to claim credit for raising the ten million dollars?" asked Leo.

"Yes, I did." There was a long silence as the two men stared at each other. Michael had spoken honestly. Leo appeared angry, but he composed himself.

"Five years ago I'd have claimed all of the credit," Leo admitted. "I just hope you understand the pressure for the team. Most of them have lived from paycheck to paycheck all their lives. Making decisions about spending one hundred thousand dollars is something they do once in their lifetime when they buy a house. Making decisions on how to spend five million dollars blows their minds."

"They all came to the right decision, though, didn't they?" asked Michael who kept a steady eye on Leo.

Leo raised his eyebrows and nodded. "I sure hope they're right. They put a lot of their faith in me, and frankly, I'm worried."

"That's why you get the big bucks," said Michael.

"Yeah," said Leo, "but there was a lot of truth to what Allen said. I could pack it in right now, close down the corporation and make a couple million dollars."

"Yeah, but none of us would," said Michael.

"Exactly!" shouted Leo. "I want to get back into the game!" Then he changed the subject. "You've had to judge personnel, being a senior accountant, correct?"

"Yes, I have," said Michael.

"I owe all these RECNAC people," said Leo. "They've helped me stay out of jail. They've helped me win the court case. Are they any good? I've got a teacher's wife as my marketing director. I've got a woman ex-cop in charge of a lingerie division. I have an ex-Army officer designing vests. I've got a retired minister, a disabled carpenter, and two Hispanic custodians as shoe salesmen. I have a school teacher selling softball bats. If anyone studying for an M.B.A. saw this motley crew, they'd slit my throat. I'd get an F if I were being graded."

"You really do have some doubts about this, don't you?" asked Michael.

"Damn right I do," said Leo.

"Okay," said Michael, "let's talk about the good points. That ex-school teacher, Larry, has done a great job with the bat manufacturers. The material that the bat is made out of is patented. And Larry had his brother, Wendell, trademark the RECNAC name."

"Larry did that?" asked Leo.

"Yes, he did," said Michael. "His brother helped him. He didn't even charge us."

"I guess he shouldn't," said Leo. "He charged me enough for the corporate case."

"In any event, Larry's got the bats in production mode. He's got a great rapport with the bat manufacturers. For ten thousand bats they want seven hundred fifty thousand dollars. However, because of Larry's enthusiasm for the bat..."

"He has that. He swears by that bat," interrupted Leo.

"The bat manufacturer says for three hundred seventy-five thousand dollars, they'll make five thousand bats C.O.D. The next five thousand, they'll ship to us when we need them and give us ninety days to pay."

"Way to go," said Leo as he reached out and shook Michael's hand. "That's the way to get other people to do our financing."

"I didn't do that," said Michael. "Larry worked it out. The bat manufacturer's president is a senior softball player. He's used the bats and thinks they're great. He's going to buy the first twenty-five."

"Larry did all that?" asked Leo.

"He sure did," said Michael. "I can't take any of the credit for it."

Leo sat there for a moment. "Michael, I'm shocked. I didn't expect Larry to have that type of financial or marketing ability."

"He has it," said Michael.

"Okay, let's move onto this lingerie thing with Theresa. Does she know what's she's doing?" inquired Leo.

"Yes, she does. Obviously, she's had the medical problems to have the inside view. She doesn't have the fashion flare that Bonnie does, but they've come up with a very good concept," said Michael.

"Will it sell?" asked Leo.

"Bonnie says the urban singles and young marrieds are going to love this vest. She said Coach will have a problem understanding that his outdoor vest is so heavily used by women."

"What about our shoe salesmen?" asked Leo shaking his head.

"You made a good decision there," said Michael. "If you're going to sell shoes to the Hispanic population, you need people like Angelo and Pablo. As a purchasing agent you see salesmen with three-piece suits and a tie selling products for the average household. They have no idea of what the average household is."

"Angelo and Pablo definitely know their constituents," said Leo.

"They both speak Spanish. These are the salesmen that we need. Bill and Allen both represent the main-line American baby boomers. Most purchasing agents completed high school with maybe a couple of years of college and think the college grad in the three-piece suit is patronizing them. Your problem is having products for them to sell."

"Tell me about it," said Leo. "What am I going to do?"

"Our vests, shoes and bats are designed and ready to go into production. It will take ninety days to get them shipped to distribution points. We've got to do our advertising when we get the product to the delivery points."

"You're telling me we're going to lose our ass for the next ninety days," said Leo.

"That's right. We've probably got twenty employees and they won't produce income for at least three months."

"That's okay," said Leo. "Our twenty employees probably won't cost us one hundred fifty thousand dollars in the next three months. They're not paid that well."

"One hundred and fifty thousand dollars. That's still a lot of money," said Michael.

"Don't think small, Michael," said Leo. "We just talked about spending ten million dollars thanks to you. I don't have QRX's deep pockets behind me, but ninety days doesn't bother me. Frankly, I think it's going to be six months."

"Six months?" Michael asked.

"Yes, I do. We can still afford six months. Nine months will be a problem, however," said Leo.

"We've got another problem," said Michael.

"Tell me about this one," said Leo.

"I got a letter from the QRX Corporation," said Michael. "You informed that dummy export-import company that was owned by Mr. Williams and Margaret Novak that we weren't going to buy their lawn chairs from them."

"Right," said Leo.

"The people who sold the lawn chairs required the QRX Corporation to be the co-signer. All those lawn chairs are piled up in a yard in San Francisco. Under the provisions of that court decree, you have to pay QRX sixty million dollars."

"Who wrote that letter?" asked Leo.

Michael shuffled through his briefcase and other papers. "Here it is. It's signed by Tom Rebul." He handed the letter to Leo.

Leo read the three-page letter. "Neither the corporate attorneys nor

Tom Rebul is aware that the export import company is owned by Mr. Williams and Margaret Novak," said Leo. "I'm sure that Mr. Williams and Novak don't know we know it," said Leo.

"How did you find out that they owned it?" asked Michael.

"I called Wendell and asked him if he would check on it. In four hours, he faxed me the articles of incorporation that listed Margaret Novak's home address as the corporate office and Mr. Williams as a shareholder," said Michael.

"Do Williams and Novak really think they're going to pull this off?" Leo asked.

"Hell, yes," said Michael. "Who's going to complain? Tom Rebul, their financial stooge? The only people who are going to complain are outside directors and SEC personnel."

"Let them sue us," said Leo.

"No, let's not do that," argued Michael. "Even if we're right, we could end up spending a bundle in attorney fees."

"You're right, damn it," said Leo. "What do you suggest?"

"Have Wendell write a letter to Tom Williams and Margaret Novak enclosing copies of the articles of incorporation," said Michael. They can either drop the lawsuit, or we will defend it in public on these issues."

"Tell Wendell to slap them with a public lawsuit if they don't get this thing resolved," said Leo.

"I think Wendell can get us a good outcome," said Michael.

"I expect some other problems as well," said Leo.

"Like what?" asked Michael.

"I wouldn't be surprised if old QRX employees try to screw us. They will tell vendors RECNAC is not a dependable vendor," said Leo.

"I expect that," said Michael, "but we can eliminate some of the problems by paying C.O.D. A lot of the corporate people from whom we're buying hold you in high regard."

"Yeah, but they sure weren't going to give me a job," said Leo.

"Leo, just don't worry so much," said Michael.

"Now look who's telling me not to worry. Five minutes ago, you had more worries than I have," said Leo.

"I guess when I tell them to you, they don't seem so big," said Michael.

Leo chuckled. "Yeah, ghosts, goblins, and even cancer all don't look so big when you're not standing alone." They both shook hands.

"Let's go eat," said Michael as they drove to Angelo's far out restaurant.

As Leo and Michael walked in, the RECNAC team all gave a shout. Leo acknowledged the noise with a raise of his hand.

"I'm glad to see you're all having fun tonight because you're all going to be working hard and for peanuts the next six months," said Leo.

"Especially me, señor," said Pablo as he raised his green card above his head.

"Señor Wendell got it for him," said Angelo. "Now he doesn't have to worry about the immigration police."

"Way to go," said Bill.

"That's interesting," said Lisa. "Two hundred and fifty years ago, Arab slave traders threw a net over my ancestors, put them in chains and sold them to Europeans who brought them to America and made them work. Now, America takes another group of people who want to work and puts them in handcuffs and then throws them out."

Leo tapped a glass for attention. "We're going to incur problems with purchasing agents who have dealt with other corporations for years. Some of our competitors will engage in smear tactics and advertising espionage. When you run into any problems like that, please bring them to my attention directly."

"Yepper," said Bill.

"Sí," said Angelo and Pablo.

"Right," said Allen.

"I want to thank you once again for your vote of confidence this evening. If this company succeeds, it will be due to your individual efforts. We'll be meeting again in about thirty days."

"Yeah!" they all chorused and high-fived each other.

Leo looked at Bonnie. "What have I gotten myself into?"

"I love ya," said Bonnie.

The letter lay on the middle of Mr. Tom Williams' desk. His super large mahogany desk was devoid of any other pieces of paper. It contained a walnut cigar humidor, a granite pen-and-pencil set, a water pitcher and two crystal water goblets. Mr. Williams touched the letter with his three thousand dollar gold pen, the way someone would touch a dead snake with a garden hoe. Margaret Novak sat in one of the nearby wing chairs, about four feet away.

"What's the problem with the letter?" she asked.

"This is a letter from that S.O.B. Wendell Nedil who is RECNAC's corporate attorney," said Mr. Williams. "They have discovered the export import company is owned by you and me. Our export-import company is being billed for sixty million dollars. QRX wrote a letter to RECNAC telling them that they had to pay the sixty million dollars."

"That's just standard business law," said Margaret.

"Right, but this damn attorney has discovered that you and I were buying these chairs for twenty million and selling them to the Leisure Services Division for sixty million dollars," said Mr. Williams. "He's caught us overcharging QRX corporation forty million dollars a year."

"What if we have overcharged?" asked Margaret. "We deserve the money."

"I know, I know," said Mr. Williams, "but the board of directors and the SEC are going to take a dim view of the fact that we made forty million dollars, one-third of which, I might add, has gone to you, Margaret."

"I deserve that for the raise they wouldn't give me," said Margaret.

"I've asked a young corporate counsel from the legal department to advise me on this," said Mr. Williams.

"Shouldn't you have outside counsel on this?" Margaret asked.

"There's no outside counsel I trust on this. They'd leak it all over *The Wall Street Journal,*" said Mr. Williams.

A buzzer sounded on Mr. Williams' intercom. He picked up the phone and said, "Send him right in please."

The door opened to reveal a six-foot, mid-thirtyish attorney with a brief case. "Ms. Novak, let me introduce you to George Johnson. George works in the Ethics and Compliance Division of in-house counsel. George, would you look at this letter, please?" asked Mr. Williams as he handed him the letter. George read the letter for three minutes and then put it down.

"Are the facts stated in this letter accurate?" asked George.

"Pretty much," said Mr. Williams casually. "In order to ensure the profitability of the Leisure Services Division, I formed an export-import company for the purposes of buying lawn chairs. We purchased them for twenty million dollars. I personally went out on a limb to ensure their arrival. The QRX Corporation co-signed the note. There was some profit made by me individually."

"This letter indicates that you made forty million dollars in profit," said George.

"That's right, but I had only the best interest of our corporation at heart," said Mr. Williams.

"I understand. As part of the Ethics and Compliance Department of corporate counsel, I must inform you that you owe QRX forty million dollars," said George.

"What do you think should be done?" asked Mr. Williams.

"It would appear that if QRX advances this suit against RECNAC, it would bring the whole subject matter under scrutiny," said George.

"What should I do?" Mr. Williams asked.

"From the corporate perspective," George stated, "QRX should not become involved in this. You will have to pay this money individually. On the other hand," he commented, "because you have suffered a loss trying to advance the corporate position, I think that you should request to be reimbursed by the board of directors."

"Mr. Johnson, I appreciate your kind comments," said Mr. Williams. "In short, you're saying that QRX should not sue. If I suffered a loss, I should ask the board of directors to reimburse us for the amount as a normal business expense."

"It would probably all be tax deductible to you," George commented, "and you may get favorable tax consequences."

"Mr. Johnson, I appreciate your kind commentary. I want to say I certainly think that you're in line for promotion to the assistant vice president level."

"I try to do my best, sir," George said. "Thank you very much." He got up and left.

"Tom, you just had our Corporate Compliance Officer in your office," said Margaret. "You informed him of a criminal violation, and he agreed not to report it. He even suggested that the board of directors compensate you for it," said Margaret. "I admire your deft touch."

"I promised him a promotion," said Mr. Williams.

"How much of a promotion?" Margaret asked.

"About thirty-five thousand dollars a year," said Mr. Williams.

"You mean for thirty-five thousand dollars he's going to stick his neck out like this?" Margaret asked.

"Of course, Margaret. Besides, the promotion will give him an extra two weeks of vacation," said Mr. Williams.

"What does this mean?" inquired Margaret.

"It means that you and I will have to go to the bank, borrow twenty million dollars and pay the lawn chair bill. Then we'll submit it to the QRX Corporation," said Mr. Williams.

"For only twenty million dollars?" asked Margaret.

"This year we won't make a profit," said Mr. Williams.

"How do we get back at these S.O.B.s?" Margaret wanted to know.

CHAPTER 20

ONE MONTH LATER the following news article appeared in *The Wall Street Journal*, buried in the last pages between two large initial public offering advertisements:

RECNAC REORGANIZES

RECNAC has announced a new line of shoes, softball and outdoor equipment and will begin a million dollar advertising campaign in selected test markets in Chicago and Texas, according to public relations director Sarah Nedil. This marketing ploy appears to be the last gasp of the RECNAC Corporation, formerly the Leisure Division of the QRX Corporation. The new RECNAC line includes both good- and best-quality shoes, new softball bats and vests.

The advertising campaign got off to an excellent start, with a barrage of billboards. The first one showed a picture of Rev. Allen Kilpatrick as he led his civil rights march for cancer, and underneath was labeled prominently:

I Wouldn't Lead A March
Without My RECNAC Shoes!

In the Texas area, the billboards had a picture of Pablo and Angelo and their families. The billboard in both English and Spanish proclaimed:

The best shoes at the best price for your families.

Another billboard had a picture of Larry. The ad was also prominently featured in the senior softball tabloids throughout the United States.

Still another billboard had a picture of Rooster—six-foot four, two hundred and sixty pounds, with big shoulders and hands, an eye patch over one eye, a leather vest and a beer gut.

The next billboard, featuring a picture of Theresa, said the following:

Had Reconstructive Surgery?
RECNAC Knows Your Most Intimate Problems and Can Provide Solutions.

The final billboard had a picture of Bill and said

Over 55? Need a
Little More
Softness on that
Older Instep?
RECNAC Knows the
Problem and
Provides a
Solution.

Approximately three months later, *Fortune* magazine reported:

RECNAC EXPERIENCES SALES SPURT

Quarterly figures released by RECNAC showed that in the second quarter of this year, sales of RECNAC shoes, sporting goods and products in its Lady RECNAC division generated almost twenty million dollars in revenue.

The sales, coming off a unique ad campaign directed at middle-aged and senior citizens, have demonstrated that RECNAC has found a niche for itself in the very competitive shoe and sporting goods division.

Six months ago financial magazines predicted its demise. After eliminating the lawn chair division, which accounted for over seventy-five percent of its sales last year, RECNAC has found a new product mix.

Leo Able's turnaround of RECNAC Corporation is going to be one of the most outstanding executive efforts since Lee Iacoca's rescue of Chrysler Corporation.

Nine months later, the entire RECNAC sales team returned to Atlanta for the second annual corporate meeting.

"Ladies and gentlemen," said Leo, bringing the meeting to order, "I just heard the results from Michael. He's projecting sales next year of over one hundred million dollars. Theresa, your undergarment line is absolutely unbelievable. It is certainly apparent you understand an existing problem. I am astounded by the public acceptance."

"Bonnie deserves as much of the credit as I do. She's the one that came up with the idea. We just took it from there," said Theresa.

"You've still done a fantastic job, Theresa," he said.

"Don't forget the outdoor vests designed by Coach. We've sold fifty-one thousand men's vests and four hundred ninety-five thousand ladies' vests with the RECNAC label. Coach Blitzkrieg is one of the top twenty-five fashion designers this year," said Theresa.

"Really," said Coach, "who says that? The National Rifle Association?"

"No," said Theresa.

"Ducks Unlimited?" asked Coach.

"No," said Theresa.

"Wild Turkey Federation?" he inquired.

"No," said Theresa.

"*Field and Stream?*" Coach asked.

"No," said Theresa.

"U.S. Trap & Skeet?" asked Coach.

"No," said Theresa.

"Who then?" he asked.

"*Seventeen Magazine,*" said Theresa. "High school girls are agog over your design."

"Oh," said a subdued Coach.

"Larry, your softball bat sales are absolutely amazing," said Leo.

"Thanks," said Larry, "but it was your idea. I saw where we could go with them. RECNAC is going to sponsor a senior citizen team, and I'm going to play on it."

"Not unless you can hit," said Coach. "I'll see that Larry does not disgrace the RECNAC bat."

"Pablo, Angelo and Bill—you are selling our shoes. I don't know why we're doing so well," said Michael.

"I ain't never sold shoes before, but I'm working with people that I like," said Bill. "Been more friend to me than anyone else. I'm not here to make money, I'm here to help you out."

"Yes," said Larry, "I've worked hard, but I'm having fun. I'm going to go play softball."

"Once again, only if you can hit," said Coach. "And we're going to bring back all the other guys."

"Not one of you has claimed credit for your work," said Leo. "Larry gave the credit to me for bats. Theresa praised Coach on the vests. Sarah devised the ad campaign. Your unselfish work attitude made all of our endeavors a success."

"I want to tell you what a good job that you've done," said Sylvia. You said your lifelong dream was to be recognized as a corporate executive who changed things. Leo, you've finally done it. Here is an advance copy of *Fortune* magazine with your picture on it. You are the Executive of the Year."

"Unbelievable!" exclaimed Leo as he looked at the proof.

"You finally understood that the business had to provide something that people needed and wanted," said Lisa.

"Why," asked Leo, "did that make me the Executive of the Year? Everyone else here has done most, if not all of the work."

"Are you going to New York to get the award?" asked Bill.

"Yes," said Leo. "I am more appreciative of getting this magazine cover from you than from anyone else in New York. For the first time in my life, I've realized that the people who worked with me made us a success." Leo was almost in tears. Bonnie touched his shoulder.

"Don't get wimpy on us," said Coach.

"Yeah," said Allen, "you're only half the jerk you used to be, but you're not cured."

Everyone laughed.

"I can't believe it. We're on our way to what we dreamed about one year ago," said Leo, wiping his eye and smiling.

"Now," said Bill. "You guys have got to help me on my dream."

"What's that?" asked Leo.

"Remember I talked about building homes for Houses for Humanity?"

"Yeah, I remember something about that," said Larry. "So what?"

"We've got to start doing some thinking," said Bill.

"I don't know how to build a house," said Michael.

"It's all done in the figuring," said Bill.

"I don't know if I can take two or three months off to build a house," said Leo.

"Leo, I spent longer than that working with you," said Bill.

"You're right," said Leo. "I owe that to you."

"But," said Bill, "you don't have to worry. We usually build a house in three days."

"What kind of a house can you build in three days?" asked Bonnie.

"It's a small house, and with a lot of dedicated help we can do it," said Bill.

"I've got to go to New York to accept this award. I'll be back in a week. I'll help you build a home," said Leo.

"Are you sure we can build a house in three days?" asked Allen.

"I sure hope so," said Bill.

At the Convention Center of the Guggenheim Museum in New York, before large groups of bankers, financiers, and their well- dressed wives, Leo and Bonnie fidgeted. Bonnie adjusted the bow tie on Leo's tuxedo.

"All the years I worked at QRX, I dreamed of being here," Leo commented. "I get cancer, almost go to jail, end up playing softball, participate in a civil rights march, and then I end up here. This is coming in the back door."

"I'm sure happy about that," said Bonnie.

"So am I." He squeezed Bonnie.

"Remember to keep your cool. Most people will be here to congratulate you. Some want to knock you down," said Bonnie.

"There's nobody like that on the RECNAC crew. There's just not that penny-ante one-upmanship," said Leo.

They were interrupted by the handsome master of ceremonies. "My thanks to the Mayor of the city of New York, and the Lieutenant Governor of New York for their remarks. I want to take this opportunity to introduce Leo Able. He joined QRX Corporation immediately after graduating from Northwestern University and remained with them until two years ago. QRX Corporation spun off the Leisure Division to him. Our magazine commented that Leo was volunteering to serve on a financial *Titanic*. He's had the laugh on us. He's turned the corporation around. He is a hallmark of the entrepreneurial spirit which made America great. Without further ado, I give you *Fortune*'s Executive of the Year, Leo Able."

Leo walked up, shook the hand of the master of ceremonies and took his place at the lectern. "Thank you very much. I appreciate this award, as it comes from a group of people whose opinion I value very much."

The MC said, "As is customary, I want to open up for questions from the audience and members of the media if they wish."

A hand rose up. "Mr. Able."

"Yes, sir?" answered Leo.

"Mr. Able, isn't it true that all through your corporate career you've been lucky? You've had people who have done a great amount of the work while you got all the credit. Weren't you fired from the QRX Corporation?"

There was a hush over the audience. There were murmurs.

"You don't have to answer," whispered the MC.

To the surprise of the audience, Leo responded, "That's true."

"What changed at RECNAC?" asked the reporter.

"I am a very lucky man," said Leo. "The people at RECNAC deserve all the credit. Larry Nedil is the genius behind our entire softball line. Allen Kilpatrick, Pablo Sirgosa and Angelo Bravo have done fantastic jobs with our recreation line. Bill Kibler and Norman Blitzkrieg have performed admirably with our outdoor line. Theresa Martinez and bonnie Able have been outstanding with our undergarment line. Every one of those ideas was conceived by those individuals."

"Do you deserve this award?" asked the reporter.

"No, it belongs to the people working with me," said Leo. "Thank you and good night."

The audience stood and clapped.

Bonnie and Leo left the award function in a limousine. Bonnie put her hand on Leo's arm. "That was a very effective way you answered that reporter. The news media are always trying to make executives look foolish. Your answer really surprised him."

"Yes," said Leo. "I was surprised by the applause. It's like watching a professional football game. One player makes a tackle because the other ten players give him the opportunity. Instead of thanking his teammates, he showboats in front of the crowd. If I had my druthers, I'd have all the RECNAC people stand with me. I just got to hold the trophy."

"That's very perceptive of you, and generous," said Bonnie.

Leo looked at her admiringly. "Bonnie, just before I got the award, one of those tabloid photographers handed me a picture of someone dancing topless on a beer truck in Chicago."

"Yes," said Bonnie.

"I looked at the picture closely. He told me that there was a rumor that it was you," said Leo.

"What did you tell him?" asked Bonnie.

"I told him I couldn't recognize anyone from that picture," said Leo.

"What do you think he was after?" asked Bonnie.

"I don't know. Something in that picture made me curious."

"What is that?" snapped Bonnie.

"The belt buckle worn by the topless dancer looks exactly like the one that I bought you at that Indian shop in Arizona. No two are alike. Bonnie, was that a picture of you?"

Bonnie looked down, and then answered, "Yes. I'm not ashamed of what I did. I just turned the whole march around," she said. "And I wasn't the only one who did."

"What do you mean you weren't the only one? Who else danced topless?"

"Sarah danced topless," said Bonnie.

"Sweet, Southern Sarah! You got to be kidding me," said Leo.

"No," said Bonnie, "and so did Theresa, but not topless.

"Theresa! Was she there?" asked Leo.

"Yes, she was," said Bonnie.

"Where did all the beer come from?" asked Leo.

"Remember you gave me fifteen thousand dollars the night before?" Bonnie asked.

"Yes," said Leo.

"I used that money to buy the beer trucks that were on the way to the Save the Octopus rally," said Bonnie. "I paid the drivers. Once they were paid, they put the beer wherever they were told."

"So that's how we had the great rally?" Leo asked.

"Yes," said Bonnie.

"Does Allen know?" Leo inquired

"No," said Bonnie.

"Does Lisa know?" asked Leo.

Bonnie laughed, "Yes, she does."

"Don't tell me she danced topless!" said Leo.

"No way, we had to protect her. She was in charge of hijacking the beer," said Bonnie.

"The wife of the reverend of a Baptist church was in charge of stealing the beer?" Leo asked.

"You've got to be pragmatic about these things," Bonnie said, blinking her eyelashes at Leo alluringly.

"So, you're telling me that if it weren't for the women's efforts, the civil rights march would have been a flop," said Leo.

"No," said Bonnie, "it just might not have been as well attended."

Leo paused for a moment as the limousine wound its way through the New York traffic. He collected his thoughts. Then he turned suddenly to Bonnie. "Did we win the fight at that café with those hard hats?" asked Leo.

"Of course we won the fight," said Bonnie. "Those three guys were out cold."

"I know there were three guys unconscious on the floor. What I'm asking is did we do it?"

"Of course we did it," said Bonnie.

"Let me rephrase my question. Of the three men who were knocked unconscious on the floor, were any of them knocked out by the REC-NAC men?" asked Leo.

"You certainly helped," said Bonnie.

Leo paused a moment, reached forward into the limousine's bar, poured himself a glass of scotch and plunked two ice cubes in it. "Who knocked out the three hard hats?"

Bonnie hesitated. Then she said, "I think Theresa hit two of them."

"Little Theresa hit two thugs and knocked them out?" Leo inquired.

"Yes," said Bonnie.

"What did she use, a baseball bat?" Leo asked.

"That's right. She hit them in the groin," said Bonnie.

"Okay," said a reflective Leo, "who knocked out the third one?" There was no response from Bonnie. Leo looked at her. "Did you hear my question? Who knocked out the third one?"

Bonnie looked Leo straight in the eyes and then, shifting her gaze to the carpet in the limousine, said, "I did, but I apologized to him."

"You apologized to that S.O.B. who was beating the hell out of me?" exploded Leo.

"I really didn't mean to hit him that hard," said Bonnie, "but he was choking Theresa. The bat somehow went right between his eyes."

"Did you swing it hard?" Leo asked.

"As hard as I could," said Bonnie. "In tennis terms it would have been called a hard overhand. I used the bat and hit him right above the nose."

"I bet that fazed him some," commented Leo.

"Yes, it did," said Bonnie, "because he let her go. He dropped to his knees and lay on the floor."

"Well," said Leo laconically, "a baseball bat to the forehead will do that. The women have made the RECNAC corporation. You wives made the civil rights march work. You and Theresa won the fight for us."

"We just try to help our husbands!" said Bonnie.

"Did we win the softball game?" asked Leo.

"You sure did!" shouted Bonnie.

"I'm afraid to ask, but I have to," said Leo. "Did we score all eighteen runs."

"Yes!" shouted Bonnie and high-fived him.

"Did we score all eighteen runs?" asked Leo.

"We just helped with three of them," said Bonnie.

"Which three?" Leo asked sternly, his face changing.

"Just the ones in the last inning," said Bonnie.

"You mean when Larry got the hit?"

"Yes, yes, that's right," yelled Bonnie. "We helped on Larry's triple."

Leo put his head down. He looked at Bonnie. "This will never go any further. Tell me what you did."

"You remember what the situation was," said Bonnie. "We had men on second and third with two outs."

"Yes, yes," said Leo struck by the fact that Bonnie actually recalled the game situation. He was bothered by her sudden knowledge. "Where did you get all this baseball expertise?"

"I bought a book. It's called *Baseball for Boobies* and I read it." She smiled at Leo.

"Okay," said Leo, "two outs, men on second and third, Larry's up. What did you do?"

"Theresa came over when Coach was talking to Larry. She pointed out that Larry was always uptight. She had put a decal of a nude woman on his bat to make him relax, but the umpire had thrown the bat out. So, just before the ball was pitched, Theresa told Sarah to unhook her bra and flash her husband."

"Sarah did that at the stadium?" asked Leo.

"Yes, but only Larry could see her," said Leo.

"All right, that gets Larry relaxed where he can hit the ball. Why didn't the right fielder catch it?"

"Theresa had another idea. She noticed that the outfielders were looking in at the plate. She had Sylvia, Lisa and me stand up and photo-flash the outfielders. Larry was told to take the first pitch so that the outfielders would be blinded by the camera flashes."

"Let me get this straight. The Reverend's wife is photo-flashing and you're photo-flashing the right fielder as the ball is pitched to Larry?" asked Leo.

"Yes! And it worked perfectly," said Bonnie. "The outfielders kept looking at us. Larry hit the ball while they were distracted. That's why that outfielder didn't get over to catch the ball in time."

"What about the next batter?" asked Leo.

"He was a good hitter. We didn't do anything. He knocked Larry in on the first pitch," said Bonnie.

"I guess this story adds a new dimension to the term 'Baseball for Boobies,'" said Leo.

"I never thought of it that way before," said Bonnie thoughtfully. "You're not going to tell anybody are you?"

Leo took a long, long, long sip of his drink and put it down. "No, I'm not going to tell anybody. Even if I did, no one would believe me." Then he reached across and gave her a big kiss and a long embrace and ran his hands gently over her body. "Bonnie, you and the rest of the wives are absolutely fantastic!"

"You know, Leo, since you've had cancer, you've really been a kinder, more considerate person than you were before," said Bonnie.

Leo looked at Bonnie. "What a terrible thing for a wife to say."

They both laughed as the limousine took them back to their hotel.

CHAPTER 21

THERE WAS NO airport in Roston, Georgia, a small community of five thousand people located in the southwest corner of the state. It was a town with substandard housing and an abundance of wood shacks left over from the sharecropper days. Most of the abandoned farmland had been purchased by wealthy Atlantans for use as tree farm and quail shooting preserves. The RECNAC Team drove into town. RECNAC working through Housing for Humanity was responsible for building a home and turning it over to the new owners at no cost.

Bill and his RECNAC workers would assemble the home in less than a week. A non-profit group would raise the fifteen thousand dollars necessary for materials and land purchase. This house was financed by the State Lawyers Association of Georgia, led by an entourage of Supreme Court and Appellate justices. The Supreme Court raised the money by levying a tax on the lawyers' clients' accounts and seized the home building opportunity as a favorable public relations gambit. In front of the building site was a large sign that said HOUSING FOR HUMANITY and listed the names of all the Supreme Court justices.

Bill and Sylvia were used to the self-aggrandizement of the sponsors. As they arrived on the job site there appeared to be two worker bees and almost thirty drones. The drones were judges and lawyers' association officers.

Shortly after Bill and Sylvia arrived, Larry, Sarah, Lisa and Allen pulled up. Michael and Theresa followed. They all shook hands and hugged each other. A few minutes later, Leo and Bonnie pulled up in his

Porsche. Leo walked up to Bill. "Here we are. What do I do?"

"The folks who put up the money are at the microphones slapping each other on the back," said Bill. "When they get finished bragging on themselves, there will be a ribbon-cutting ceremony. Then we'll go to work and build this house."

"You know how to do this, Bill?" asked Leo.

"Yep," said Bill. "I've been doing it for twenty-five years for rich people. This here is just a fifteen hundred square-foot, five-room house. I could build it by myself."

"Really," said Larry.

"Yepper," said Bill.

Sylvia nodded her head in agreement. "If they have the subcontracting crews, Bill can knock this house out in three days."

"A lot of good that'll do," came a voice.

They all turned around. Bill said, "Hey, this is a good thing we're doing. We're building a new house for folks who lived in a shack."

"I have no problem with your building a house. I don't want to see those S.O.B.s taking credit for it," he said, and pointed to the Supreme Court justices.

Leo studied the sixtyish man with thin graying hair, wearing a red baseball cap with ROSTEN SEED & FEED COMPANY embroidered on the front. "What's your problem?"

The man held out his hand. "My name is Patrick Jefferson. I'm an attorney."

"That's okay," said Larry. "My brother is a lawyer."

"What's your problem with those judges over there?" asked Allen.

"I'll tell you my problem with them," said Patrick. "About five years ago, a guy named Johnson sued a mortgage company because they were charging him sixty-five percent interest."

"Sixty-five percent interest!" said Michael. "That's usury! Didn't he know he was getting charged that?"

"Those Supreme Court justices said sixty five percent interest was immoral and improper, but legal in Georgia," said Patrick. "Almost eight thousand families have lost their homes because they could not pay their house payments."

"What do we care?" commented Bill. "We came here to build a house."

"They are using this house as a publicity stunt to cover up their past decision," said Patrick.

"Not my fight," said Bill. "Who is in charge?"

"The lawyer with the pressed overalls," said Patrick as he pointed to him with his finger.

Bill walked up to the man in the new pressed carpenter overalls, and said, "I'm here to build a house."

"Are you part of the RECNAC crew?" asked the lawyer.

"Yepper," said Bill. "We are ready to go."

"Not so fast," said the lawyer. "You all have to sign releases absolving the state lawyers association and the judges of all liability in case somebody gets hurt."

"Okay," said Bill. "Give me the piece of paper to sign."

"What does RECNAC stand for?" asked the lawyer.

"It's an organization of prostate cancer survivors," said Bill. "We're all in remission."

"You're all cancer survivors?" asked the astonished lawyer.

"Yepper," said Bill.

"I'll have to check on this," said the lawyer as he scurried away to talk to a judge.

"Is there a problem?" Larry asked as he, Allen, Leo and Michael walked over.

"I don't know," said Bill. "I just finished explaining to that lawyer in the fancy carpenter overalls that we were all cancer survivors. He appeared shocked and ran off."

They all looked over to see the lawyer in animated conversation with one of the judges. They both turned and walked over to where the RECNAC crew was standing.

"Judge, this is Bill. He is the RECNAC foreman," said the lawyer.

"Glad to meet you, Bill," said the judge. He looked at the rest of the RECNAC crew. "I understand you're all cancer survivors."

"That's right," said Leo.

"I think it's great that you're willing to try to build a house," said the Judge.

"We're not going to try to build it. We will build it," said Bill.

"Yes, I can see you feel that way," said the judge patronizingly.

"I'm getting back in the game. I'm a carpenter foreman and REC-

NAC will build this house," said Bill.

"I'm sure you mean well," said the judge, "but our reputation is on that sign," as he pointed. "We don't want you or us to look bad."

"We won't make you look bad," promised Bill.

"I'm sure you'll do your best," said the judge.

"We are ready to start," said Bill.

"Go ahead then," said the judge. "Rest assured, if you can't finish the job, it's all right. I've arranged to have some state maintenance crews here in five days to complete the house." Then the judge walked off.

"That guy is unbelievable," said Leo.

"Watch your language," said Allen smiling, "but that judge does need a lot of prayers."

RECNAC has got to build this or we're going to have egg on our faces," said Bill.

"But there are only twelve of us," said Leo.

"That's enough. Will you help me?" Bill asked.

"Sure thing," said Leo. "How long is it going to take us?"

"Seventy-two hours," said Bill. "I'm gonna tell those television folks right now."

"Wow!" said Sylvia, "I think Bill is a little mad."

"Let's hear what he's got to say," said Sarah.

Bill walked over to the television camera crew. "I figure you're here to film this house being built."

"That's right," said the TV reporter.

"We're the workers. We're fixing to build this house in three days," said Bill.

"Seventy-two hours?" inquired the TV reporter. "It takes seventy-two hours for those Supreme Court justices to clear their throats."

"We'll have it built. This is Housing for Humanity. We'll have this fella and his family in this house in seventy-two hours."

"Who are you?" the TV reporter asked.

"I'm Bill Kibler. RECNAC is here. We're gonna build this house."

"What's RECNAC?" asked the TV reporter.

"Come back in three days," said Bill.

The cameraman turned to the TV reporter. "I've heard of that name before. I recognize two of those people over there. That guy with that real fancy-looking wife."

"How do you know it's his wife?" asked the TV reporter.

"She's got a ring on her finger," said the camera man.

"Oh, yeah," said the reporter.

"I've seen that guy somewhere before," said the camera man.

"Like where?" the TV reporter asked.

"*Money* magazine, *Fortune* magazine, something like that," said the camera man.

Bill turned and walked over to the local supply coordinator. "We're fixing to start. You got all the materials lined up?"

"Yeah," said the supply coordinator.

"We'll have this house all framed in and roofed by tomorrow morning. At sunrise, have the electricians and plumbers ready to go," said Bill.

"You're crazy. You're never going to have this thing framed and roofed in by tomorrow morning," said the coordinator.

"I'm hog-sloppin' mad so just back off and watch us. Are those the blueprints?" asked Bill.

"Yeah," said the coordinator.

"Gimme them." Bill picked them up from the startled supply coordinator.

Bill walked over to RECNAC. "I told the reporters we'll have this house built in seventy-two hours. Tomorrow morning you'll have this house framed and a roof on. The subs start tomorrow morning at seven o'clock. While they're working we'll put the siding on. The women will paint."

"Who's going to paint?" Bonnie asked.

"You are," said Bill.

"You been taking lessons from Coach Blitzkrieg?" said Bonnie.

"I phoned him. He's on his way," said a very determined Bill.

Angelo made a sign of the cross.

Bill called them over to his pickup truck. "Let's get cracking. Let's unload my truck." Bill carried out an array of equipment that most of them had never seen before. He walked over to the power pole and plugged in his air compressor, electric saw, table saw and pneumatic stapler.

He then cut two-by-four spacers. He laid the sills on the ground, and told the RECNAC team to put two-by-fours the distance of each one of the spacers. In a short period of time, they had the front and back wall all laid down. He laid the sills on the exterior cinder block and across the piers. After that was done, he distributed plywood that was laid across the rafter to the sub-flooring on the first floor. After they had nailed the exterior wall portions, they stood them up.

He checked the blueprints. He laid out two sets of two-by-fours for the front door and back door. He then went across with a saw, and just on eye, cut across all the window heights. He put in the door sills and window placements. In less than four hours, they had the whole first floor framed up and windows and doors roughed in. They broke for lunch. He had the crane install the roof trestles. They nailed the roof trestles and spaced them, and the house was framed top to bottom by five o'clock. They were all tired, but Bill wouldn't let them rest. He got the plywood for the roof.

"Keep nailing up there," encouraged Bill. "We can't work on the roof after the sun goes down. We're wasting daylight."

"Wasting daylight," said Larry. "Who is he, John Wayne?"

"Keep working," said Michael, his T-shirt wet clear through. "We get to quit when the sun goes down."

"It's times like this I hate daylight savings time," said a perspiring Leo.

"I'm beat," said Bonnie.

"I don't mind putting this roofing board up, but I have no idea how to shingle a house," said Larry as he manned the pneumatic stapler.

By sunset, they had the roof on. "I guess it's time to go home now," said Larry.

"No way," said Bill. "We've got to finish the interior partitions tonight."

"Oh, no," said Leo. He tried to beg off. "I'm really beat."

"We're finishing the interior partitions tonight," said Bill. "Then we're done. They'll do the rough plumbing and electrical tomorrow. You'll hang the insulation and the drywall after they get through."

"You mean if we work till midnight, we're off until four o'clock in the afternoon?"

"No," said Bill. "Come back at dinnertime. We've got to nail on the exterior siding."

"I don't do nailing," said Bonnie. "It's bad for my hands."

"You'll be doing the painting," said Bill

"Bill, can we do this in seventy-two hours?" asked Sylvia.

"If I don't die first. I know you don't believe it," said Bill, "but I'm damn gonna do it."

They pitched in and worked until midnight. All the exterior and interior walls were framed and the roof was on.

"Be back here at twelve o'clock," said Bill, "and expect a twelve-hour day."

They all left grumbling. Even Leo was too tired to complain about the motels. They all crawled into their beds and slept.

At seven o'clock the next morning, Bill greeted the electrical, plumbing and HVAC crews. He showed them the plans, and they went right to work.

"You've got all three crews working at one time," said the electrical foreman. "When is this house going to be completed?"

"Two days from now," said Bill, "so all your crews have to be back here for the finish work tomorrow morning."

"No way," said the plumbing foreman. "You can't insulate, drywall, sand and paint this place in twenty-four hours."

"Yep," said Bill, "maybe you're right. How about showing up at eight o'clock day after tomorrow. Can you do the finish work in three hours?"

"Is there a race?" asked the air conditioning man.

"Sure is," said Bill.

"Who's in the race?" asked the air conditioning man.

"My group of old people, called RECNAC," said Bill. "We're trying to beat those judges by building a house in seventy-two hours."

"How long did it take them to build a house?" inquired the plumbing foreman.

Bill pointed. "It took them eleven months to put up the sign."

"Screw them judges. They're all pious ass hypocrites," said the electrical foreman. "If you've got it all ready, we'll finish in three hours."

"Fair enough," said Bill as he shook the foreman's hand. The workmen plunged into their tasks.

At noontime, the RECNAC people drove up, bleary-eyed. Bonnie wasn't wearing any makeup.

"Is that you, Bonnie?" asked Sylvia.

"Yes it is," said Bonnie.

"I hardly recognize you," said Sylvia.

"You mean without my makeup," said Bonnie.

"Yes," said Lisa.

"I didn't know you had freckles," said Sarah.

"It's my most intimate secret," said Bonnie.

"What's the slave driver got ready for us today?" Lisa asked.

"That's harsh," said Theresa.

"We really need help," said Sylvia. "Bill's working our people to death. I don't think we can keep up the pace."

"Let's ask for help. Those reporters are going to be here today. I'll ask them to help us," said Theresa.

"What good are reporters?" Sarah asked.

"They can get us instant help," said Bonnie.

They started painting. About an hour later, a young reporter showed up. Theresa turned to the women. "I'll go talk with her."

Theresa talked to the television reporter and told her that since all the judges had left, RECNAC was building the house alone.

"What's RECNAC?" the reporter inquired.

"It's *cancer* spelled backwards," said Theresa. "I want you to ask every person who's had cancer to come here and bring tools."

"This is a small TV station," said the reporter.

"We don't need a thousand people," added Sylvia. "Just get us twenty people who can drywall, paint and do finish carpentry. We'll have this house finished day after tomorrow."

The TV and radio reporters broadcast the appeal. Around four o'clock, twenty pickup trucks showed up. The drivers asked for the supervisor. The electricians pointed to Bill.

"Are you building this house?" asked a heavy-set, seventy year old.

"Yes," said Bill.

"Our oncology doctor told us to help you out," said the seventy year old.

"What's your trade?" asked Bill.

"We've got six finish carpenters and five drywall hangers."

"Six," a man shouted as he got out of his pickup.

The seventy year old turned around. "Six hangers, three drywall mudders, three drywall finishers, and a whole bunch of laborers."

"Can you hang insulation?" asked Bill.

"Yep," said several of the new arrivals.

Bill pointed to the insulation lying on the floor. "Get your staple guns, hang it up, then hang the drywall. Let's get crackin."

Bill walked over to Sylvia. "Who sent for help?"

"I did," said Theresa.

"We didn't need a whole bunch of workers," said Bill.

"They're all RECNAC people," said Sarah.

"Then that's okay," said Bill smiling.

"Besides," added Bonnie, "my nails were starting to split. My manicurist is going to hate me."

Bill looked at Sylvia for a translation.

"It means, Bill," said Sylvia, "that this work is hurting her hands, and mine as well. We're not used to twelve-hour days."

"You used to be," said Bill.

"Yes," said Sylvia, "but I'm a little older."

Bill rolled his eyes. "Tell me about it."

"Anyway," said Theresa, "you've got additional workers to bring this house in on time."

"Thanks," said Bill. "We did need extra people." He kissed Sylvia on the cheek.

"We're going to have lunch," said Lisa.

"The siding has got to go up. You've got to paint the first coat today," said Bill. "But," he turned to Bonnie, "you can put on rubber gloves. Your hands won't get busted up. Go to a drug store and ask for the gloves."

They all left for lunch. "I hope they have some cute little places to eat," said Bonnie.

"Give it a break," said Sarah. "We're lucky if they've got a McDonald's."

"Yes," said Theresa, "if we're working like this, we don't have to worry about calories."

Bonnie asked one of the local workmen where they could find a good place to eat.

"Millie's. Best place!" he said, wiping some sweat from his chin. "It's in a pink double-wide, about a mile out on the four-lane." He pointed the way. "You can't miss it."

Bonnie looked at the workman as if he were speaking Chinese. Bonnie turned to Sylvia for a translation.

"Gotcha," said Sylvia, "out on the highway a mile, two mobile homes fastened together with pink vinyl siding." They followed Sylvia's direction, drove to Millie's and walked in.

Millie walked up to the workers. "Hey, you're new in town. I bet you're part of that crew that's building that new house."

"Yes, we are," said Sarah.

"Glad to have you here. Television reporters and judges come in here. Our business has really been good. I'm going to be sorry when the house is done," said Millie.

"It's supposed to be done tomorrow afternoon," said Sylvia.

"What can I get'cha today?" asked the waitress.

"I'd like a club sandwich on rye bread, thinly sliced ham and very fresh lettuce, with fried bacon and fresh tomatoes," said Bonnie.

The waitress looked at Bonnie. "Honey, this here's Roston, Georgia, and we haven't got all those highfalutin city ways. We got fried chicken, tomatoes, okra, corn and turnip greens with mashed potatoes and gravy."

"How many fat grams are in that meal?" asked Bonnie.

"Plenty, honey," said the waitress, "and you look like you could use a few extra pounds, skinny as you are. The food's good for you." She looked at Lisa. "Tell them about Southern cooking."

Lisa responded, "I'm born and raised in Chicago. This is my first trip to Georgia. I don't know anything about Southern cooking."

"Oh," said Millie. "It's good food. It'll stick to your ribs. You can go on out and wrestle an alligator and not run out of energy. I'll bring six specials over to the table. Y'all want some iced tea, right?"

"With lemon?" asked Bonnie.

"With lemon," said Millie shaking her head as she walked away. She walked behind the counter and yelled to the cook, "Six specials, with the works!"

"Bill would be proud of us, the way we're eating," said Sylvia. "They're working a lot harder than we are. I'm still surprised at how hungry I get."

"Bill's really on a tear," said Sarah.

"Yes, he is," said Sylvia. "He's like all our husbands. He's out to prove something to himself and to the world."

"What's that?" asked Bonnie.

"They want to prove that they can do their jobs," said Sylvia. "They want to prove that they don't have to be just put on the shelf because they have cancer."

"That's right," said Lisa. "After Allen got cancer, they made him an assistant and they put him on the shelf. He was determined that his march was going to succeed. I was determined that he was going to be successful at it."

"Leo's still mad inside," said Bonnie. "QRX canned him. He had an opportunity with RECNAC that he never would have had with QRX."

"It's the same with Larry. He's proving that he shouldn't have been put out to pasture. Every time he makes a sale, he feels vindicated that the Board of Education was wrong. Deep inside, he has a really hostile attitude about the way he was treated."

"That's sure what's edging Bill," said Sylvia. "I've never seen him work like that. He's proven that he's a good supervisor by building this house with lots of untrained people in three days."

"That's the way Michael feels," said Theresa. "They really never gave him an opportunity to do anything at his company when he had cancer. Now look what he has done for RECNAC."

"Who would have ever thought Michael could raise ten million dollars to start the company?" Bonnie asked. "RECNAC owes a lot of its success to Michael."

"Each one of our husbands, or boyfriends," said Sarah looking at Theresa, "has done so much better because he got pushed."

"I'm really proud to be able to see this," said Lisa.

The waitress walked up. "Here are your specials," she said, and she systematically clunked the heavily laden plates in front of each of the women. "Eat hearty," she said and walked off.

Bonnie looked at the food, picked up a fork and started shoveling it into her mouth. Lisa watched in amazement. "Bonnie, you're eating like a field hand."

"Let's eat this food and get out of here. We have alligators to wrestle," said Bonnie.

Next morning, with the use of all the crews, the house was close to being finished. At nine o'clock the final electrical and plumbing was being installed. At noon the house was completely finished. Leo had contacted a landscaping company. While RECNAC was finishing up inside, the landscapers put plants by the doors, harrowed the front yard and laid down centipede sod.

Bill hugged Leo. "That's a nice touch."

"When we bought our house, they'd laid the whole yard in five hours. All they have to do is water it and it'll take hold," said Leo.

"It's too bad," said Bill, "they don't have an irrigation system."

"That would be pushing it," said Leo. "They're going to have to do some of the house maintenance themselves. They're a young couple, and they'll be able to do it."

"You're right," said Bill.

At twelve-thirty the local television and newspaper reporters were present. There were reporters from the Atlanta newspaper, plus television stations from Atlanta, Columbus and Tallahassee. Leo had arranged for the additional television coverage.

Bill presented the keys to the family, a couple about thirty-five years of age, with three children. The father, who walked with a cane, was missing a leg that he'd lost in a farm accident.

Leo had ordered a much bigger sign. It read: "This Housing for Humanity Project was built by RECNAC. It took the judges eleven months to put up their sign; it took RECNAC three days to build the house."

"Nice sign, Leo," said Larry.

"Way to go," said Michael and Allen.

"They were pious hypocrites. They deserve this," said Leo.

"You've got that right," said Patrick. "I'd like to tell those TV reporters what I think."

"Don't do that," said Larry.

"The publicity will be enough," said Michael.

"I guess you're right," said Patrick, "but I'd still like to punch them in the nose."

"Bill," said Leo, "I can't believe this. I have done more work and had more fun in seventy-two hours than I can remember."

"What about our honeymoon?" smiled Bonnie.

"That lasted ninety-six hours," said Leo exuberantly, "but it's right up there."

"Allen whispered to Larry, "Leo almost put his foot in his mouth.""

"Hey," said Michael, "Let me have your attention. Theresa and I would like to make an announcement. We're going to be married."

"Really?" said Bonnie. "That's great."

"Oh congratulations," Sarah said to Michael.

"You old fox, you," said Larry. "I wondered if you were ever going to get around to it."

"Congratulations," said Allen.

"Where are you getting married?" asked Bill.

"You mean, like a church?" asked Allen.

"Even the city would help," said Bonnie.

"We're going to get married in Winslow, Arizona," said Michael.

"Send us invitations and we'll all be there, if I can live through these aching muscles," grumbled Larry.

They all waved good-bye to Michael and Theresa as they drove off.

"Ain't young love great!" exhorted Bill. "Bet they'll be he-ing and she-ing."

"Speak for yourself Bill," said Sylvia. "I'm going to bed, to sleep. Understand, Bill?"

"Yes Ma'am," answered a subdued Bill.

"Don't forget your sales quotas," reminded Leo. "Monday is a work day."

"What a slave driver," groaned Sarah.

CHAPTER 22

THE WEDNESDAY AFTERNOON flight into Sky Harbor Airport in Phoenix, Arizona, carried the RECNAC team. They had drinks on the airplane, and there was a spirit of frivolity and mischief. The airline hostesses finally put them in the back of the airplane. One hostess shook her head and admonished them that the motorcycle group in front was disturbed by their rowdiness.

Bring those bikers back here," bragged Bill.

"I'll clean their clocks," said Allen.

"Big blowhards," said Leo.

"I'll deck that noisy gang," said Michael.

I'm not starting this fight," said Larry.

They acted subdued until Bonnie asked the stewardess, "You get any lately?"

The stewardess' face turned red. They all laughed. She stomped off toward the front and told the other hostess, "Don't let those people back there have anymore drinks."

The second hostess replied, "They're all cancer patients. They've probably only got ninety days to live. Let them have a good time."

"Oh, I didn't know," the stewardess said.

"They're traveling to see one cancer patient marry another. Two cancer patients getting married," said the hostess. "They might not live to see their first anniversary."

"That bad, huh?" said the stewardess.

"Would you marry somebody who had cancer?" asked the hostess.

"Definitely not," said the stewardess. "I'll give each of them a free drink."

When RECNAC landed at Sky Harbor Airport, they rented two vans. They were having so much fun that Allen had to be the designated driver. The men rode in one van. Sylvia was the designated driver for the women.

"I'd like to hear what the men are talking about," said Sarah.

"Wouldn't that be interesting," said Bonnie.

"You don't think they're going to talk about sex?" asked Theresa.

"They're not talking about anything else," said Sarah.

"It'll probably be dull," said Bonnie.

"Now wait a minute," said Theresa. "I don't think Michael is going to be like that."

"Weren't you married before?" asked Sylvia.

"Yeah, sure. But that guy was a crumb, a slob," said Theresa.

"Was he like that when he proposed to you?" Bonnie asked.

"Oh no," said Theresa. "He was romantic and everything else. Do you think Michael is going to change after we get married?"

"Only for the better," said Sarah.

"You've got to be kidding," said Bonnie.

"I noticed, ever since Larry got cancer he's more kind and considerate," said Sarah.

"You're right," said Bonnie. "I noticed that about Leo. He's not the ruthless, mean businessman he was before."

"What a despicable thing for a wife to say!" said Lisa, and they all laughed.

"Looking back," said Sarah, "I've kept a statistical sheet of what happened to us since we met two and a half years ago."

"Really," said Lisa. "What kind of statistics? Business? Personal? What?"

"Before our husbands met at the Mayo Clinic two and a half years ago, none of them had any criminal arrests, not even traffic tickets."

"Yeah, so what?" said Theresa.

"As far as I can see, none of us had ever been involved with the police before. Right, Bonnie?" asked Sarah.

"Of course," said Bonnie. "I was a cheerleader in high school and college."

"That's right," said Theresa. "Bonnie graduated magna cum laude, with a minor in business."

"No way," said Lisa. "We thought you were a cocktail..."

"Bimbo," said Bonnie.

"Don't jump off the handle," said Sarah, "I'm trying to get to my statistics."

"Let's hear your damn statistics," said Bonnie.

"We don't use that word," said Lisa.

"Sorry," said Bonnie.

Sarah pulled out her note pad and went over the stats.

"In any event, if I total it up, in the two and a half years that we've been involved with cancer, we've had one criminal violation and two court trials, without any convictions."

"Don't forget the cafe fight with the hard hats," said Lisa.

"We've really kept the judges busy," said Bonnie.

"We don't want to brag about this to our children," said Sarah.

"No," said Sylvia, "but we can brag about it to our grandchildren."

Later, Lisa said, "Let's get down to the serious stuff."

"Right," said Bonnie.

"Theresa, we want to see the wedding dress. We want to see the lingerie you've picked out for Saturday evening."

"Yeah," said Sarah. "How much did you spend at Victoria's Secret?"

"And who designed the wedding dress?" asked Bonnie.

The men, who were riding in the van behind the women, were having a good time. Leo had arranged for a double cooler that contained two suitcases of beer.

"That looks mighty good, but we're going to have to let the windows down so it's warm enough to enjoy it," said Larry.

"Sí," said Pablo, "and I hope they've got some limes. We can really enjoy this."

"What?" said Leo. "I get an air-conditioned van and you're going to roll down the windows so you're hot enough to drink beer?"

"That's how you do it," said Angelo. "That's why we always ride in a pickup. You suck a lime; you have a beer. Unless, of course, you want some premixed margaritas. I have a few here."

"Right on," said Leo. "I could have a premixed margarita."

Pablo dipped a paper cup into the ice, then into a salt box, and poured a premixed margarita into it.

"Is there an open container law in Arizona?" asked Larry.

"I don't know," said Bill. "Why do you ask?"

"There's a police car behind us with a flashing light."

"Wow," said Allen.

"Stay cool," said Leo. "We'll see what happens."

Allen pulled over to the side of the road. An Arizona state patrolman walked up to the driver's side. "Good afternoon, sir," the patrolman said to Allen, noticing that Allen was dressed in a business suit with a minister's collar. "I couldn't help noticing that your passengers appeared to be drinking beer."

"Wouldn't think of it," said Larry.

"No way," said Leo.

"Not us," said Bill.

"I'm on my way to my wedding," said Michael.

"Okay. I take it that the driver is your chauffeur. Is that correct?" asked the trooper.

"Yes," said Leo, "he's our designated driver."

"No," said the trooper, "I mean, is he a chauffeur?" the patrolman inquired.

Rev. Kilpatrick caught on right away. "Yes," said the Reverend. "I am the chauffeur."

"If you're being driven by a chauffeur, in a commercial vehicle, alcohol consumption is permitted," said the patrolman.

"This is a commercial vehicle," said Rev. Kilpatrick. "It is owned by Ace Rental Car Company, and I am the assigned driver for these five men."

"Well," said the trooper, "in that case you can proceed on down the road, since you are a hired employee."

The patrolman cautioned all the passengers: "I understand you're on the way to a wedding, but you must have a modicum of decency. No throwing beer cans out the window."

"Sí, señor," said Pablo. "We are the maintenance men. We have a bag here so that we can recycle the beer cans. We have the aluminum concession on this vehicle."

He turned to Leo, who looked to be the most prosperous, and said, "Is this your vehicle?"

"Yes, it is officer. I have a chauffeur and two maintenance men in the back whose job is to pick up any disposable materials and recycle them," said Leo.

"You mean, sir," said the officer, "that you have one chauffeur and two associates to haul you and these other four men?"

"Yes," said Leo. "I am the chief executive officer of the Recreation Company of North America."

The trooper replied, "I've never heard of it."

"I will have my party roll up the windows and conduct themselves more appropriately," said Leo.

"Thank you, sir," said the trooper. "Enjoy the Arizona highways."

With that, the patrolman made a U-turn and headed in the other direction.

Allen drove off. Bill said, "Leo, how the hell did you pull that off?"

"There was a little bit of bull," said Leo. "I'm sure he was sympathetic to Michael getting married."

"You kept your cool," said Michael.

"Looks that way," said Leo.

"Way to go." Pablo and Angelo high-fived each other in the back of the van.

"Don't forget my part," said Allen. "I really played the chauffeur."

"You sure did," said Leo.

"Way to go," said Bill, "and you got us out of a lot of trouble."

They passed the women's van that had stopped when the patrol officer had stopped Allen.

"You think they got a ticket?" asked Sarah.

"No," said Bonnie. "Leo talked him out of it."

"No way," said Lisa. "Allen laid some religion on them."

"What could the cops have stopped them for?" Theresa asked. "As long as they didn't throw beer cans on the highway, they weren't in trouble anyway."

"It's a good thing that trooper didn't hear Sarah reciting their criminal charges."

"Or ours either," said Sarah.

As they drove on, Coach said, "Hey, did I ever tell you about my war experiences?"

"Is this the one where you carried two privates and a sergeant on your shoulders through a twenty-mile minefield?" asked Michael.

"In a twelve-inch snowfall?" asked Leo.

"No, it was a seventy-mile-per-hour sand storm," said Allen.

"Last time you told it, it was a four-inch monsoon rain," said Bill.

"Screw you," said Coach.

"Hey, did I ever tell you about jump mastering the ARVN Airborne at Ap Dong?" asked Larry.

"About twenty times," said Leo.

"Okay," said Larry. "Let me tell you this joke. There's this couple—Michael, you'd better pay attention—that were on their honeymoon."

"Right," said Michael.

"They were in the dark. They had a tube of K-Y Jelly and some Ben-Gay. They got it mixed up."

"You're not going to tell us that story," said Leo.

"Not now," said Allen. "I can't hear that one again."

"We're almost on the outskirts of Winslow," said Michael. "Keep a lookout for the motel."

"Right," said Leo. "Don't forget, tomorrow night we're going to have a RECNAC corporate meeting that will take place about an hour before the rehearsal dinner."

"What rehearsal dinner?" asked Michael.

"You've got to have a rehearsal dinner, Michael. Since your parents are deceased, we will host the rehearsal dinner," said Leo.

"Really?" said Michael. "I'd forgotten all about a rehearsal dinner."

"We're going to have it on Friday so that you have time to get yourself organized," Leo said.

"Yeah," said Coach, "we don't want you to let us down. We expect you to perform spectacularly."

Bonnie had arranged the rehearsal dinner to start at seven-thirty p.m. The RECNAC meeting was at six o'clock. Everyone arrived on time. The RECNAC crew comprised seventeen individuals.

Leo called the meeting to order with "Ladies and Gentlemen" and he signaled to the waitress "no drinks at this time." There was a murmur of discontent. Leo maintained his posture. "This is serious." They all quieted down.

"As you all know, two and a half years ago, we met for the first time at the Mayo Clinic. We all had to return to our homes and come back sixty days later. In the interim, all of us were fired, retired, demoted or put out to pasture. Since that time I'd like to tell you what we have accomplished. We won a nationally publicized softball game, led a huge civil rights rally, started a new corporation and built a house for humanity. But let's not forget the very significant contributions these wonderful ladies had in each accomplishment."

"I had a great time," said Allen. "And I'll never forget the face of that Supreme Court judge."

"And now we're here for Michael and Theresa," said Leo. "Every one of us has turned out to be as lucky as can be. After checking with our accountants, I am going to give a five percent stock ownership to Theresa, Coach, Bill, Larry, Sarah, Bonnie, Pablo, Angela, Allen, Lisa and Michael."

"You've just transferred fifty-five percent of the stock," said Bonnie.

"That's right," said Leo.

"You've only got forty-five percent. They could vote you out. What do I get?" Bonnie asked.

"You got me," said Leo.

They could fire you," said Bonnie.

"Hell, yes," said Larry. "But who would have the business leadership in this organization?"

"That's exactly my point," said Leo. "I get all the credit, and you've done all the work. I don't know what this company is worth. We've done one hundred million dollars in sales. If we're lucky we'll have ten million dollars in profit. I'm not paying taxes on all of it."

"Yepper," said Bill. "It went up mighty fast. I hope it doesn't go down just as quickly."

"It's been more fun than the Persian desert," said Coach.

"That's the end of the corporate meeting," said Leo. "We're a very small company by American standards. I just wanted to take this opportunity to transfer the stock."

"Since you gave us the stock, you've got us locked in so we can't quit," said Michael.

"You got that right," said Leo.

"You mean we'll have to keep working like we have been for the next five or six years?" asked Sylvia.

"You didn't want to retire," said Leo. "Be glad you have something to do."

"I don't want this interfering with my softball tournaments," said Larry.

"Yeah, I've got some sporting clays tournaments to win," said Coach.

"I know," said Leo. "Unlike the corporations where everybody just wants to make money, we don't have to do it. I enjoy what I'm doing. When I look at some of these other executives, I say to hell with them."

"Can I still drive my 1991 Suzuki to corporate headquarters?" asked Larry.

"Yes you can," said Leo, "but you've got to wash it at least once a month."

"Sí, señor, that's right," said Pablo. "I'm doing well. I don't want anybody to know that I'm making money. I traded down my 1990 car for two 1980s. I don't want young men coming after my daughters for my money."

"Unlike New York, we believe in one-downsmanship," said Michael.

"Yeah," said Allen. "Not many people want to know that their minister is rich."

"Maybe they'll let you preach two Sunday sermons a year at Mount Moriah Church," said Leo.

"This is great," said Michael. "I'll be able to pay for Theresa's dress."

"No problem," said Bonnie. "Theresa will be able to pay for it herself."

"No tricks on us now that we're getting married." Michael looked at Sarah. "You have a penchant for mischief. So does Bonnie."

Sarah and Bonnie looked at each other in complete surprise.

The waitress walked in and said, "All the guests have started to come in."

"Bring them all in. It's time for the rehearsal dinner."

Theresa's relatives came on in. The RECNAC crew immediately sprang into their gracious manners mode and welcomed everyone.

All the RECNAC people showed up at eleven a.m. at St. Cecilia's Church in Winslow, Arizona, for the ecumenical service. Father Patrick Mendoza and Rev. Allen Kilpatrick presided at the ceremony.

Theresa's relatives numbered about two hundred and Michael's about fifteen, plus the entire RECNAC crew. Enough to fill up the small church. Theresa's sisters and nieces were in the wedding party. Theresa looked gorgeous in a white silk wedding gown, and Bonnie was just thrilled.

"It's really gorgeous," said Sarah and Lisa.

"Her grandmother got married in that dress, and I worked with a seamstress to make it a little more modern. It really turned out nice," said Bonnie.

"Yes," said Sylvia, "and the contrasting light green color on the bridesmaids is really great. The flower girl is just beautiful."

"That's Theresa's niece," said Lisa.

"There's a reception right after this. Then they're leaving on their honeymoon," said Sarah. "They'll be out of here by four o'clock. We've got to do something to make this memorable."

Theresa's relatives had provided a fabulous reception. Two tables about forty feet long were laden with chili con-queso dip, quesadillas, soft and hard tacos, chicken wings, veggie and deli trays, meatballs, marinated chicken shish kebabs, sliced meat, a wondrous variety of rolls, wedding cookies and lady fingers. It was outdoors, and the Winslow weather was just fantastic.

At three-thirty it was apparent that Michael and Theresa were trying to extricate themselves from their friends, their relatives and RECNAC. Leo had placed a smoke bomb in the car that Theresa normally drove. She was aware that something would probably be done to their car, and adroitly had arranged for a relative to take them to their escape vehicle. Leo, with a few twenty dollar bills, had managed to corrupt her relatives. As she went to her backup vehicle, two officers of the Winslow police department walked up to Michael.

"Are you Michael Yret?" one officer asked.

"Yes, I am," said Michael. "I just got married to Theresa here this afternoon."

"We heard that. We have an extradition warrant from the Governor of Texas. You're wanted on a bigamy charge. We've been watching you. You can't come here and marry one of our young maidens and expect to get away with it."

"What?" said Theresa.

"Stick out your hands." Michael stuck out his hands and the two police officers slapped handcuffs on him. The officer looked at Theresa. "I'm sorry ma'am. We've just arrested the Texas Gigolo."

"There's got to be some mistake," said Michael, as the officers put him into the police car.

Theresa was flabbergasted. Just then Bonnie and Sarah walked up to her. "They've just arrested Michael," said Theresa.

"Really, what for?" asked Bonnie.

"They said he's the Texas Gigolo," said Theresa, breaking down in tears.

"The cad!" said Sarah.

"You cannot ever trust a man," said Bonnie.

"But you can trust yours," said Theresa, still crying.

Lisa walked up. "Have you finally wised up to that four-flushing Michael?"

"Hard to believe," said Sylvia.

"It's those quiet ones all the time," said Rev. Allen.

"I don't know if my brother can get him out of this one," said Larry, "but I'll have him try."

"How come all of you are right here, right now?" asked Theresa.

"We're just here to help you out," said Bonnie. "Which way did you come in?"

Theresa caught on. "Dammit, Bonnie. Where's Michael?"

"He's right around the corner, waiting for you. You've got your car. You're on your way to the airport."

Everyone shouted, "Have a good time!" Theresa ran around the corner. Michael was out of the patrol car. The police officers were laughing as they put him in his own car.

"I should have known," said Theresa, "being an ex-cop, that they would pull some crap like this. Get away from here as fast as you can," she ordered Michael.

Michael's tires screeched for about the third time in his life as he drove away.

Theresa's niece came up and pulled on Larry's suit coat sleeve. "Do you have cancer like Aunt Theresa does?"

Larry looked at the six-year-old child. "Yes," he said.

"Are Aunt Theresa, Uncle Michael and you going to die?" asked niece.

Larry, Allen, Sarah and Sylvia were shocked by the question. Allen was mouthing an answer when Larry responded.

"Someday…but when you are as old as we are, have cancer, and it comes to dying, we are all in the on-deck circle."

"Hope the batter in front of me fouls off five thousand pitches," said Allen.

"But Mr. Larry," said Theresa's niece, "you only get three fouls in softball."

"We're playing baseball rules," said Larry.

"I'll pray on that," said Allen. They walked off to the parking lot.

"I just want to get back in the game," said Larry. And he did.

ABOUT THE AUTHOR

Prostate cancer survivor Terry Leiden has been a practicing attorney for thirty-eight years. He specializes in consumer bankruptcy law. He also is a player and coach on the Triumphs 65 softball team.

He and Sara, his wife, live in Augusta, Georgia, and have three grown sons—Zane, Yale and Eric.

Get Back in the Game is his first published work of fiction.

To order copies of *Get Back in the Game* as well as other titles from Harbor House, visit our Web site:

www.harborhousebooks.com